GIRLS FROM DA HOOD 5

GIRLS FROM DA HOOD 5

KEISHA ERVIN
BRENDA HAMPTON
EDD McNAIR

www.urbanbooks.net

Urban Books, LLC
1199 Straight Path
West Babylon, NY 11704

ISBN-13: 978-1-60162-152-8
ISBN-10: 1-60162-152-3

First Printing September 2009
Printed in the United States of America

10 9 8 7 6 5 4 3 2 1

Distributed by Kensington Publishing Corp.
Submit Wholesale Orders to:
Kensington Publishing Corp.
C/O Penguin Group (USA) Inc.
Attention: Order Processing
405 Murray Hill Parkway
East Rutherford, NJ 07073-2316
Phone: 1-800-526-0275
Fax: 1-800-227-9604

Diva
Definition: A female version of a hustler.

Queen Pynn

Keisha Ervin

Prologue

"Ooh, just like that!"

"You like that, ma?"

"Yes, baby! Lick it just like that!"

Doing as he was told, Ahsim placed the tip of his tongue on Q's clit while she looked on with sheer appreciation. She couldn't wait for him to taste her. Gazing back up at her, Ahsim flicked his tongue across her clit at a feverish pace. Q never knew that the feel of someone's tongue on her clit could be so good. Her husband of five years, Sean, never made her feel this way. He said that giving head was something a real man would never have to do to please his woman.

But the way Ahsim worked his tongue in and out of her pussy proved Sean's theory to be wrong. Dead wrong, as a matter of fact. Ahsim's tongue felt like a feather fluttering ever so lightly across her pussy. Q had no other choice but to rub his head and moan. Ahsim always made sure to take his time when pleasing her. Never once did he rush through their lovemaking. Slow and steady was always the pace.

None of their encounters were ever the same. Whenever and wherever was their motto. At any given moment, Q could find herself bent over the couch or on top of the kitchen sink getting fucked. This time she and Ahsim were in her and Sean's bed getting it on. She was buck naked except for a pair of red patent leather stilettos. Her legs were spread-eagle in the air.

She was always guaranteed to cum at least twice, when fucking Ahsim. The man knew how to handle a pussy. His tongue, fingers, and dick worked her into a frenzy every time. Deciding that she was ready to cum, Ahsim targeted her spot on the right side of her clit. He licked and sucked until Q couldn't take it anymore.

"Ooh, baby, stop. I can't breathe," she yelled. "This shit feels so good!"

"You want me to stop?" he asked, daring her to say yes.

"No, baby! Please don't stop! I don't want you to ever stop! Ooh . . . yes . . . I'm cumming! I'm cumming!" Q shrieked as she rotated her hips in a circular motion.

Cum slithered from the lips of her pussy onto his tongue. Ahsim savored every drop. Q's entire body shook as she came all over her thighs and sheets. Then, before Q or Ahsim knew it, someone came bursting through the door.

Part One

Put It On Her

A hsim sat on the edge of the couch with his hands clutched firmly together, his face stony. By instinct, he surveyed his surroundings. Everything seemed fine on the surface, but Ahsim knew better. He wouldn't have been called if nothing were wrong. His job was to protect the wealthy and the elite with his life. This particular client was willing to pay top dollar for him to do just that.

Before arriving at the Pynn estate, Ahsim had done some research on the man who'd called requesting his services. Sean Pynn was a well-known Midwest rapper. Since his debut album in 2002, he'd produced hit after hit. He'd won numerous American Music, Grammy, and Billboard awards. *The Source* magazine named him the hottest rapper alive, but as the old saying goes, mo' money, mo' problems. Sean's cocky, disrespectful attitude and boastful ways garnered him legions of fans, legal issues, and enemies.

Sean hadn't been on the scene even a year before

things began to go downhill. In 2002, he was convicted of attacking an employee on the set of a music video. He was sentenced to thirty days in jail and community service. Two years later, he was arrested on a weapons charge and sentenced to five years' probation.

Months later, he was arrested on a violation of his parole. In 2007, Sean almost ended his career for good. He was accused of sexually abusing a woman in a hotel room. Sean vehemently denied the charges, but was sentenced to two years in prison. During that period, he was dropped from his label and flat broke due to legal fees. He'd tried shopping some of his unreleased material to other labels, but nobody wanted to sign him because he was such a liability.

After serving twelve months, Sean was released from the penitentiary due in large part to the help and influence of Rocco "Roc" De Luca. He was the CEO of Murder Mob Records and a well-known mobster. Roc was a huge fan of Sean's work. He posted $1.5 million bail pending appeal of the conviction; in exchange, Sean was obligated to release five albums under Murder Mob Records.

Desperately wanting to be released from jail, Sean signed the contract without even knowing what half of it meant. Upon his release, Sean immediately went back to recording and beefing with other artists, mainly fellow Midwest rapper Grip. Sean claimed in an interview that Grip was trying to copy his style and didn't write his own rhymes. Grip then responded with a dis record titled *Sucka Niggaz*.

The two men went back and forth on wax and in interviews for months, but after coming face to face at the 2008 BET Awards, things got heated. Sean walked up to Grip during the red carpet taping and hit him in the face. After that it was on. Both men and their camps were escorted from the premises and denied access to the show.

For a while things died down; that is, until Grip came with the ultimate dis, claiming that he fucked Sean's wife.

That's were Ahsim came in. Sean wanted to believe his wife, but he didn't, so he hired a bodyguard who would report back to him daily on her comings and goings. Ahsim checked his watch. After being greeted at the door by the housekeeper, Rosa, he had been escorted into the living area and told that Sean would be down in a second. Fifteen minutes later, Ahsim was still waiting for him to make an appearance. He had five more minutes. After that Ahsim would be up. He didn't give a fuck how much money he was being offered. Luckily for Sean he came striding into the room with just a minute to spare.

Within a matter of seconds Ahsim had him fully sized up. Sean's swagger was topnotch. With the looks and confidence of NFL player Reggie Bush, he knew he was the shit. That afternoon he sported a pinstriped Etro suit and a pair of Ermenegildo Zegna Leonardo loafers. The Audemar Piguet watch he rocked spoke for itself, but Ahsim could tell that, underneath it all, Sean was still a street nigga to the heart.

"Sorry for the hold up," Sean explained. "I just got out of a meeting. Ahsim, right?"

"Yeah." Ahsim stood up.

"You good." Sean waved him off, unbuttoned his suit jacket, and sat down.

"Mr. Pynn—"

"Call me Sean."

"Sean, I was informed by my company that you were in need of my services."

"Yeah, I'll be out of town for a week and I need someone here I can trust to look after my wife, Queen. She's a little hard-headed but she is never to go anywhere alone, even if she insists. Ya dig?"

"I got you." Ahsim nodded as he noticed a voluptuous figure glide down the spiral staircase.

She was unlike any women he'd ever seen before. Everything about her said "proceed with caution," but Ahsim was willing to take the risk. It was like they were in a silent movie and she was his leading lady. Her skin was the sweetest shade of butterscotch. Long, coal black hair cascaded past her shoulders and down her back. That day, she wore it over to the side in a partial bun. Three-carat diamond earrings gleamed from her ears.

She possessed catlike brown eyes, lashes that went on for days, high cheekbones, and succulent pink lips. Her shape was reminiscent of Jessica Rabbit. The black, one-shoulder Herve Leger dress she wore highlighted her 34 D breasts and hugged her plump ass just right. Sean sat back in his chair and crossed his legs.

"Ahsim, I'd like you to meet my wife, Queen."

"Hello." She extended her hand, giving him a once-over glance. "Please, call me Q."

"Nice to meet you, Q." Ahsim took her delicate hand into his and almost didn't want to let go.

"I didn't know we had company." Q stood beside her husband and placed her left hand around his shoulder.

"And I ain't know we walked around not wearing our wedding rings. Where the fuck is yo' ring?" Sean shot with his face screwed up.

"Calm down. I just finished washing my hands. I must've left it upstairs on the sink," Q tried to explain.

"Yeah, a'ight," he sneered. "But check it; this Ahsim, your new bodyguard. He'll be keeping an eye on you while I'm out of town, touring."

"An eye on me," she repeated. "What am I, five? We never discussed me having a guard. I'm a grown-ass woman. I can take care of myself," Q spat, offended.

"Am I confused about something? Last time I checked, I took care of you. You don't take care of me."

"All I'm saying, Sean—"

"Look," he interrupted, raising his hand, "don't make me come outside myself in front of company. You're getting a guard and that's it. Do I make myself clear?" he questioned without even looking in her direction.

"Perfectly," she replied, storming off.

"And put your fuckin' ring back on!"

Once Q was out of earshot, Sean reached into his suit jacket, pulled out a Cohiba cigar, and lit it.

"I know it may seem like I'm going hard on her, but Queen means a lot to me." He took a pull from the cigar then exhaled the smoke. "I mean, it's obvious she's beautiful, but if anything were to happen to her or if you were to touch her in any kind of way, I don't know what I might do." Sean gave Ahsim a warning glare.

Ahsim studied his expression before replying. He didn't want to lose his cool and say the wrong thing, but Sean had him fucked up. He wasn't Q, or just some flunky on Sean's payroll. He was a man. A man who didn't take too kindly to threats.

"Trust me; Queen will be in very good hands wit me."

Queen Pynn

Q sat in front of her gold vanity and brushed her hair with her back to the mirror. She hated seeing her reflection. Instead, she focused her attention on her exquisite bedroom designed by Kara Mann. The entire room was designed with a contemporary feel to it. The focal point was the bed. It sparkled in a blanket of platinum, with a towering headboard made of clean lines detailed with understated tufting. An Opera armchair and an Ixelles

Collection wing chair added an extra dose of spice to the space.

But all of the fancy furniture in the world couldn't hide the fact that she was unhappy. Over the past seven years Q had lost herself. She was no longer the church-going girl from the North side of the Lou with a voice like velvet. The media portrayed her as a cheating, gold-digging wife. It didn't matter that she once had dreams of stardom or that she'd known Sean before he had millions.

The media didn't know that he was prone to violent outbursts. They didn't know that before the platinum plaques, Sean had been so poor he couldn't book his own studio time, or that Q loved him so much that when he asked her to strip (on top of going to school and being a cashier), she did so in support of his career. They didn't know that he'd sheltered her to the point that she had no friends and could barely communicate with her family. They didn't know that she drowned herself in numerous charities just so she could be away from him. The media was blind to the fact that behind Sean's megawatt smile lay a cold-hearted, malicious man. Despite it all, Q hoped that one day the man she fell in love with would return, and things would go back to the way they used to be.

Out of the corner of her eye, Q saw Sean enter the room. She didn't even acknowledge his presence. Instead, she set down her brush and began rubbing La Mer Body Crème into her calves and thighs. Staying quiet usually avoided any arguments or drama, so Q held her tongue and prayed that for once God would make her invisible.

"So what you gon' act like you don't see me?" Sean asked from behind with his hand inside his pants.

Q looked into the mirror at him. There was no denying it: Sean was finer than a muthafucka. Dressed simply in a wife beater and jeans, he was 220 pounds of absolute wonder. The muscles that rippled down his physique were like works of art painted by Van Gogh. But all of that went out the window once she noticed the remnants of white powder on the tip of his nose.

"Hi, Sean," Q replied dryly.

"You got a' attitude?" Sean stood behind her.

"No, ain't nothing wrong with me."

"Well, fix yo' fuckin' face then." He mushed her in the back of the head then walked away. "You know what?" He spun back around. "I'm about sick of you and yo' shit. Why you always gotta disrespect me, huh?"

"Disrespect you how?"

"In front of the bodyguard and shit! I'm out here grindin' hard in these streets. Tryin' to take care of you. Make sure you a'ight and you got the nerve to question me about the muthafuckin' choices I make?"

"Sean, I wasn't tryin' to question you." Q kept her voice steady as she turned to face him. "All I was tryin' to say is I don't understand why I gotta have a body-guard with me twenty-four hours of the day. That's silly."

"No, it ain't, when niggas out here claimin' they fucked you!"

"How many times do we have to go over this? I didn't fuck him!"

"So now I'm joke?" Sean stepped back with a surprised look on his face. "You think you gon' play me? What you think; 'cause you went to college you better then me?"

"What are you talkin' about?" she shot, slamming down the lotion.

"I'm tired of muthafuckas like you think 'cause you read a book once or twice in yo' life that you know some-thing. I know shit too, Q!" Spit spewed from his mouth onto Q's face.

Disgusted, she slowly wiped her face and said, "I never said you didn't."

"Well, why is it every time I say something you gotta question me? It's bad enough I go into these meetings with these crackers, tryin' to broker a new deal and they look at me like I'm some dumb nigga! I ain't tryin' to be signed to Murder Mob forever!"

"So after all the stuff Roc has done for you, you just gon' up and leave?" Q asked, flabbergasted.

"You damn right!" His upper lip curled as he looked at her like she was crazy. "Fuck that pasta-eating mutha-fucka! He done made hella money off of me! Them crack-ers over at Sony offering me 30 mil just to sign wit'em and I'm gon' do it! Shit, I already got over a hundred songs recorded and ready to go!"

Q exhaled slowly and shook her head. Sean was the most ungrateful man she'd ever met. Roc had gone out of his way to help him in his time of need, and now that he was back on his feet Sean was going to shit on him.

"Then I got yo' big ass over here thinkin' you hot shit 'cause *Maxim* named you number fifty-five on they hot list. Don't let that shit go to yo' head, Q. You was number fifty-five, bitch!"

In the beginning, Sean talking to her crazy hurt like hell, but after years of hearing the same ol' shit over and over again, Q had become immune to his abuse.

"Sean, why don't you just lay down and go to bed," she suggested. "You're high and trippin'."

"Fuck that! You my bitch. I do what the fuck I wanna do." He walked up and stood in front of her. "I made you." Sean caressed her cheek softly. "You ain't going no-where . . . and we both know why, don't we?" He grabbed her cheeks and squeezed them together. "You wouldn't be shit wit' out me. I got yo' ass off the pole. Now look, you don't want for nothing. Ain't that right, baby?"

"Sean, you know the only reason I stripped in the first place was 'cause you asked me to." Q gazed into his eyes, visibly upset by his words.

"And I appreciate that in you." He unzipped his pants and pulled out his dick.

It was rock solid.

"You see how hard that is?" He placed it up to her full lips. "'G'on and make it disappear for me."

"Not now, Sean, c'mon." Q turned her head, revolted by the idea.

She didn't know where or in who Sean's dick had been.

"You can't do that for me?" He traced her cheek with the tip of his dick.

"Not tonight. I don't feel like it."

"C'mon, it ain't gon' take that long. I'm ready to bust now." He turned her face back toward him.

"I said no, Sean." Q pulled away again.

"Just lick the tip then." Sean forced her head forward.

"Nah uh now, c'mon, stop." She yanked her head back, then pushed his hand away.

The next thing Q knew, Sean had slapped her so hard she was holding her cheek.

"Don't ever put yo' muthafuckin' hands on me!" he warned.

Tears instantly formed and spilled out of Q's eyes.

"Fuck is on yo' mind?" he shot with a deranged look in his eye.

"I'm sorry," she sobbed.

"You sorry all right and you gon' suck my dick!"

Q's bottom lip trembled as she stared into Sean's bloodshot eyes. The man she once knew was no longer there. He hadn't been there in years. The monster who stood before her was what he'd become. She wanted to plead with him, but begging would only infuriate him more, so Q reluctantly took a hold of his dick and placed it in her mouth. The taste was bitter like salt as she bobbed her head back and forth.

"Ahh," Sean moaned with his eyes closed and his hand on the back of her head.

Q knew in order to make him cum quick she would have to deep throat his dick. The only problem was Sean's dick was so big it could barely fit into her mouth. Opening her mouth as wide as she could, Q eased his penis inch by inch past her tongue and to the back of her throat.

"Shit," Sean groaned as his dick began to thump.

At any second he was sure to explode. Q hated the taste of cum. She most definitely didn't want Sean cumming in her mouth so she tried to maneuver her way back, but Sean had such a tight grip on her head that she was unable to move or breathe.

"Fuck, I'm cumming," he exclaimed, fucking her mouth like it was her pussy.

Q tried to push him off of her but to no avail; cum shot down the back of her throat. Unable to breathe and unwilling to swallow, she began to choke. Sean came down from his orgasmic high and noticed her turning blue. He quickly pulled his dick from her mouth. Q coughed repeatedly while spitting up his semen in her hands.

"Look at you." Sean shook his head, revolted. "Go in the bathroom and clean ya'self up," he ordered. "I want some pussy."

Q wiped her mouth and got up. Everything in her wanted to haul off and punch the shit out of Sean, but that would only further escalate things. The last time she'd gotten enough courage to fight back she'd landed in the hospital with two broken ribs and a contusion on her forehead. In order to keep Sean's reputation squeaky clean, his publicist had spun the story to make it seem like she'd been in a minor car accident. No, Q wouldn't fight back. She'd continue to be the devoted wife she was until there was a way for her to break away from Sean for good.

Queen Pynn

Rays from the sun shone through the bamboo blinds and onto Q's face like stripes as she opened her eyes. She'd barely gotten any sleep. Sean had her up half the night doing what he called making love. They'd had sex in every position imaginable. Sean was so crazed with jealousy that while hitting it from back, he slapped her hard on the ass and asked repeatedly if Grip liked it that way too. Q took his taunts in stride and willed herself not to cry.

It wasn't fair that she was caught in the middle of a silly rap beef. Sean was her husband, and since day one she'd been his ride or die chick, but deep down inside she knew there was only so much more she could take. Sean's abuse was getting worse as his coke habit escalated. Surprised not to hear him snoring loudly beside her, Q turned her head to his side of the bed and found it empty. She was shocked. Despite Sean's rude remarks and sadistic ways, it kind of bothered her that he could've left without saying a word. In search of answers, Q got out of bed and put on her robe. To her surprise, as soon as she opened the door she spotted Ahsim sitting, reading the Post Dispatch newspaper.

Q was never one to be taken in by a pretty face and a smile, but Ahsim's mocha-colored skin and kissable lips caused her heart to skip a beat. He was fly as hell and his swagger was just right. Ahsim stood six feet three inches tall. He was 195 pounds and built like a West Indian god. The low-cut Caesar with waves he rocked blended like water into his perfectly lined and trimmed beard. His eyes were chestnut brown and shaped like diamonds.

That morning, he had donned a blue and orange Mets cap cocked slightly to the left; a blue bubble vest; blue, black, and white plaid lumberjack flannel; dark denim jeans; and a pair of blue and cream Chuck Taylor–inspired Diesel sneakers. His whole existence was intoxicating and should've been illegal in all fifty states. When he stood up, his legs were slightly bowed. Q just knew that a chocolate python lay on the inside of his pants.

"What are you doing sittin' outside my door?" she finally asked.

"My job," he answered, never taking his eyes off the paper.

"My husband hired you to guard me, not stalk me."

"Your husband hired me to keep an eye on you twenty-four hours of the day, so if you have a problem with that I suggest you take that up wit him."

Q looked at Ahsim like he was crazy. His cocky attitude might've intimidated others but he had her all the way fucked up.

"Let me explain something to you." She placed her hand on her hip and pointed her finger in his direction. "While you're on staff you will respect me and if you can't, I won't wait until my husband comes back from tour. I will fire you my damn self. Now do you understand that?"

Ahsim focused his attention on her. Q had completely forgotten that she wore no bra. Her brown nipples were hard, and poked through the satin fabric of her robe. Liking what he saw, Ahsim simply hit her with a crooked grin, resumed reading the paper, and replied, "I got you, ma, but check it: you ain't hire me so you can't fire me. Ol' boy don't even give you that much power so don't even flatter ya'self; and by the way, you might wanna cover ya'self up."

Q glanced down and remembered that underneath her robe she wore nothing. Slightly embarrassed, she quickly folded her arms across her chest.

"Speaking of my husband," she tried to continue as if nothing had happened, "have you seen him?"

"He left a couple of hours ago. What, you ain't know?" Ahsim asked, shocked.

"If I did I wouldn't have asked." Q was obviously hurt.

When she and Sean were first married, he would've never left without saying good-bye. She cherished his kisses and hugs before he walked out the door, but now all of that was a distant memory.

"He did have the chef prepare you a really nice breakfast, though." Ahsim tried to ease some of her pain.

"It's good. Tell the chef I'm not hungry. If anybody needs me, I'll be in my room getting dressed. You and I will be out for the rest of the day."

Queen Pynn

Q and Ahsim quietly sat opposite each other in the back of a silver Phantom. Q, her eyes concealed by a pair of black Balenciaga shades, tried her best to pretend as if he didn't exist. But the way his tongue toyed with the toothpick between his teeth only made her wonder what other kind of freaky tricks his tongue could do. The Jean Paul Gaultier cologne he wore wasn't helping much, either. The scent was Q's favorite. The song "Sex and Candy" instantly came to mind.

Crossing her legs tight, she closed her eyes and prayed that the erotic twitch in her clit and the forbidden thoughts in her mind would cease. Thankfully, the sound of a text message coming through on her phone helped distract her. Q flipped her cell phone open, saw who the sender was, and rolled her eyes. Not in the mood to talk, she shut her phone without replying. Ahsim noticed her reaction and took a mental note. Just as Q placed her phone in her bag, Ahsim's cell phone began to ring. He checked the screen, saw who the caller was, and answered.

"Hello?"

"What's going on?" Sean asked while inhaling smoke from a blunt.

"We're heading downtown right now. Q wanted to do a little shopping."

"That's what's up." He exhaled the smoke from his lungs. "Let her buy whatever she wants."

"Baby, hurry up and get off the phone." Ahsim could hear a woman whine in the background.

"Is that my husband?" Q screwed up her face, pissed.

Ahsim stalled for a second, then answered, "Yeah."

"Let me speak to him." She reached out her hand.

"Uh—"

"What you mean uh? Hand me the phone!"

Ahsim remembered that he was there to do a job, not play mediator, so he obliged Q's request without hesitation.

"Thank you," she snapped, snatching the phone from him. "Hello?"

"What's up, babe?" Sean wiped his nose.

He'd just finished doing a line of coke.

"So you mean to tell me you can call and check in wit' a muthafucka we barely know and not with me, your wife?"

"Calm down. I was gon' get at you later."

"You was gon' get at me later?" she repeated in disbelief. "Sean, you didn't even say good-bye to me when you left. Anything could'a happened to you when you got on that plane."

"But it didn't," he replied as the woman he was with kissed his neck. "I'm all right. You all right?"

"No, I'm not all right," she snapped.

"Sean." The woman stressed his name. "I want some dick."

"Hold up! Who the fuck was that?" Q yelled, ready to explode.

"Yo . . . let me hit you later." Sean eyes were at half-mast as the woman began to unzip his Yohji Yammamato Y-3 jeans.

"Sean, if you hang up this phone, I swear to God . . ."

"Q, chill out. I'ma call you in a minute; and answer the fuckin' phone."

"Sean!" Q shouted as he hung up. "I know this mutha-fucka didn't!" She took the phone away from her ear and looked at it.

Embarrassed, hurt, and humiliated weren't even the words to describe how she felt. Q wished that she had it in her to be on some ring-the-alarm shit, but her days of running in behind Sean and his latest mistress were over. She was tired of trying to prove herself worthy enough of his love. He would never see all things she kept locked inside her heart strictly for him. Q wasn't willing to play the broken-hearted girl anymore.

Swallowing the lump that had crept up her throat, she kindly handed Ahsim his phone, and sat back. Ahsim wanted desperately not to feel any kind of emotion for her, but the single tear that slipped down her cheek made him want to take her off to a distant land, where love was like breathing and hurt and pain didn't exist.

"You a'ight?" he asked, concerned.

"I'm fine." Q quickly wiped her face, determined not to let another tear drop.

For a while, she gazed out the window silently as Ahsim pondered why she stayed in such a fucked-up relationship. Sensing what was on his mind, Q opened up and said, "Things weren't always like this, you know. Sean used to be the sweetest man I ever knew, but once the money started rollin' in, he changed. I've been tryin' so hard to find my way back to the man he once was, but these days I don't know if it's possible."

"Yo." Ahsim looked at her. "I ain't even tryin' to get off into y'all relationship like that 'cause I ain't no therapist and it ain't none of my business but . . . can't you see you the only one tryin'?"

"Well, that's easier said then felt."

"Chicks fuck me up." He smirked.

"Chicks fuck you up and what?"

"It's nothing." He shook his head. "My fault, I shouldn't have even said that."

"It's cool, we talkin'." Q shrugged her shoulders with an attitude. "Say whatever it is you got to say. I'm grown, I can handle it."

"A'ight," Ahsim complied. "Y'all chicks will fight tooth and nail to hold on to a no-good muthafucka who treats like you shit. Make all the excuses for him in the world and he still got another chick suckin' his dick; and where you at? Sittin' in the car, cryin'."

"Excuse you." She snapped her neck, offended.

"No need for the pleasantries, ma, you excused. And if you catchin' an attitude 'cause I hurt yo' feelin's then I'm sorry, but I'm just statin' facts."

"First of all, my name ain't ma. It's Queen and I haven't given you permission to relax your standards. Second of all, you ain't statin' shit 'cause you don't know what the fuck you talkin' about." Q leaned forward furious. "And I shouldn't have ever asked your opinion. You ain't spittin' nothin' but a bunch of hired-help bullshit . . .

so do us both a favor; shut the fuck up, do your job, and guard something."

"Check this, Queen," Ahsim barked back. "I may be a guard, but I'm a man first and the man in me will not allow you to get away wit' all the rah-rah you just spat. The next time you speak to me, speak to me with respect. Otherwise, don't say shit. You so busy tellin' me what to guard. How bout you guard yo' heart, guard your emotions, guard you settling for less, and guard yo' mouth," Ahsim leaned close to her face.

Their lips were only inches apart.

"Now do you understand?"

Q rolled her eyes and leaned back against the seat. Pissed, she folded her arms across her chest. She would never admit it, but the reality was that everything Ahsim said was right. It ate her up inside. Instead of sticking up for herself, time and time again she excused Sean's intentions and pretended that everything was okay. She was the only one trying, and what made it even worse was coming to the realization that she was the only one in love.

"Ralph," she called out to the driver.

"Yes, ma'am." He glanced at her through the rearview mirror.

"Turn the radio up. That's my song."

"Sure thing, ma'am."

Ralph quickly turned up the volume. He hated to see Q upset. Ralph was willing to do anything within his power to make her happy. "Diva," by Beyonce, thumped from the speakers, hyping Q up. *Fuck all these niggas*, she thought as she pulled out her Dior cosmetic mirror. Q was about to do her, and that meant hitting the stores and spending an obscene amount of money on shit she didn't need. Ralph pulled up to the curb slowly. Once the car was parked, he got out and opened the coach doors.

Ahsim stepped out first to make sure their surroundings were safe, and to tell the store owner they were there.

After that was taken care of, Ralph signaled to Q that it was okay to step out. A light drizzle fell from the sky, but Ralph had everything covered. Before Q's foot even hit the pavement he'd already pulled out one of the two umbrellas conveniently located in each of the rear doors. Not a single hair on her head would be out of place. All eyes were on Q. Men stopped mid-stride just to catch a glimpse of her thick thighs, while some women admired and others tuned up their faces. It didn't matter. At that moment, she felt as if she were the superstar.

Dressed casually chic in a wife beater, gray stone-washed skinny jeans, and five-inch, black suede peep toe Christian Louboutin ankle boots, Q knew she was the bitch. Her hair was pulled back in a sleek ponytail. She wore no makeup, a pair of diamond stud earrings, her wedding ring, and a black patent leather Valentino purse with rosettes on the front.

Q ignored the onlookers and made her way through the doors. City Chic Boutique was one of her favorite stores in the Delmar Loop. She especially loved that it was black-owned, and it didn't hurt that the owner, Renee, was pretty nice, too. It didn't matter what time of the day it was she would always shut down the store for Q so she could shop by herself.

"How are you miss?" Tabitha hugged her and air-kissed both cheeks. "You look nice as always, and the boots are sick."

"Thank you, girl. Love the top." Q stepped back and appreciated the shirt Tabitha wore. "Please tell me it's one of your own."

"And you know it. Kaycee," Tabitha called out to one of her employees.

"Yes."

"Show Q where this top is. I have to make a phone call." Tabitha turned back to Q. "Let me know if you need anything."

"I will. Thanks, Tabitha."

"Look at you lookin' fly." Kaycee smiled as she escorted Q to the shirt rack.

"Thank you. I just threw on something today."

"I feel you, girl. I did too, but tell me; who is that fine-ass nigga you got wit' you?" Kaycee pointed.

Q glanced over her shoulder at Ahsim. He stood by the door in a b-boy stance still toying with the toothpick in his mouth. It fucked her up that he didn't try to hide the fact that he was admiring her frame from behind.

"That's Ahsim, my new bodyguard."

"I know you're happy. Shit, he can guard me any day." Kaycee licked her lips and blew him a kiss.

"Kaycee, please." Q rolled her eyes. "I am a married woman."

"Well, I'm single, horny as hell, and ready to fuck, so please give him my number. As a matter of fact, I think I'll do it myself."

With her shoulders pulled back, Kaycee switched over to Ahsim and sparked up a conversation. Q pretended not to care as she roamed the racks and shelves of clothes, but the thought of Ahsim being interested in someone other then her tortured her pride. Jealous, Q snuck a glance from the corner of her eye. Ahsim smiled as Kaycee placed her hand on his arm. Q loathed the fact that staring at him alone ignited a fire inside her heart that only he could put out. Spotting Kaycee coming her way, she swiftly turned her head.

"Homeboy is a winner for real," she announced gleefully.

"That's what's up," Q replied dryly. "You get his number?"

"Yeah, and I will be callin' him tonight."

"Good for you. Now, come on and ring me out. I got some other places I need to go."

In less then fifteen minutes, Q racked up $5,000 worth of merchandise. Half of the stuff she hadn't even really looked at. *Fuck the recession*, Q thought. Tabitha was ecstatic. Q tried her best to hide her attitude, but it was useless. She couldn't get a grasp on what kind of game Ahsim was playing, but she for damn sure was going to find out. Their next stop was a lingerie store called Soma Intimates. Once again, the owner loved Q so much that he was willing to close the store just for her.

As soon as she entered she was offered a complimentary glass of Dom and strawberries. Q drank the entire glass in one gulp. With a fresh glass in hand she went into the dressing room. Five pieces of lingerie and heels had already been picked out for her. Q stripped down and tried on the first one. It was a dusty blue, pleated, satin teddy with an elastic waist and lace trim. The teddy was made like a jumper. The panty part highlighted her voluptuous ass perfectly. She just had to know if Ahsim liked it, too.

"Ahsim," she called from inside the dressing room.

"What's good?"

"If I ask your opinion will you give me an honest answer?" she quizzed.

"Haven't we tried that already today?"

"Please."

"Depends."

"On what?" she asked, sliding back the velvet curtain.

Ahsim couldn't believe his eyes. Every part of him wanted Q in the worst way. Her honey-colored physique had more dips and curves then a roller coaster ride. Q stood in front of the full body mirror with her back to him. Ahsim couldn't help but notice just how fat her ass was.

"So what you think?"

"It's a'ight." He tried to play it cool. Ahsim couldn't let Q see him sweat.

"Really," she remarked, shocked.

"You asked for my opinion."

"Okay," she smirked, reentering the dressing room.

Q closed the curtain behind her. If Ahsim wanted to play games, she was gonna play right along with him. Q pulled the rubber band from her hair, allowing her hair to fall past her shoulders. The next outfit she tried on was a black, sheer lace babydoll dress. Lightly lined under-wire cups accentuated her breasts, pushing them up just right. Underneath, she wore a matching sheer lace g-string. This time, instead of going barefoot, she placed on a pair of black patent leather four-inch stilettos with a pointed toe.

"You ready?" she asked as the flame he'd ignited burned.

"Yeah," he answered, unprepared for what he was about to see.

Q pushed back the curtain and posed. Sheer appreciation was written all over Ahsim's face as he stood up straight and adjusted his dick. There was no denying it. Q had him hook, line, and sinker. All she had to do was the say the word and he'd fulfill her every desire. The curves of her hips were begging to be caressed. Ahsim could visualize himself cupping her breasts while placing erotic kisses from her collarbone to the heartbeat of her clit.

"You like?" She smiled wickedly.

"Ahh . . ." He flicked his hand back and forth, pretending not to be fazed. "You stepped up yo' game a li'l bit."

"A li'l bit," she repeated in disbelief.

"I mean, it look better then the last outfit."

Displeased with his answer, Q slammed the curtain shut once again. Ahsim was playing to hard to get, but she always caught her prey. She wasn't going to give up until she had Ahsim on his knees. The final outfit she tried on was a black lace, sheer cutout teddy. There were no straps; just a black string that tied around her neck like a halter.

The halter connected to a lace bra. sheer Black material streamed down the center of her stomach. Once the material reached her waist, it turned into a g-string. Q's goods were out for the world to see, but the only eyes she wanted on her were Ahsim's. This time, Q didn't make an announcement as she stepped out. She would allow her body to do all the talking.

Ahsim didn't even know that she was back in the room until he suddenly glanced up and saw her standing there. Q slowly sauntered toward him. The smell of her Viktor & Rolf perfume enticed his nose. Q was a Playboy bunny, Jet Beauty of the Week, and Eye Candy of the Month rolled up into one perfect woman. Ahsim loved that she wasn't runway-model thin, but tantalizingly thick in all the right places. Her stomach was as flat as a board, but her titties and ass were more then a mouthful. Q turned her back to his chest and pulled her hair over to the side, revealing her neck. Her plump ass was pressed up against Ahsim's hard dick. It seemed to get longer by the second.

"You mind untying this for me?" she asked seductively.

Instead of obliging her, Ahsim leaned down, gripped her waist tight, placed his lips on her ear and whispered, "I don't know what type of game you playin', but I'm the wrong nigga to fuck wit', so I suggest you take yo' pretty ass back into that dressing room and get dressed so we can get the fuck up outta of here."

Ahsim couldn't help but nibble and lick her ear just a little bit. The sensation sent shivers down Q's spine.

"And hurry up," he demanded, slapping her ass.

Doing as she was told, Q made her way back to the dressing room. She didn't know what part of the game this was. None of her tricks were working. Ahsim had her sewed up and there was no way she could get out. Ahsim, on the other hand, stood back and marveled at the way her ass cheeks bounced as she walked. It was going to take everything in him not to cross the line and lay it on her.

Part Two

Boogieman

Ahsim lay on his back, asleep in a pool of sweat. He tossed and turned repeatedly but to no avail. The white sheets that lay on top of him clung to his skin like a woman's grasp during sex. Thoughts of Q invaded his memory's museum. He'd summoned her there, into his dreams. Inside his nightmares was the only place they could be lovers without consequence. There he was, standing at the start of a long corridor that seemed to have no end.

To the side were rows and rows of mirrors trimmed in gold, going in different directions. He was trapped and it was freezing cold. Ahsim clenched his fist tight and began to walk slowly. With each step, mirages of Q appeared. Inside the mirrors, she floated above a pit of flames. A sinister grin graced the corner of her lips as she reached out for him.

Ahsim was captivated by her scarlet eyes. He should've been scared, but she was the most beautiful boogieman he'd ever seen. His conscious told him not to, but he stepped closer. He wanted to be where she was; but the closer he got, the colder he became. The touch of her hand would be the death of him. Ahsim looked down. Q could sense his hesitation.

"Come here," she said in the sweetest tone.

Ahsim promptly focused his attention on her again.

"I need you," she whispered as a tear made of blood traced her cheek.

The sadness that filled her eyes made Ahsim want to kiss all of her pain away. Fuck it, he'd played with fire before. Q was a guilty pleasure that, given the chance, he'd forever indulge in. This time nothing, not even the flames, would stop him from being close to her. Ahsim took hold of her fragile hand and stepped inside the burning blaze of fire. Finally, they were together.

Q grasped his face, gazed into his eyes, and smiled. Before Ahsim could realize his fate, her cold lips were upon his. The kiss was sensual; her tongue flicking against his. Then, suddenly, the blood in his veins became ice. The longer the kiss lasted, the harder it became to breathe.

Ahsim desperately wanted to fight, but dying never felt so good. Q had him locked within her web and no matter how hard he tried he would never get out. Just as Ahsim was about to take his last breath, he woke up. Frantically, he searched the room with his eyes. He was alive. It was all just a dream. Ahsim rubbed his eyes. He had to get Q out of his mind. There was no way he was going to let her cloud his judgment.

Sitting up, he ran his hands down his face and exhaled. His mouth was dry and he needed to take a piss. Ahsim looked down and realized that he needed a fresh set of sheets, too. Pulling the cover from over him, he got up. A newly rolled blunt called his name from the nightstand. Ahsim picked it up and tucked it behind his ear.

It was one of those summer nights that was so hot, the central air alone wouldn't do. He walked to the window and allowed what cool breeze there was outside to come through. Before he could make it to the bathroom, muffled voices by the pool caught his attention. Ahsim stared out the window in search of where the voices were coming from, but the trees in front of him blocked his view. Able to recognize Q's voice, he heard her shout, "No." On impulse, he reached for his gun and headed out the door. Ahsim ran down the steps and went out the back way that led to the pool. As he turned the corner he aimed his gun.

"Don't move," he ordered.

Q jumped and spun around.

"Ahsim, what the fuck are you doing?" she yelled, holding a towel in front of her naked body.

"I heard voices. I heard you yell 'no.' " His eyes darted around the pool area in pursuit of the other person.

"Are you fuckin' crazy? Put the gun down. I was singing a fuckin' song."

She bent down and picked up her iPod. Ahsim noticed that lying on the ground next to her foot was a platinum ring designed as a crown.

"See, 'you holdin' up traffic, green means Go,' " she sang.

Ahsim put the safety back on and placed the gun by his side.

"I could've sworn I heard you talkin' to someone." He continued to search around suspiciously.

"Well, no, I wasn't." She rolled her eyes. "I was about to take a swim, like I do every night."

Q dropped her towel and allowed her toned body to glisten under the moonlight. She'd never been ashamed of her body, so for Ahsim to see her naked was nothing. Ahsim tried to look away, but once his eyes centered on her raspberry nipples it was murder she wrote. Q sneered and sauntered toward the pool. Before Ahsim could blink, she'd dipped into the pool and disappeared under the turquoise water. Never one to miss a good show, he walked to the opposite end of the pool and sat down.

His feet dangled in the water like bait. Ahsim pulled the blunt from behind his ear and lit it. The herbal medicine inside calmed him down on the first hit. Buzzed, he glanced around and soaked up the view. The backyard was reminiscent of a Tuscan villa. It was completely closed in by hundreds of flowers, bushes, shrubs, and trees. Soft yellow lights gave the space a mellow feeling. Five wooden beach chairs and a fire pit sat on the opposite end of the pool, facing him.

There was even an outdoor bed, and a sofa. Q soared through the water, causing a rippling effect to spiral toward him. Unknowingly, she'd become his addiction. He thought of her every second of the day. Ahsim took another pull from the blunt and watched as she swam between his legs. Q came up from the water and placed her hands on his knees. Her long hair clung to the nape of her neck.

What she was about to do was wrong on so many levels, but the urgency of wanting him outweighed any common sense she possessed. She wanted to know what he liked, what he needed, what he wished for. Any fantasy he came with, she'd provide. She'd feed him, fuck him, taste him, suck him, it didn't matter. Q's eyes roamed over his physique. The tattoos that covered his chest and arms were pleading to be assaulted with wet kisses. Ahsim read her mind and put his hands under her arms to pull her up.

Beads of water dripped from Q's body as she gazed into his coffee-colored eyes. His arms were wrapped securely around her waist. The hard bulge inside his hooping shorts caused her clit to twitch. Tired of playing a game of cat-and-mouse, Ahsim pressed his full lips against hers. Q immediately became caught up in the warmth of his mouth. His kiss was spellbinding.

As he rotated between sucking her top and bottom lip, Ahsim manipulated the skin of her back with his fingertips and said,"Let me make love to you." Q's body fell limp in his embrace. She had to stop before things went too far, but the folds of her flesh yearned for him to stroke her clit slowly with his tongue. Setting aside the naughty thoughts in her mind, she pushed him back.

"What's the problem?" Ahsim asked, wanting more.

"I'm sorry. I should've never let things go this far. I'm trippin'." She paced back and forth. "If my husband ever finds out . . ." Her voice shook. "Oh my God, I gotta go."

Q snatched her towel and ran up the walkway, ashamed. Ahsim stood alone, wondering how things had spiraled out of control. Confused, he walked over to the ring and picked it up. It seemed oddly familiar. He just couldn't remember where he'd see it before. Determined to find out, he placed it inside his pocket and made his way back inside the house.

Queen Pynn

The next morning, things were awkward between Q and Ahsim. They barely said three words to one another, and when Sean called to check up on her, Q almost pissed on herself. Along with coke, Sean could sniff a liar from miles away. Ahsim had to choose his words just right, or Sean would be on the next flight home ready to kill both their asses. Thankfully, Ahsim played it cool. Sean didn't suspect a thing. Q took a look at herself as she stood in front of a full-length mirror.

It was the one Sunday a month she got to see her family. That morning they would be attending services at Unity Chapel Baptist church. It was the same church Q attended as a child, where she used to sing lead in the choir. She had to be on point. Q thought she looked elegant in a white fitted button-up shirt and gold, gray, and tan high-waisted pencil skirt. The sleeves of the shirt were rolled up, revealing her gold Frank Muller watch. A thin, gold, three-layered necklace that reached the top of her skirt accessorized the ensemble even more. On her feet, she rocked a pair of gold metallic, watersnake Jimmy Choo platforms.

Q donned her Oliver Peoples shades, grabbed her white, quilted Marc Jacobs bag, and signaled to Ahsim that she was ready to go. Not a word was spoken between them as they headed to Q's family church. Neither could find the right things to say, although so much needed to be said. Church services lasted two hours. Afterward, the entire family had lunch at Q's grandparents' house.

Q hated that her family still lived in the hood. Sean refused to give her any money to buy her grandparents a new home. The north side of St. Louis was filled with violence. Every other day someone got killed. Crackheads roamed the streets at night.

Young black girls fell victim to teenage pregnancy while young boys sold rocks for sneakers. Plus, the fact that her grandparents' house wasn't up to par didn't help much. The roof was caving in. There were numerous leaks in the ceiling. Anytime there was a heavy rain, their basement flooded. They had no central air. The only relief from the heat came from an air conditioner in their bedroom window.

Her mother wasn't doing any better. Due to the recession, she'd lost her job and was forced to move in with her parents sharing a room with Q's brother. It pained Q to the core to know she had the means to help her family but because of her selfish husband she wasn't able to. Q's immediate family consisted of her mother, Taylor; seventeen-year-old brother, Jay; grandfather, Ty; grandmother, Earlene; and Great Aunt Erniece. Earlene and Erniece were identical twins. They were seventy-one years old, but still as hip as they were in their younger days. After saying grace, the entire family, including Ahsim and Ralph, sat around the table eating and conversing. The topic of the moment was T.I. and his impending jail sentence.

"Now, that's some bullshit and you know it, Earlene," Erniece barked. "The hip-hop police been after T.I. since *Trap Muzik*. They knew then that what he was spittin' was the truth."

"I ain't say that the police hadn't been watchin' him, but the boy shouldn't been buying all them damn guns. That's what you get guards like Ahsim for," Earlene replied. "I gotta give it to him. His li'l ass do be talkin' that gangsta shit. He say, 'Just gimme some cocaine and somewhere to slang and I'm *straight*.' You can't tell me that ain't no real shit right there." She pounded her hand against the table, amped.

"You know who I like?" Q's brother Jay jumped in.

"Who?"

"Jay-Z."

"Aw, yeah." Earlene put down her fork and closed her eyes. "When I heard that 'Show Me What You Got' he had me, baby! Now, he ain't much on the eye—"

"Nah, he ain't," Erniece cut her off.

"But he smart," Earlene continued.

"Sho nuff," Erniece nodded. "*Banonsay* knew what she was doing when she hooked that retarded-lookin' muthafucka. She said, 'Fuck good looks; when I'm old, fat, titties hangin' down to my knees like Aretha, this nigga gon' be able to take care of me. Feed me all the Popeye's chicken I want.' "

"You got that right," Earlene agreed, laughing.

"Have you heard his song with John Legend?" Q asked before taking a sip of her lemonade.

"Girl, you know that's yo' Aunt 'Niece boo."

"Talk about a muthafucka that's fine." Erniece rolled her neck. "Every time I see him on the television, my panties get moist."

"Aunt Niece, that's enough." Q scrunched up her face as Ahsim laughed uncontrollably.

"Let him come to St. Louis. I'ma be in the front row, wit' my panties off, swingin 'em in the air. That lil' yellow nigga ain't gon' know what hit 'em; and he can dress."

"Yes, sir," Earlene concurred. "The man stay sharp."

"Sharper than a muthafuckin' switch blade."

"A'ight, Aunt 'Niece, Uncle Fred gon' find out you cheatin' on him and go crazy," Jay teased, referring to his aunt's ex-boyfriend.

"Shit." She screwed up her face. "Boy, please, Fred can kiss my ass."

"You ain't gotta front, Aunt 'Niece. We know you still love Uncle Fred."

"I ain't thinkin' about Fred and Fred ain't thinkin' about me."

"So, Ahsim," Q's grandfather spoke up. "How do you like guarding my granddaughter so far? I hope she ain't been too much trouble."

"Just a little bit," Ahsim joked.

"Q, you ain't been giving this man a hard time, have you?"

"Just a little bit." She looked at Ahsim and smiled.

Being around her family seemed to loosen the tension between them.

"Well, I'm just happy she got somebody to keep her

safe," Earlene commented. "Lord knows that good-for-nothin' Sean ain't gon' do it."

"Earlene, that's enough," Ty ordered.

"Nah, Ty, I got to speak my piece. It's because of him Q need a guard in the first place. Got all that money and walkin' around here actin' like a fool."

"He look like a goddamn monkey's ass," Erniece backed up her sister.

"Smell like one, too."

"All right, Mama." Taylor gave them both the evil eye.

"I'm just sayin'—"

"Well, you've said enough."

"All right, all right." Earlene raised her hand in defeat.

"Where is Sean, by the way?" Jay asked.

"Touring," Q answered, trying her best to hide her pain.

"Well, how come he ain't take you wit'em?" Erniece questioned.

"Auntie, wives don't really go on tour with their husbands. Besides, I trust Sean," Q lied.

"Shiiit, you's a good one, niece. Let 'em fuck wit' a bitch like me. He'll have a tracking device stuck up his ass."

"This conversation is officially over." Taylor got up from the table to empty her plate.

After dinner, Q and Ahsim sat on the porch enjoying the cool summer air. Ralph stood outside the car, puffing on a cigarette. A couple of neighborhood kids raced around playing tag. Rays from the sun seemed to dance across Q's face as she crossed her arms and embraced herself. Her entire presence was like the wind: soft, cool, and free. So many thoughts and secrets lay behind her slanted eyes.

Ahsim wanted to know the real woman behind the

magnetic smile. He had to make her see that she could trust him. She had no reason to run. Q was a rose ready to bloom. All she had to do was open her eyes and realize that she was worth so much more. There was a man out there who would love her for her, and, given the opportunity, Ahsim wanted to prove that he was that man.

"Your family is crazy as hell," he commented.

"Yeah, but I love 'em anyway." Q laughed as her cell began to ring.

The number came up on the screen as restricted, so she didn't answer.

"So you grew up on Holly Avenue?"

"Born and raised."

"That's hella crazy. My peoples live right off Carter."

"Get out of here. Really?" Q asked, amazed.

"Yeah." Ahsim nodded.

"Wonder why we never ran into each other?"

"That's a good question." His eyes roamed over her physique.

Q turned away and smiled.

"I'ma be honest wit' you, Q. I thought you grew up wit' paper."

"What made you think that?"

"The way you carry yo'self. You fly than a mutha-fucka."

"Thanks," she giggled. "But, nah. My peoples making it, but they ain't got much. I wish I could do more but," she inhaled deeply and shook her head. "About last night—"

"You good, ma," he cut her off. "Your secret safe wit' me."

"But that's what I'm afraid of. Secrets can cause a lot of problems."

"Quit trippin'. All we did was kiss; it's nothing."

"Yeah, okay," Q rolled her eyes and laughed. "Don't front; that kiss had you weak in the knees."

"Man, please." he waved her off.

"A'ight, we'll see." She turned and sashayed back into the house. "We'll see."

Queen Pynn

It was one of those lazy Monday afternoons that felt like Sunday. Rain poured heavily from the sky. Q sat cross-legged on the couch underneath a chocolate wool throw. The sound of rain tapping against the windowpane soothed her. Q picked up her favorite mug filled with green tea and took a sip. The relaxing drink warmed her insides. Content, she placed the cup back on a coaster and picked up the remote.

For a while, she roamed aimlessly through the channels until she came to the E! network. *The Daily 10* was on. Q stretched her legs and leaned her back against the arm of the couch. The show was down to its last ten minutes of airtime, but Q still didn't want to miss it. The number two story was whether Lindsay Lohan and Samantha Ronson were still together. Q chuckled to herself. Lindsay hadn't had a hit movie in years and still managed to be newsworthy.

The number one story would be on after the break. While a commercial for Rothman Furniture played, Q wondered if she should have the chef make her something for dinner or go out. The sound of her cell phone ringing distracted her from her thoughts. Q recognized the number on the screen and sucked her teeth.

"What?" she answered with an attitude. "I ain't got nothing to say to you," she spat. "When I wanted to talk you was too busy wit' that bitch, so be wit' the bitch . . .

No, you don't love me. Yeah, okay, whateva," she shot, hanging up the phone. "He got me fucked up."

"Who got you fucked up?" Ahsim asked, taking a seat next to her.

"Nobody." She folded her arms under her breasts and resumed watching television.

The Daily 10 was back on.

"The number one story for the day is," Sal Masekela said into the camera, "while partying in Miami, Midwest rapper Sean Pynn was caught all over Czech supermodel Jasmine Kurkova."

Video footage of the two of them kissing popped onto the screen.

"The two were seen over the weekend in Miami at Club Mansion. Now, you ask what makes this newsworthy. Well, Sean is married . . . and has been for quite a while to *Maxim* magazine hottie Queen. We here at *The Daily 10* wonder how Mrs. Pynn feels about this."

Q's heart sank to her knees. She'd tried to be blind to Sean's cheating ways, but he'd never embarrassed her like this before. Over the years she'd heard through the grapevine of his trysts with R&B superstars and A-list actresses, but none had been made public knowledge. Q only had herself to blame. The more time she let pass, the further down she became on his to-do list.

She noticed the calls he'd get that would cause him to leave the room, but she looked past them. She wanted to curl up in a ball and cry, but crying never kept him home anyway. Nothing she ever did got through to him. This time Sean had taken things too far. Public humiliation was the worst kind of pain Q could endure. He'd shattered her heart, and nothing he could ever say or do would mend it again.

"I can't believe this muthafucka," she spat, turning off the TV.

"Damn ol' boy doing it like that," Ahsim said, dumbfounded.

"Really?" Q looked at him like he was stupid.

"My bad. I ain't mean it like that," he apologized. "So what you gon' do?"

"What can I do? I signed a stupid prenup that says if I leave I get nothing. As long as I'm Sean's wife I'm entitled to everything. So fuck it, I can't leave. I'm not going back to the fuckin' hood. Been there, done that. Besides, that crazy muthafucka already said if I try to leave he would kill me, so you tell me what I should do."

"Go to the fuckin' police."

"I already tried that. The police won't listen to me and neither did Sean's mother or father. When I tried to talk to them they basically gave me their ass to kiss. And what fucks me up the most is his parents didn't even believe in him at first. They thought rappin' was a waste of time, but now that Sean is rich, guess who his biggest fans are."

"That's fucked up. I mean, the only advice I can give you is to leave, but obviously that's not an option. So I don't know what you can do." He massaged his chin thoughtfully.

"I just wish I could get away from this muthafucka. It's like he's just determined to hurt me." Q's bottom lip trembled as tears streamed down her face. "I wish I could kill him."

Suddenly, the house phone began to ring. A moment later, Rosa, the maid, came into the sitting room.

"Miss," Rosa said, "it's your mother."

"Tell her I'm busy. I'll call her back later," she cried.

"Okay."

"Yo, Q, chill out." Ahsim rubbed her knee. "Cryin' ain't even you."

"I know, it just hurts." She covered her face with her hands as the phone rang again.

"I'm sorry, ma'am, but it's a reporter on the phone from *US Weekly* magazine. She wants to know how you feel about the footage."

"How does it look like I feel, Rosa?" Q snapped, heated. "My husband is off somewhere fuckin' some Czech bitch and the whole world knows about it! How in the fuck would you feel?"

"Rosa," Ahsim intervened, calmly. "First, tell the reporter no comment. If anybody else from the media calls, tell them that Mrs. Pynn will not be taking any phone calls, a'ight?"

"Yes, sir." She turned to leave.

"And Rosa."

"Yes, Mr. Ahsim." She turned back around.

"Give me and Mrs. Pynn a minute alone."

"Sure thing." She closed the door behind her.

"Now, back to you, beautiful." Ahsim scooted closer to Q. "You are way too fly to be sweatin' some lame-ass nigga."

"No, I'm not." She sniffed as he caressed her cheek with his thumb.

"I know it hurts, ma, but feelin' sorry for yourself ain't gon' change the situation."

Q took a hold of Ahsim's hand.

"Well, help me get over it then." She shamelessly kissed the palm of it.

"Fuckin' me ain't gon' stop the pain, either." He took her face into his hands and passionately kissed her lips.

"No, but it'll make me feel good," Q whispered, placing a trail of kisses down his neck.

Ahsim swiftly pulled his T-shirt over his head, then removed her tank top. Filled with desire, he gazed into her eyes and slowly peeled down her leggings. To his surprise, she wore no panties or bra. Ahsim stripped off his clothes and knelt before her. Q parted her legs and welcomed his tongue on her clit.

Ahsim slithered his tongue like a snake over the lips of her pussy. Q closed her eyes tight and enjoyed the sensation. Her freshly manicured nails massaged his head as he licked and bit her clit with manic aggression.

"Ahsim . . . shit," she purred.

Ahsim made his way up. He pushed her breasts together and began manipulating her nipples with his tongue. Her breasts were his favorite part of her. Q tried to be ladylike, but the way his tongue flicked across her nipples drove her insane. She couldn't help but touch herself. Forbidden thoughts of all the freaky things she wanted to try crammed her mind. Ahsim teasingly slid his dick up and down the center of her wet slit.

Q ached for him to enter her. She was beyond aroused. As the tips of her fingers played with her clit, Ahsim grabbed his hard dick and inserted himself deep within her valley. Q's hand immediately went from her clit to his back as her eyes flew open and she gasped. Ten inches of chocolate, brown sugar was slowly rockin' her pussy to sleep.

Q scratched his back in agony and moaned, "Ooh, daddy, you feel so good."

A cornucopia of pleasure and pain traveled throughout her pelvis, all the way down to her toes. Each stroke sent her to the moon where her breasts kissed the stars. Their warm bodies melted into one another, becoming one. Before Q knew it, she'd been flipped over. Her hands gripped the arm of the couch in anticipation of him entering her again. Sticky white cream saturated Ahsim's dick. The visual turned him on even more. Q's pussy was the best. Back inside, he sped up his pace.

"Ahh," she yelled, overtaken by the size of him.

"You gotta be quiet, ma," he said as she caught his thrust and threw it back at him.

"I can't," Q whined. "It feels too good. You gon' make me cum, baby. Ooh."

Ahsim leaned forward and placed his hand over her mouth so no one would be able to hear her screams. Together they both came. A rush of energy surged through their bodies. Ahsim fell limp onto Q's back, her breasts cupped in his hands. Q breathed in and out. What she and Ahsim had just created was sinful and decadent, but the thought still remained: why did she feel so empty?

Queen Pynn

Ahsim lay on his back with his right hand under his head and his left on the curve of Q's hip. She straddled him, riding him slowly. The woman was a beast in the bedroom. They'd been having sex all night. Now, it was early afternoon and Q still couldn't get enough of him. Q was riding a wave of ecstasy. She'd called on God in every language known to man. Ahsim fucked her so good that she was willing to give him anything. She'd give him candy, buy him diamonds, and feed him breakfast in bed. He could have all her money. Whatever he wanted he could have, as long as he didn't take his dick away.

"Ooh, I love this dick." She eyed him hungrily and bit her bottom lip.

"Show me how much you love it then," Ahsim challenged.

"Anything for you, daddy." She smiled, while easing her way down.

Q took his rock solid dick into her hands and placed it inside her wanting mouth. Every lick was sinful and pleasing to her palette. The rigid veins of his dick thumped against the bud of her tongue. Ahsim couldn't contain himself. If Q continued to suck his dick with such reckless abandon, he was sure to explode.

"Fuck . . . I told you to show me, but damn," he groaned.

Hearing his reaction only turned Q on more. She wanted him to cum, so she bobbed her head at a faster pace.

"Ahh," he moaned loudly as she deep-throated his dick.

Q sensed that he was about to cum, so she eased him out of her mouth and flicked her tongue across the tip. Ahsim was done, finito, finished. Cum shot from his penis onto Q's hands. She happily jerked his shaft until every last drop was out.

"Goddamn, you the shit," he panted heavily.

"I aim to please." She winked, then got up to go to the bathroom.

After washing her hands and rinsing with mouthwash, she pulled her hair up into a loose ponytail. Q felt happier then she had in years. She and Ahsim connected on an emotional and physical level. He understood her feelings, and the way he made her body quiver took her attraction for him to new levels. Q turned off the light and went back into her bedroom. Ahsim sat on Sean's side of the bed, beckoning her.

"No, baby, we gotta get up, time for us to get dressed." She grabbed a T-shirt and threw it on.

"You right," he reluctantly agreed.

"I know I am." She sauntered over and tenderly pecked his lips. "Ooh, I got a' idea." She jumped back, excited.

"What's up?"

"We should get out of town for day or two while Sean is still gone. Maybe go to Chicago or something. That way we don't have to hide or sneak around."

"That don't sound to bad." Ahsim stepped into his boxers. "Maybe—"

"Mrs. Pynn." Rosa tapped on the door.

"Yes?" Q covered Ahsim's mouth.

"Your husband is on the phone. He'd like to speak to you."

"Okay, I'll take the call from the phone in here."

"Sure thing, miss."

Q removed her hand from Ahsim's mouth and crept over to the door. She had to make sure the coast was clear; it was.

"Oh my God." She frantically spun around on her heels and faced Ahsim. "Has he called you? I bet you he has. He's gonna wonder why you haven't answered the phone."

"Calm down." Ahsim picked up his phone. "You spazzin' for nothing. He ain't even called me."

"Thank God." Q placed her hand on her chest and let out a sigh of relief.

Nervous as hell, she sat on her side of the bed and picked up the phone.

"Hello?"

"Baby," Sean cried into the phone.

"What, Sean?"

"I know you mad at me but I can explain. The paparazzi set me up. They Photoshopped that shit, I swear. I put that on everything I love; I ain't fuckin' with that bitch. You know I wouldn't do you like that."

Q exhaled and rolled her eyes to the ceiling.

"The paparazzi can't Photoshop a video tape, dummy."

"I'm tellin' you, baby, it's some new technology out there. That wasn't me." He tried his best to convince her. "But look I need you to do me a favor."

"I knew it was something," she scoffed. "What do you want now, Sean?"

"I need you to release a statement saying that although you and I are going through a difficult time, you believe in me one hundred percent and that you ask that the media give us our privacy," he slowly read from the paper in front of him.

"I wish I could," Q hissed.

"C'mon, baby, get off the bullshit."

"The only reason you even on this phone is because your publicist told you to call," she spat. "You don't give a fuck about me. This wouldn't be the first time you've dipped out on me or the last, so how about you do us both a favor and tell the truth for once in your life."

Ahsim sat behind her, pleased to hear her stick up for herself.

"You right," Sean shockingly agreed. "I ain't gon' even front. It was me, but fuck all that. You my bitch. I was just fuckin' that broad. I was gon' get right back. I swear to God, Q, from day one you the only chick that's been able to capture my heart."

Q inhaled deeply and held her breath.

"Tell me you still love me." Sean just had to know.

It took everything in her to spit out the words but she did anyway. "I love you." She let out an exasperated breath.

"That's my girl," Sean responded, relieved.

"You gon' release that statement for me?"

"Mm-hmm."

"That's what's up," he said, pleased. "I love you."

"Yep."

"Holla," he said before hanging up.

Q shook her head and hung up too.

"I hope you just told that nigga you loved him to buy some time," Ahsim spoke up as soon as she got off the phone.

"Buy some time for what?" Q asked, perplexed. "We discussed this. I can't leave him. Plus, this shit is fucked up anyway," she realized. "I just fucked you in the bed me and my husband share. I can't keep on doing this wit' you."

"That's really how you feel?"

"Yeah, this shit is foul." Q inhaled deeply, then ran her fingers through her hair, overwhelmed. "Besides, you don't wanna fuck wit' a chick like me. I'm no good."

"Look, ma." Ahsim stayed cool, calm, and collected. "I like you—"

"Ahsim," Q cut him off.

"Shh." He placed his index finger on her lips. "I'm talkin'. I'ma do you a favor and fall back. Give you a minute to figure things out. When you have everything figured out, come holla at me."

And with that said, he grabbed the rest of his things and left her behind, speechless.

Part Three

Supreme Bitch

Q was accustomed to hiding her feelings. Her way of life was to keep her cards close to her chest and never reveal her hand. But lately her emotions were spinning out of control. Ahsim had come into her life and reminded her of how love was supposed to feel. For a long time it had been only a one-sided emotion. Plain and simple, Ahsim was the truth. Q just couldn't allow him to get the best of her. Fuckin' with him wasn't a part of her plan, and he for damn sure wasn't going to be the reason she got sidetracked.

Plus, sticking by her husband's side was becoming harder to do by the day. Instead of dealing with his infidelity with a glass of wine and a shopping spree like she'd done in the past, she'd had to face it in front of the world. That afternoon, she was attending a charity luncheon at which she would be presented an award for her commitment and contributions to the Boys and Girls Club of St. Louis.

Q knew there would be a bunch of bitter, lonely bitches snickering and talking shit behind her back. She had to remind herself that half the ladies' husbands were cheating on them, too. Once her hat was on straight, Q grabbed her Carlos Falchi clutch purse and headed to the door. Ahsim stood waiting for her, posted like a king.

She hadn't laid eyes on him since their discussion earlier that day. His hair was freshly lined and cut by the in-house barber. A toothpick hung from the corner of his mouth. There was nothing special about his outfit, but the simplicity of it caused the lips of her pussy to coat with cream. Ahsim looked good as hell in a white T-shirt, slightly baggy, dark denim jeans, and all-white shell toe Adidas. A gold rosary hung from his neck.

"You ready?" he asked with somewhat of an attitude, taking the toothpick from his mouth.

"Yeah," she replied with a lustful hint in her eye.

"Have a good time, miss." Rosa smiled, opening the door for them.

"Thanks, Rosa."

Q stepped outside into the bright July sun. To her surprise, in the driveway were three different cars: a 2009 black Mercedes-Benz SLR McLaren, silver Maybach 62, and a Koenigsegg CCX, which was the third-fastest car in the world. Each car was filled with designer bags from Chanel, Bergdorf Goodman, and Barneys New York.

"They're all from Mr. Pynn," Rosa gushed, thrilled.

Q was overwhelmed with a mixture of emotions. A part of her was flattered by the expensive gifts, but the part of her with some sense knew that no amount of cars or clothes would be able to make up for his betrayal or the excruciating pain in her heart.

"Send it all back," she demanded.

"Are you sure, ma'am?" Rosa asked, astonished.

"Positive," she replied getting into the car.

A slight smile crept onto Ahsim's face as he headed around the opposite side to get in. He was glad to see that Q couldn't be bought with materialistic bullshit. Twenty minutes later, they arrived at the Chase Park Plaza Hotel. Ahsim stepped out and surveyed his surroundings. Everything on the surface seemed cool so he turned and reached for Q's hand. As soon as she stepped out of the Phantom, the whispers about Sean's infidelity began. From behind her shades she could see the other women gawk and stare.

She knew damn well it wasn't because of what she wore. The peach/apricot tiger print Rachel Roy dress and gold Versace slingback heels were to die for. For a second, Q wondered if should she climb back in the car and go home. Maybe it was too soon to show her face.

"Q." Roc's Brazilian girlfriend, Annalisa, approached her with open arms.

"Anna." Q ran into her arms.

"Are you okay? I heard about what happened on the radio this morning."

"You along with everyone else in America," Q replied sarcastically. "Nah, I'm good. Have the chickens started cluckin' yet?"

"You know they have, but fuck 'em. Next week it'll be one of their husbands in the news and we'll be talkin' about them."

"Right," Q chuckled.

"Nevertheless, you look beautiful."

"Thanks, so do you," Q said honestly. Annalisa and Giselle Bundchen could have been twins. "The double platform Christian Louboutins are off the hook, sweetie."

"I just bought 'em yesterday." Annalisa flexed her foot. "Now, come on. You got a' award to accept." She linked arms with Q and escorted her in.

The Khorassan Ballroom was breathtaking. It was the largest event space the Chase offered. A mixture of square and rectangle tables were elegantly designed with pink floral embroidered linens, bountiful floral center pieces, and organza chair coverings. Twenty-foot birch trees strung with pink petals and votives added a little touch of spice to the room. Q and Annalisa sat together along with Nelly's girlfriend, Ashanti, and Chingy's latest jump-off.

"Did you write a speech?" Annalisa inquired.

"I wrote a li'l something down." Q took a sip of her cucumber water.

"I don't know if you heard yet," Anna said, unfolding her napkin and placing it in her lap, "but Grip wrote another dis record about Sean."

"Oh my God. I wish they would just stop."

"Who you tellin'. The whole thing is ridiculous and out of control. They're both good at what they do and they're both gettin' money, but somebody just has to be the king of the Midwest."

"It's silly."

"I just hope things calm down before somebody gets hurt. Lord knows we don't want another Tupac and Biggie on our hands."

"All we can do is pray for the best, girl," Q declared.

"Speaking of praying for the best," Anna whispered as the MC for the event called for everyone's attention. "I've been having my own share of problems, too, with Roc."

"Problems like what?"

"His ass is cheatin' on me again."

"With who?" Q looked at her, stunned. "Please tell me not that one girl. What was her name?"

"Dena; nah, it ain't her. This some new mystery bitch. I can't find out shit about her. All I know is they been fuckin' around for a minute and I'm starting to think whoever this chick is, he must really like her."

"Anna, please." Q dismissed her with a wave of the

hand. "You said the same thing about Dena, but look how that shit turned out. He copped you a five-carat purple diamond ring and gave Dena his ass to kiss."

"Yeah, but that was then. This new chick really got her claws in him. He won't even make love to me no more."

"Are you serious?"

"Yeah." Annalisa choked back the tears that begged to spill from her eyes. "I don't know what to do anymore. I've tried everything. I've tried lingerie, lettin' him fuck me in my ass," she whispered. "I even suggested a three-some with another girl but he still won't give me the time of the day. I just wish I could get rid of this bitch. Awhile ago I followed him."

"For real," Q responded stunned. "Did you find out anything?"

"No, my dumb ass ended up losing him at the light," Annalisa giggled. "I did go through his phone and get her number."

"Did you talk to her?"

"No. Every time I call the number she won't answer the phone."

"Hmm . . . Well if you need my help finding out who this chick is I'll help you," Q offered.

"Thanks, Q, but how you gon' help me without gettin' caught?"

"Girl, please, don't sleep. I'm the type of bitch they never saw coming."

Queen Pynn

Q had been dreading this day all week. It was Friday: the day Sean came home. He'd only been back a couple of hours and was already getting on her nerves. Sean stood over her, yelling and spewing spit with a bottle of Grey Goose in hand. He drunkenly pointed his finger in her face as she gazed absently at the plush carpeted floor. Q didn't even have it in her to argue back. All of her energy was gone. Besides, half the stuff he was saying he wouldn't even remember once he sobered up, so she simply tuned him out and let him say whatever it was he had to say.

"So, what, you don't love me no more?" He flung his arm, spilling vodka on the floor.

"I never said that."

"Then what the fuck are you sayin'?" he yelled.

"Can you please stop yellin' at me?"

Sean stepped back and looked at her.

"On the real, Q, you can stop wit' the innocent act, straight up. You always tryin' to make me look like the bad guy. Yo' ass be on some foul shit, too. Let's not forget how you stole a hundred-fifty Gs from my bank account. I should've killed yo' ass then. You's a dirty bitch and both of us know it."

"I didn't steal shit," Q shot, fed up.

She was sick of him thinking that just because he put a ring on her finger and some clothes on her back, she was obligated to be treated like shit.

"I'm your wife." She pointed toward her chest. "I'm entitled to that money. Besides, all I was tryin' to do was help my family. You know my grandfather's sick."

"Boo-hoo-hoo." Sean put his hands up to his eyes and pretended to cry. "Poor Q. I think the police will think differently. What you did is called theft, sweetie, but fuck all that. Why you change yo' cell number? I've been tryin' to call you."

"No, you haven't."

He paused to gather his thoughts. "How the fuck," he said, "you gon' tell me what I did. I did call yo' muthafuckin' ass."

"No, you didn't. You must have me confused wit' that other bitch," Q spat sarcastically.

"Hold up." He checked his phone, stumbling backward.

Sean scrolled through his call log and saw that he had been dialing the wrong number.

"Damn, you sholl is right. I was callin' Tameka the whole time but fuck all that. Ain't nobody tell you to change your fuckin' number. Call T-Mobile and have them change it back."

"I can't."

"What the fuck can you do?" He cocked his head in disgust. "You can't cook. You can't suck dick, you fat. All you know how to do is run yo' muthafuckin' mouth." He mushed her in the head, causing her neck to jerk back.

"Mr. Pynn," Rosa interrupted.

"What the fuck is it, Rosa? I'm so sick of yo' fresh-off-the-boat ass, I don't know what to do. Can't you see me and my wife having a conversation?"

"Your barber is here, sir. He's waiting for you downstairs."

"That's what's up." He perked up, excited. "A nigga about to get fresh." He danced, rocking his booty from left to right.

"And Mr. Ahsim would like to speak to you."

Q's heart skipped a beat. She wondered what he could possibly want to talk to Sean about.

"A'ight, a'ight." Sean shooed Rosa away as he stood in front of the mirror and did a number of jailhouse poses.

Once he was done, he looked at Q and took another swig from the bottle.

"I'ma deal wit' yo' ass when I get done."

Q sucked her teeth and watched him leave the room. Sean's cruel words didn't mean much to her. He'd said far worse in the past. Plus, he was high off God-knows-what. Q walked down the hall and entered her private dressing room as if nothing were wrong. The entire glam squad was there ready to doll her up. She and Sean were having dinner with Roc so he could discuss being released from his contract.

"So, how you want your hair?" Delicious, her beautician, asked.

"You can give me some soft Chinese-cut bangs and loose curls."

Downstairs, Sean sat with his eyes closed and neck back. His barber was shaving his neck with Cade shaving cream and a straight razor. Ahsim stood in the doorway with his hands in his pockets. He'd heard Sean and Q's entire verbal exchange. The killer in him wanted to take the razor and slit Sean's throat. Ahsim placed the thought aside, cleared his throat, and said, "Yo, Sean, can I holla at you for a second?"

"Go 'head." Sean tried his best not to move.

"I know you and Q going out, so I was wondering could I have the night off? I got this li'l shorty I'm tryin' to get wit'."

"You good, my guard Big Black is here."

"Good lookin' out. You and Q have a good time," Ahsim turned to leave.

"You do the same. And, Ahsim," Sean called out.

"What's up?"

"Everything been cool?"

"Yeah . . . Q straight. I think you worrying for nothing," Ahsim assured.

"I feel you, but you gotta keep your eye on her. Q can be a li'l sneaky muthafucka when she wants to."

Queen Pynn

"I am a diamond cluster hustler-Queen bitch supreme bitch-" Q rapped as she applied a coat of clear MAC lip gloss to her lips.

She was finally dressed and ready to go after three hours. It sickened her that she would have to put on a fake smile and act as if she and Sean were as happy as could be. The love they once shared was dead and gone, and destined never to return again. He was as heartless as Kanye's song. Every night when she closed her eyes to go to sleep, she saw him in her nightmares.

"Q," he yelled from bottom of the stairs. "Bring yo' ass on. The car is waiting."

Q curled her upper lip. She was starting to really hate his guts. Irate, she flicked her hair behind her shoulders and descended the steps. She expected for Ahsim to be there, marveling at her strapless, gold Dolce & Gabbana dress and black, peep toe Jimmy Choo heels, but he wasn't. To her disappointment, only Sean, his pot'nah, Mo B, and Big Black were there.

"Damn, it took you long enough," Sean complained, visibly high by his dilated pupils. "I swear to God, Q. I just got diagnosed with smack'um disease and you look like my first candidate."

"Whatever, Sean. Where is Ahsim?" she questioned, worried.

"On a date. Now, come on. We already half an hour late."

Queen Pynn

Mihali's was a distinctive premier chophouse and bar with stunning sultry décor. The restaurant served more than 400 different wine selections, and on the weekend there was live entertainment. Underground soul singer Timothy Bloom was performing that night. The maitre d' escorted Q and Sean to their table, where Roc waited.

Roc stood up to greet them. There was no way Q could deny his sex appeal. He wasn't an around-the-way hood-boy who rocked a wife beater and jeans, but a mobster who donned only the finest Italian suits. Roc was the type of man who made your pussy sing songs of erotic bliss. He was a thirty-seven-year-old, six-foot-one, 225 lb., all-the-way live, full-blooded, Italian god. His skin was golden tan and his sky-blue eyes were the prettiest Q had ever seen. A light, scruffy beard outlined his cheek and jaw. The Armani Privé suit he rocked was handstitched and tailor-made to fit.

"My man." He hugged Sean patting his back. "You're late, but it's good to see you."

"My bad." Sean stared at Q. "Shit got hectic back at the crib."

Roc could smell the liquor on his breath from a mile away.

"It's my fault we're late. It took me longer then I thought it would to get dressed," Q said.

"Well, I must say the wait was worth it." Roc took her hand and softly kissed the outside. "How are you, beautiful?"

"Fine, thanks." Q blushed.

"Where is Annalisa?" Sean questioned.

"Ahh, we broke up, man." He smirked.

"Really?" Q spoke up, surprised.

"Yeah, I think I'm in love with someone else."

"Damn, I'ma have to call Annalisa and see how she's doing," she said, wanting to know what went down.

"You know my homeboy, Mo B," Sean chimed in.

"Yes" Roc shook his hand.

"Have a seat, baby," Sean pulled out Q's chair.

Q gazed around the restaurant before sitting to make sure he was talking to her. It fucked her up how in front of others Sean could be so nice and kind. No one would believe that the entire car ride over to the restaurant, he had cussed her out like a dog while doing lines of cocaine. Q had been called every foul name in the book.

"So, Sean," Roc said, sitting down, "I see you started hittin' the bottle early. I thought we discussed that." He sounded displeased.

"Ahh, you know." Sean wiped his nose, nervous. "Ain't nothin' wrong wit' a li'l sip now and then. As a matter of fact, let me show you a token of my appreciation by ordering us a bottle of wine." Sean raised his hand and signaled to the waiter.

"Yes, sir?"

"I'd like to order a bottle of your finest wine."

"Would a 1995 Chateau Margaux do?" the waiter asked.

"I don't know what the fuck that is, but yeah, I'm wit' it."

"I'll have a bottle brought right over."

Once their orders were placed, everyone sat around the table quietly eating their first course, except Sean. He'd suddenly lost his appetite. Maybe it was because he'd taken two trips to the restroom to sniff coke. During the course of the meal, Q couldn't help but steal glances at Roc. His eyes were amazing. She could get lost in them eyes forever.

"Sean." Roc wiped the corners of his mouth with his napkin. "What's up? I know you didn't invite me to dinner to talk about nothing."

"Nah, nah, my bad." Sean remembered what they were there for. "What I wanted to say was, uh . . ." he looked around the table nervously. "I've produced two triple platinum albums in the last year-and-a-half. We've made a lot of money, but I just feel like it's time for me to move on. Sony is offering me a nice deal. They even willing to buy me out of my contract wit' you. And, I mean, don't get me wrong, I appreciate everything you've done, but I just think I'll have a better look over there."

"A better look, huh?" Roc sat back in his chair and laughed. "Murder Mob ain't good enough for you no more?"

"I'm not sayin' that—"

"Shut up," Roc cut him off and leaned forward. "Just to let you know, a little birdie already told me about your deal with Sony. But let me remind you of something: when yo' black ass was piss poor and couldn't get a record deal for shit, I saved you. Them Jew muthafuckas didn't want to touch you, but now that you back on top they checkin' for you and yo' gullible ass fallin' for it. Well, let me explain something to you. You signed a five-album deal. You've only delivered two, which means you got three more to go, but even after that I get first right of refusal over your next album, so it looks like you'll be a Murder nigga for life."

Sean's nostrils flared. It was taking everything in him not to reach across the table and choke the shit out of Roc. If it weren't for the .45 he was sure Roc had tucked in his waist and the three henchmen by the door, he would have.

"This burnt pizza muthafucka got us fucked up." Mo B jumped up.

"I suggest you get a hold of your friend," Roc warned as he resumed eating his food, unfazed.

He wasn't the type to talk smack. He just twisted caps.

"Cuz, chill out," Sean demanded.

Mo B ice grilled Roc, but did as he was told.

"Yo, Roc, all that callin' me out my name and shit ain't even necessary. I came here to talk to you like a man, so respect me as one, 'cause frankly, I could've been on some foul shit like you and signed the contract without giving a fuck. "

"Explain to me how I treated you foul?" Roc sat back in his chair and cocked his head to the side.

"When I signed wit' you I expected you to be fair. I trusted you, and you played off that shit. I ain't understand them words in that contract. I was just a nigga tryin' to get put on. You ain't have to do me like that. You making most of the profit, Roc. Yo' take already bigger then mine and you still taking from me. That shit ain't fair and you know it."

"You a funny guy." Roc pointed his fork toward Sean and chuckled.

"This cat straight take us as a joke," Mo B shot, amped as hell.

"Yo, I'm done." Sean threw down his napkin and stood up.

The effect of the cocaine was making him feel like Superman. At that moment, he could care less that Roc was affiliated with the mob.

"And I'll tell you what. I ain't fuckin' wit' you no more. I'm signing wit' Sony and that's that. If you got a problem wit' it then buck . . . otherwise, this is done."

"Do what you gotta do and see where it takes you, but I suggest you do yo'self a favor and live." Roc lit a Bolivar cigar and stared at Sean.

The cold glare in Roc's eye sent chills throughout Sean's body. Roc wasn't a man who made idle threats.

"C'mon, Q," Sean said, never taking his eyes off of him.

Inside the limo, Sean leaned back against the seat and loosened his tie. Anger was written all over his face. Q was unsure of what to say or do. Sean was so on edge that anything she did might set him off, but she didn't care. For once Sean had gotten what he deserved. Happy with the outcome, she placed her hand on his shoulder.

"Get the fuck off me." He shrugged his arm away. "It's your fuckin' fault I'm in this position in the first place."

"What?" She looked at him, puzzled.

"Cause of yo' stupid ass we was late! If we would've got there on time maybe I would've had more time to make him see where I was coming from! And besides," he said, looking her square in the eyes, "the whole time that muthafucka was going off on me you ain't say shit! You just sat yo' fat ass there," Sean said as he used his index finger to mush her in the side of the head, "and kept on eatin'! What the fuck was the point of you being there? Your presence was useless. You could've said something to back me up!"

"Sean, you cannot blame this on me," Q shot, not having it. "You the one that want to switch labels—"

"Look," he snapped, cutting her off. "When I ask you to talk, that's when you speak! Until then, shut the fuck up!"

Q sat back against the leather seat with her arms folded across chest, fuming. Everything in her wanted to haul off and knock the shit out of Sean. But fighting him wouldn't solve anything. Q was smarter then that. There were other ways to get back at Sean, and she knew just how to do it.

Queen Pynn

Alone with her thoughts, Q took a puff from a Virginia Slim menthol cigarette. Darkness surrounded her while demented thoughts filled her head. Salty tears rolled down her cheeks as she gazed out into blackness. It was one in the morning. Everyone, including Sean, was asleep. Q couldn't close her eyes if she wanted to. Not as long as Ahsim was gone. She wished that she never let him hold her. Without him she was at her loneliest, but with him she couldn't be herself.

Q knew she could only be with Ahsim for so long. He'd eventually see her for who she was. She'd been hit and lied to for too long to take love seriously. To her, love was a losing game that only fools played. Only one person made her feel whole. She'd give her all to him. Q wished to the stars above that she had a bottle of gin to ease her pain. Even a good blunt would do. She would rather be pumped off drugs then drown in her own tears. Her life was a mess.

Q cheated herself out of happiness time and time again as if it were okay. Things couldn't continue the way they were. She needed to get her feet on solid ground, but no matter what she tried she always returned to black. The only way she could see the clear blue sky was if Sean were gone. Q could hear the sound of Ahsim putting his key into the lock. Taking one last pull from the cigarette, she put it out and sprayed air freshener.

Q didn't want anyone to know that she smoked. It was a dirty little secret of hers. Ahsim stepped into the house and the scent of his Gaultier cologne filled the room. The smell drove Q crazy. She had to have him.

"You know what time it is?" she snapped.

"The last I checked almost ten minutes to two." He walked into the living room and stood behind the couch. "Why you sittin' in the dark?"

She ignored his question. "Did you enjoy your date?"

"It was cool, did you?" Ahsim took off his jacket and placed it on the back of the couch.

"I didn't go on a date and you know it."

"Well, you had me fooled."

"Did you fuck her?" Q demanded to know with a look of lust in her eyes.

"That's a bit personal, don't you think?"

"It's a simple question. Either yes or no." Q stood up and got in his face.

Her full breasts were pressed up against his chest.

"Did you fuck ol' boy?" He kissed her lips roughly.

"No."

"A'ight, then." Ahsim began to unzip the back of her dress.

"Why you actin' like you don't like me no more?" She wrapped her arms around his neck.

"I ain't actin' like nothin'. You the one said we need to chill out."

"Stop bringing up old shit." She kissed his lips passionately.

After that, nothing else mattered. The electricity between them was inevitable. Ahsim was back in Q's arms where he belonged. Thoughts of her sweating with her ass up filled his mind as he unbuckled his pants. There was no other place that he'd rather be. Ready to do his thing, Ahsim gripped her waist and pushed her against the wall. There they made love quietly until neither could physically go anymore.

Part Four

Back to Black

"Celebrity Photos, this is Frank. How can I help you?"

"We still on?"

"Yeah," Frank agreed eagerly.

"What time will you be there?"

"At twelve o'clock as you requested."

"Cool . . . And remember, make it seem real."

Queen Pynn

Q bobbed her head and vibed to the beat. "She Got Her Own (Miss Independent Remix)" by Ne-Yo featuring Jamie Foxx and Fabolous was playing, hyping the ladies up. The Loft was packed. It seemed like everybody in the Lou was in the spot. From wall to wall there were playas and thugs. Chicks strutted around the club their noses in the air, doing their best impression of *America's Next Top Model* contestants. Q covered her mouth and laughed.

It was funny how every female in the spot felt that she

was the number one bitch every nigga wanted to get with. Q sat at alone in the VIP section of the club with an apple martini in hand. She was determined to have a good time. Sean was out of town for the night doing a show in KC. Finally, she and Ahsim would have a night alone without him breathing down her neck. She couldn't wait for Ahsim to return from the bar so they could hit the dance floor.

All of the pent-up frustrations she'd bottled inside were dying to be released. Q pulled out her gold Sephora compact mirror and checked her face. As always, she was on point, but her lips needed a fresh coat of gloss. Q grabbed her tube of Stila lip glaze and glided it across her bottom lip. Smacking her lips together, she noticed a male figure approach her table.

Q closed her mirror and focused her attention on the man. To her surprise, it was Grip. Q's heart rate immediately increased. She swore if she looked down she would see it beat through her chest. Grip was the type of nigga that you loved to hate. He was ruggedly handsome in a Lil Wayne kind of way, but that didn't stop her from hating his guts. His outlandish accusations had made her life a living hell. *How dare he come near me as if everything were all good?* she thought.

"What's good, Q?" He licked his lips suggestively.

"Not a damn thing." Her upper lip curled.

"C'mon, ma, don't be like that." He caressed her cheek.

Q tried her best to catch his hand with her teeth, but missed.

"You feisty tonight, ain't you." He grinned.

"Spell feisty," she spat, aggravated by his presence.

"I miss you."

"An' . . . wrong."

"I know you miss me too," he whispered softly into her ear.

"Have you ever been evaluated? 'Cause you are certifiably crazy."

"Excuse me, Mrs. Pynn," a photographer from Celebrity Photos said.

"Yes."

"Can I get a picture of you and Grip?" He held the camera up before she could reply.

"No." She put up her hand to block her face. *Where is Ahsim*, she thought.

"One picture ain't gon' hurt." Grip wrapped his arm around her shoulder and posed.

"If you don't get yo' ass away from me!" Q jerked her arm away as the photographer proceeded to take her picture anyway.

"Just give me a kiss for old time's sake." He leaned in, his lips inches away from hers.

"I said move." She pushed him as Ahsim came toward them.

Ahsim promptly recognized Grip and pulled out his gun.

"Get yo' ass outta here!" He pushed the photographer away.

The photographer didn't care. He'd already gotten his shot.

"Yo, my man." Ahsim yoked Grip up by the collar and placed the cold, steel tip of the gun to his head. "You need to fall back."

"You got one second to get yo' hands off me," Grip warned.

"Or you gon' do what?" Ahsim took safety off. "That's what I thought. Now understand this: Mrs. Pynn ain't got nothin' for you. As a matter of fact, anytime you see her I suggest you look the other way. 'Cause if you don't, I'ma be in yo' fuckin' face and you won't live to rap about it."

"Yo, Q, I suggest you get yo' man," Grip said in a menacing tone.

"Ahsim, it's cool." She tugged on his arm, scared.

Ahsim tightened his hold on Grip's collar, then let him go.

"Get the fuck outta here," he barked.

Grip heatedly fixed his clothes, then looked at Q and smiled.

"Call me later."

"Please," she snarled as he walked away.

"You a'ight?" Ahsim caressed her cheek, concerned.

"Yeah, he's an asshole."

"You wanna go home?"

"I think it's best." She picked up her purse, pissed that her one night without Sean was ruined.

Queen Pynn

The room was quiet. Everything was still, like an Ingrid Michaelson song. Shades of grey outlined the room. The curtains in Q's bedroom were closed, making it seem as if it were night, although it was actually mid-afternoon. She lay curled in the fetal position, knocked out. Her long, black hair was sprawled over the satin pillowcase like a fan. She was in such a deep sleep that she didn't hear the sound of heavy footsteps enter through the door.

Even the sound of the curtains being forced back with aggression didn't alarm her. Sean stumbled over to the bed humming a dirty rap song, drunk out of his mind. He had something in store for Q. Quietly, he took hold of her hair, wrapped it tight around his fist, and yanked her out the bed. Startled, Q's eyes popped open as the follicles of her head burned.

"I'ma kill you." Sean dragged her across the floor.

The excruciating pain of her hair being ripped from her head caused Q to wail out in distress.

"I knew you was fuckin' him!"

"What the fuck are you talkin' about?" She tried to remove his hand from her hair, but to no avail.

"Yo' scandalous ass been up to no good this whole time. I can't believe I let you make a fool outta me!" He slapped her face hard.

The intensity of the hit caused her bottom lip to split open and squirt out blood.

"I didn't even do nothing! What are you talkin' about?"

Sean let go of her hair and got on top of her.

"Bitch, you fuckin' him!" He squeezed her cheeks with his hands tight.

"Fuckin' who?"

"Grip!" He punched her in the eye. "The shit all over the Net! I'm out of town making money and you in the club takin' pictures with this nigga!"

"It wasn't even like that," she cried.

"Stop lyin'." He let go of her face and pounded her head into the floor.

"I'm not!"

"I fuckin' hate yo' ass! You gon' die today, bitch!" He began to choke her.

Q tried prying Sean's hand away but his clasp was too tight. To her dismay, the more she put up a fight the harder it was for her to breath. She could see stars. Death was approaching but she had to hold on. After all her hard work things couldn't end now.

"Mr. Pynn." Rosa rushed in the room. "Ralph," she screamed. "Come quick! He's killing her this time!"

Ralph, along with Sean's pot'nah Anrico and Mo B, came to Q's aid. It took all three men to pull Sean off of Q.

"Get the fuck off of me." He pushed them all away.

Q held her throat and gasped for air.

"I want yo' ass outta here by the time I get back." He pointed his finger towards her and left. Anrico and Mo B followed.

"Are you okay, Mrs. Pynn?" Rosa sat with her on the floor.

"I don't know why he treats me like this," Q wept.

"Me either, dear, me either."

"I can't take this anymore."

"What the hell is going on?"Ahsim raced into the room, panicked.

The sight of Q's face answered his question. Anger seethed through his veins. The left side of her face was crimson, she had a black eye, her bottom lip was busted, and Sean's fingerprints were plastered around her neck like cement.

"You said you wouldn't let him hurt me," she sobbed.

"What happened?"

"Where were you?" she countered.

"I was out jogging. Why did he do this to you?" He leaned down and wiped her hair from her face.

"He thinks I'm cheating on him with Grip! The pictures the photographer took are all over the Internet and he thinks I did it on purpose. You have to tell him it isn't true or else he's going to kill me! I just know it!"

Queen Pynn

Q eyes fluttered open. Unlike earlier in the day she wasn't awakened by a violent attack. The room was stark grey. She could hear rain tap against the window. Her body ached in places she didn't even know existed. It hurt to even blink, but the white box tied with a yellow ribbon brought tears to her eyes. Sean often tried to buy her affections after he'd beaten her. Normally she would feed into his ploy to win her back, but not this time. Her heart couldn't take another gift sent from the devil. The sight of it made her stomach turn. Fed up, Q pushed the box off the edge of the bed.

"You ain't gon' open it?" She heard Ahsim say from behind.

Q slowly turned on her side. To her surprise, he was sitting in a chair beside the bed. Seeing his face brought a slight smile to hers, but it quickly faded once she remembered the state of her lip.

"How long have you been sitting there?"

"Since you fell asleep. Did the pain pills help any?"

"A little. Where is Sean?"

"He and Mo B went to the studio. He said that they'd be there for a couple of hours. I explained to him what happened, though. He knows that Grip set you up, if it matters any."

"It doesn't." She looked away. "'I just want him dead."

Ahsim sat quiet, unsure of how to reply.

"Will you just lay down with me?" Q gazed somberly into his eyes.

"Of course."

Ahsim got up and lay behind her. With his strong arm wrapped around her waist, Q could finally breathe again. No word in the English dictionary could describe how he made her feel. He showed her the beauty of trust and friendship. He saw that outside of her physical beauty, she also possessed class and smarts. Sean never appreciated those things in her. Q was beginning to wonder if he ever loved her at all. There was no way he could have when she made it so easy for him. Soon it would be time to pack her bags and go.

Queen Pynn

With her eyes concealed by oversized Prada shades, Q sat alone at a table for two. She was dressed to impress in a gorgeous watermelon-colored Carmen Marc Valvo scoop neck, empire-waist dress and nude, patent leather, peep toe Jimmy Choo. It was a cloudy Sunday afternoon, but Mosaic, a modern/fusion restaurant, was crowded with people dying to taste the one-of-a-kind fine cuisine. Q, on the other hand, didn't have an appetite at all. After being ridiculed and beaten, things in her life only got more chaotic. One night while at The Venue, Sean stood in the men's restroom with his legs parted, holding his dick, taking a piss.

He could barely stand up he was so drunk and high. Sean was so fucked up, the room was spinning. Off his guard, he ignored the sound of the restroom door creaking open, and continued to pee. Sean assumed that one of his boys was nearby so he wasn't worried about anyone trying to harm him. Poor, naïve Sean had no idea that danger was lurking right over shoulder. Finished handling his business, Sean went to flush the urinal when a cord was placed around his neck.

Instantly, he fought to remove the cord, but to no avail. The assailant's grip was too strong. The next thing Sean knew, he was being dragged across the room. The air in his lungs was decreasing by the second. Sweat poured from his beat red face while drools of spit slid out of the corner of his mouth. Before he could no longer breathe, the person attacking him whispered in his ear, "Next time you'll think twice before crossing Roc, muthafucka."

With that being said, Sean was let go and dropped to the floor. The attacker left before Sean could even get a glimpse of his face. After that, Sean was more paranoid then ever. He doubled their security team. Neither he nor Q could go anywhere without a guard. Q glanced over her shoulder two tables away at Ahsim and a new guard, Cash, who sat watching her and the door's every move. Hearing the restaurant's door open, they both focused their attention at the entranceway.

There, standing looking around the restaurant for Q, was Annalisa. As usual, she looked beautiful. That afternoon she wore a leopard-print, tiered-ruffle dress by D&G, but there was unavoidable sadness in her eyes. Q raised her hand in the air and signaled for her to come over. Spotting her friend, Annalisa released a warm smile and headed her way. Q happily stood up and greeted Annalisa with a hug and an air kiss to the cheek.

"How you been, mama?" Q asked as they sat down.

"Well, I'm sure you've heard by now that me and Roc broke up." Annalisa placed her Bottega Veneta purse down beside her.

"I did. Are you okay?"

"I just can't believe it." Annalisa shook her head in disbelief. "I mean, a part of me seen it coming but I never really thought it would happen. We've been together for a little over three years. I thought I was going to marry this man, but this new chick that he fuckin' evidently has something that I just don't have."

"First of all, you can't think like that. You and Roc breaking up just means that your relationship ran its course. It wasn't meant to be. He's obviously found the person he wants to be with, so now it's time for you to do the same. Like my mama always says, 'Don't cry over spoiled milk. Go out to the store and get you new one,' " Q joked.

Annalisa couldn't help but laugh too.

"Girl, you are silly." She crossed her arms and rested them on the table. "I guess you're right."

"I know I'm right," Q replied as the waiter came over and took their orders.

Once their drinks were at the table, the two women chatted some more.

"So what's been going on wit' you?" Annalisa took a sip of her ice tea.

"Girl, you don't even wanna know." Q waved her hand.

"Talk to me. What's going on?" Annalisa said, genuinely concerned.

"This is what's going on." Q slid down her shades so Annalisa could see her slightly healed black eye.

"Oh my God," Annalisa gasped, shocked. "Who did that to you?"

"My husband." Q placed her glasses back on.

"Why?"

"Don't tell me you're the only person on the planet who hasn't seen the picture of me and Grip."

"Girl, I don't know what's going on. I've been too busy dealing with my own drama."

"Well, about a week ago I was at the Loft, and Grip and some photographer approached me, trying to get a picture of us together."

"For real?"

"Yes, I was pissed the fuck off." Q rolled her neck. "Like the dude is straight-up crazy and delusional. The shit he's been doing is borderline stalkerish. But, of course, I'm the one who comes out lookin' like a slut because of it."

"That shit is crazy." Annalisa sat with her mouth open, stunned. "So let me guess, when Sean saw the pictures, he went berserk?"

"Yeah." Q nodded. "Homeboy lost his mind. This crazy muthafucka woke me up out of my sleep, whopin' ass."

"I never saw Sean as the abusive type."

Q laughed.

"Nobody does. He hides it from the public well."

"So why don't you leave him?"

"I want to, believe me I do, but—"

"Uh-uh," Annalisa cut her off. "There is no buts and no excuse for letting a muthafucka pound on you. What you need to do is come up with a plan to leave, and do it. If you need my help I'll be glad to assist you any way I can."

"You're right," Q had to admit. "There is no excuse. I have to leave him."

Right then and there, at that moment, Q had it set in her mind that Sean would never be able to put his hands on her again. It was just a matter of time before he was out her life for good.

Part Five

Black Widow

Q sat with her legs crossed inside Gotham Studios. The setting was very intimate. Soft lights illuminated the space. In front of her was a recording and mixing board. Keyboards, drum machines, an MPC, Mac computer, and speakers were also in the room. Sean bobbed his head and zoned out to the hypnotic beat that was playing. Q couldn't stand being around him, but to see him at work was fascinating. Sean was a genius at making hit records. Once the beat played and he connected with it, rhymes instantly came to mind.

He'd jump into the booth and magic would happen. What fucked people up was that he never wrote anything down. Q still couldn't understand why he wanted her in the studio with him. She felt totally out of place. She and three groupies who fawned over her husband relentlessly were the only women there. The rest of the people were Sean's homeboys from the north side.

Q loathed being around them. They were nothing but a bunch of freeloading hooligans up to no good. The studio Sean was renting out for $10,000 an hour had been completely trashed. Bottles of Heineken, Moët, Ace of Spades, and leftover take-out containers were everywhere. Weed smoke hovered over their heads like clouds. The whole atmosphere was like a bad scene from a Shorty Lo video. Q would much rather be spending her time with Ahsim, making love. Whenever they had a spare moment alone they went at it like wild animals. They'd made love all over the house, but now here she was stuck in hell with Sean and his goons. Q tapped her foot against the wooden floor as she counted down the time. They'd only been there two hours, but she was beyond ready to go.

"Huh," she groaned, popping her gum.

"What the fuck is you huffin' and puffin' for?" Sean spun around in his chair, annoyed by her attitude.

"I'm ready to go. Why couldn't I have just stayed home?"

" 'Cause I wanted you here with me. We husband and wife, ain't we?"

"Unfortunately," she mumbled under her breath.

"Well, act like it," he replied, unaware of her comment.

"Ay, Sean." Mo B poked his head into the room. "I think you need to turn the radio on. Grip on *The Beat* talkin' mad greasy about you."

Sean rolled over to the stereo and turned it on. Everybody in the studio became silent. Q unconsciously held her breath. Nervous butterflies filled the pit of her stomach.

"So, Grip, what's up?" Shorty, the radio host, asked. "You going hard against my man. Sean a good dude. Why can't y'all just squash the beef?"

"Man, fuck Sean." Grip spoke into the microphone. "That nigga's a fag. I mean, can't y'all see that he's fake? The nigga's the rap version of T.D. Jakes."

Shorty tried to keep his composure, but couldn't help but laugh.

"You wild, man. But why you have to go and say, and

I quote, 'You's a misdemeanor, don't let the Nina hit you and split yo' beam up. Fuck them punks wit' you, we hit yo' team up. Y'all niggas is hurtin', that publicity stunt is not workin'.' "

"Yeah, I said it, what?" Grip spat, not giving a fuck. "It is what it is. I fucked his wife and I'm fuckin' him in the game. Understand," he said, stressing his words, "I'm not gon' argue wit' no nigga. Like I said, come see about me. It ain't no secret where I be. That nigga Sean is a studio thug, flat out! This ain't shit but Young Buck all over again. Except for I ain't fifty. I will kill that nigga and you can quote me on that."

"Wow," Shorty said, dumbfounded by his words. "So you don't see no ending to the beef?"

"Nah," Grip said. "Not until the nigga say sorry."

"You crazy, G, so be honest wit' me. You messing wit' Sean's old lady or not?"

"Man, please. I skeeted over Superhead and kept it moving."

"Okay," Shorty said. "Let's go to a commercial break."

Sean switched off the radio. He was furious. Q could practically see smoke coming out of his ears.

"You see how this shit making me look?" he questioned her, furious.

Q gulped, swallowing the lump in her throat. Not wanting to cause a scene, she remained quiet.

"Yo, Sean, we gotta do something about this nigga, cuz."

"Don't worry." He nodded, taking a pull from the blunt. "I'ma handle this shit tonight."

Queen Pynn

Sean was sitting on top of the world. Fuck that, the world was his. He and his crew were posted up in the

VIP section of Society. Twenty scantly clad women ful-filled their every desire. Blunts were being passed. The finest champagne was popped, toasts were made. Cigars were lit. Club-goers on the lower level couldn't take their eyes off of him.

This was the life. He was as high as a kite and loved every minute. The bottle of Goose in his hand only added to his buzz. For a nigga that was once considered black and ugly as a child he'd come a long way. Sean took a lengthy swig from the bottle and swallowed hard. Grip said to come see about him, so he had.

There was no way on God's green earth he was going to get away with saying the things he'd said. Sean was a man full of pride. His reputation meant everything to him. No man was going to be able to disrespect him and live to tell about it. Sean even went as far as to leave his security at home. He couldn't be seen as a studio thug to his fans. There was only about an hour before the club was supposed to close and Grip still wasn't there. *Maybe he ain't a super thug after all,* Sean thought. His theory was proved wrong when Grip and his homeboys came strolling through the door.

"Yo,' Sean, there go yo' man," Mo B said in his ear. "What you gon' do?"

Sean pulled out the pearl handle .22 tucked in his waist and checked the clip. It was full. Ready to handle his biz he put the gun back inside his pants and walked down the steps. His pot'nahs were behind him. The crowd parted like the Red Sea. People wanted to see an altercation. Nobody was willing to miss a showdown be-tween two of hip-hop's favorite rappers. This would be a once-in-a-lifetime event. Sean stepped to Grip, who leaned against the wall.

"Talk that gangsta shit now, nigga." He mean mugged him.

"My man, I'm warning you. Get the fuck out my face."

"Nah, nigga fuck all that. Come see about me." Sean pulled out his gun.

Grip lowered his head and laughed.

"This nigga laughing at you, cuz," Mo B continued to amp Sean up.

Sean was really pissed. Grip stood up straight and got in his face.

"This ain't even you, fam. Don't let yo' man soup you up to get killed, so I'm advising you either put the gun up or do something."

Sean could see in Grip's eyes that he wasn't playing or willing to back down. Pulling guns out on cats wasn't his thing, but Sean couldn't come off as a punk. He had to do something. Maybe he should snuff him.

"That's what I thought," Grip shot before he could make up his mind. "Now if you'll excuse me . . . pardon my back."

Grip signaled to his homeboys while ice grillin' Sean as they began to walk away.

"You just gon' let that nigga leave?" Mo B looked at him like he was soft.

"Man, fuck that nigga." Sean waved him off. In the end, killing someone wasn't worth ruining his life or career.

"Nigga, fuck that." Mo B took the gun from his hand and let off a shot aimed at Grip.

The next thing Sean knew, everything was moving in slow motion. People were running and screaming, ducking for cover. The music had stopped playing. He stood frozen in fear as he watched Grip dodge the bullet and pull out his own gun. With the precision of a trained killer, he aimed for Mo B's head. Thankfully for Mo B, he saw the shot coming and headed for the floor. Not ready to die, he stayed low to the ground and headed for the closest exit, leaving Sean alone.

He was fucked. Things were never supposed to go this far in the beginning. All he wanted was some publicity for his album. Guns were never supposed to be drawn. Their beef was to be strictly on wax, at least in his mind. Now here he stood, seconds away from death. Sean's entire life flashed before his eyes. Q was the first person who came to mind. Maybe if he would've treated her right he wouldn't be in this predicament. Grip stared at him with pure hate in his eyes.

"This for Q, nigga," he spat before unloading five shots into his chest.

Each bullet felt like venomous poison. Sean fell back and landed on the floor with a thud. He'd always thought that the last thing he'd hear before dying would be the cry of his loved ones, but all Sean could hear were sirens nearing as he lay in a pool of his own blood.

Queen Pynn

"Ooh, just like that," Q whispered, barely able to breath. "You like that, ma?"

"Yes, baby! Lick it just like that!"

Doing as he was told, Ahsim placed the tip of his tongue on Q's clit while she looked on with a look of sheer appreciation on her face. She couldn't wait for him to taste her. Ahsim gazed back up at her and flicked his tongue across her clit at a feverish pace. Q never knew that the feel of someone's tongue on her clit could feel so good.

Ahsim's tongue felt like a feather fluttering ever so lightly across her pussy. Q had no other choice but to rub his head and moan.

Deciding that she was ready to cum Ahsim targeted

her spot on the right side of her clit. He licked and sucked until Q couldn't take it anymore.

"Ooooooh, baby stop I can't breathe," she yelled. "Ooooh! Ahhhhhhhhhhhhh! This shit feels so good!"

"You want me to stop?" He asked, daring her to say yes.

"No baby! Please don't stop! I don't want you to ever stop! Ooh . . . yes . . . ahh . . . I'm cumming! I'm cumming! Ahhhhhhhhhh!" Q shrieked, as she rotated her hips in a circular motion.

Cum slithered from the lips of her pussy onto his tongue. Ahsim savored every drop. Q's entire body shook as she came all over his face and sheets. Then, before she or Ahsim knew it, someone came bursting through the door.

"Mrs. Pynn." Rosa rushed in, unaware of what was going on.

"What the hell is it, Rosa?" Q quickly covered herself up.

"I'm sorry, ma'am." She turned her head and shielded her eyes with her hand. Rosa wasn't that surprised by Q and Ahsim's affair. She'd noticed stolen glances between the two of them, but had kept her mouth shut.

"I have terrible news, Mrs. Pynn: Mr. Pynn is dead!"

Queen Pynn

Q anxiously fiddled with her Chanel glasses as she sat alone inside a cold, sterile interrogation room. The florescent light above her head flickered on and off. For the first time in her life, she was scared. Funeral arrangements hadn't even been finalized and she was being brought in for questioning. Q examined her surroundings. The green and grey paint on the walls was peeling.

The table at which she sat was black with names, numbers, and hood slang etched into it. A huge mirror faced her. Q was pretty sure that on the other side there was someone watching her every move. Unexpectedly, the door swung open and the detective strolled in. Swallowing the lump in her throat, Q smoothed down her hair and sat up straight.

The detective was immediately captivated by her beauty. The photos on the Web didn't do her any justice. She was way prettier in person. Her smooth, raven hair was flat-ironed straight with bangs. She was simply but chicly dressed in a wife beater, sleeveless gray cardigan, black skinny jeans, and leather ankle boots. A purple, white, and black scarf hung from her neck, while her $15,000 Birkin bag rested on the table beside her hand.

"How are you, Mrs. . . . ah," the detective stuttered, glancing down at his file.

"Pynn," Q replied.

"Mrs. Pynn, I'm sorry. I knew that. I'm Detective Johnson." He stuck out his hand for a shake.

Q begrudgingly took his hand into hers.

"I apologize for the circumstances, but, unfortunately, we have to be here."

"I guess." She shook her head. "Can you . . . tell me how long this is going to be? I have to find a suit to bury my husband in."

"I'm sorry for the inconvenience, but I actually can't tell you how long this will take. I'll try to get you out of here as quickly as I can."

Q looked away and sighed.

"You do understand the gravity of this situation?"

"Of course I do." She looked the detective square in the eyes. "My husband is dead." Her bottom lip quivered as she began to cry.

"I'm sorry. I didn't mean to upset you." He handed her a tissue.

"Thank you." She wiped her nose.

"Mrs. Pynn . . . Did your husband own a gun?"

"Yes."

"Did he ever threaten to kill you with it?"

"Yes, but what does this have to do with anything?" She sniffed.

"We just want to know if your husband was known to have a violent temper, that's all. Now, did he ever hit you?"

"Yes, on occasion."

"Did you ever file a police report?"

"No."

"Why not?"

"Because I was afraid no one would believe me."

"Hmm." Detective Johnson paced the room. "Well, that's all for today. If I have any more questions, I'll be sure to get in contact with you."

Q got up and grabbed her things.

"Oh, before I forget, the trial against Mr. Wright begins in a couple of months. Don't be surprised if you're called in to testify on your husband's behalf."

"Okay." She nodded, opening the door.

Ahsim was outside waiting for her. He'd been questioned, too.

"Mrs. Pynn," Detective Johnson called out.

"Yes."

"Would you care for a smoke? You looked kind of shaken up." He pointed the box in her direction. "Maybe it'll calm you down."

"No, thank you. I don't smoke."

"You ready?" Ahsim took her hand.

"Yeah."

"How did everything go?"

"Good . . . I guess."

Queen Pynn

Never in life did Q expect that laying her husband down to rest would be so hard. Sean wasn't the most pleasant man to deal with while he was on earth, but to see him laid up in a coffin, stiff as a board, caused a piece of her to die as well. Despite their hardships, he was her husband. At one point she'd vowed to love him forever and forsake all others. Q didn't know how she would go on. The love and support of her family and his fans was what brought her through. On the day of the funeral, fans of Sean's lined the streets to pay their respects. Q by no means knew he would be so missed.

At night was her only time to cry. During the day she was bombarded with radio, magazine, and television interviews. The media coverage of Sean's death was overwhelming. Wherever she turned, someone was talking about his untimely death. The fact that Grip was on trial for his murder only intensified things. If it weren't for Ahsim, Q knew she would have lost it. During the craziest moments he kept her sane, but Ahsim wouldn't be able to hold her hand and guide her down the right path this time.

The Old St. Louis County Courthouse was packed with photographers and news crews. Each pew in the courtroom was stuffed with people. After Rosa's testimony, Q would have to face the jury alone. Annalisa had already taken the stand and testified that Grip had gone way beyond a rap beef and turned things into a crazy, sadistic game of cat-and-mouse. Q watched intently as Rosa was sworn in.

"Mrs. Rosa Sanchez, you have been the Pynns' maid for how long?" District Attorney Jonathon Banks asked.

"For almost eight years." Rosa clenched her hands tightly together.

"And have you ever witnessed any odd or indecent behavior between Mrs. Pynn and the defendant, Mr. Wright?"

"Oh, no." She shook her head emphatically. "Mrs. Pynn
would never associate with a man like him. He's crazy, I
tell you. For the past year, Mr. Wright has been calling and
calling, harassing Mrs. Pynn. At night she couldn't sleep
because of it. You wouldn't believe how much stress his
behavior has caused."

"Thank you, Mrs. Sanchez. You may now step down
from the stand."

"Mr. Simmons," Judge Meyers said from the bench.
"Who will be your next witness?"

"Your Honor," Grip's attorney announced, "I would
now like to bring Mrs. Pynn to the stand."

Q gulped hard. This was it, the moment she'd been
dreading. All eyes were on her as she made her way to
the witness stand, dressed in a chiffon bubble skirt, black
turtleneck, and tights. After being sworn in by the bailiff,
she took a seat on the hard, wooden chair. She and Grip
caught each other's eyes as his attorney approached the
stand. He mischievously winked his eye. Q rolled her
eyes and ignored him.

"Mrs. Pynn," Mr. Simmons said.

"Yes."

"Do you know my client?"

"No, not personally."

"No," he repeated. "You sure?"

"Yes, I'm quite sure."

"You and my client have never spent any time alone
with one another?"

"Hell, no, I wouldn't be caught dead alone with him,"
she spat as the courtroom gasped.

"Yo, she lyin'," Grip shouted.

"Order in the court," Judge Meyers yelled. "Simmons,
get a hold of your client."

"Yes, sir." Mr. Simmons glared at Grip. "As I was saying, you and Mr. Wright have never spent any alone time together?"

"No."

"So, you've never seen this before?" Mr. Simmons held up a platinum crown ring.

"Yeah, I've seen him wear that in his videos." Her heart raced.

"So this ring wasn't left at your house a couple of months ago?"

"No, of course not."

Ahsim looked on, knowing that she'd just lied.

"You mean to tell me that you and my client have not been having an affair?"

"No!"

"Bitch, you fuckin' lyin'!" Grip jumped up from his chair.

"Order, order, order!" The judge banged his gavel. "Order in the court! If I hear one more peep out of your client, I am going to hold him in contempt! Do you understand?"

"Understood," Simmons agreed.

Grip's two other lawyers got him back in his seat and tried their best to calm him down.

"No, but she lyin'." Q could hear him say.

"Mrs. Pynn you never told Mr. Wright that you wanted him to kill your husband because you were tired of him abusing you?"

"Mr. Simmons, as I said before, no! Your client is obsessed with me!" Q shot from her chair. "He's been harassing me for over a year. It's all over the news. He writes all these crazy songs about me. He's nuts. He's a freak! He even threatened on the radio that he would kill my husband. Anybody who listens to hip-hop music knows that I'm tellin' the truth. The only reason he killed my husband was to get him out of the picture so in some kind of sick way he could be closer to me! Sean wasn't the best man in the world, but he didn't deserve this."

"I swear to God I'ma have you killed, bitch!" Grip jumped over the table trying to get to her.

"See," she screamed, as the bailiff and two guards tackled Grip to the ground.

The courtroom erupted in pandemonium.

"So we have an innocent man on trail for murder, a dead body, and you," Mr. Simmons yelled over the noise. "Something just doesn't seem right here! No further questions!" He threw his hands up in defeat.

After a week of testimony and a day of deliberation, the jury came back with their verdict. Q sat with her head down. Her leg violently shook as she awaited the verdict. Ahsim was next to her, holding her hand tight.

"The jury in the case of the State of Missouri against Reginald Wright finds the defendant guilty of murder in the first degree," the foreman announced.

Grip bit down on his bottom lip, determined not cry. None of this was supposed to go down this way. Shaking his head, he turned and glanced over his shoulder at Q. She brought her face up, laughing. Nobody caught the expression but him. He boiled with anger. Grip kissed his family good-bye, and vowed to get revenge one day.

Epilogue

A few days later, Q and Ahsim were on the island of Bora Bora inside their overwater bungalow making passionate love. They were the only ones there. For hours they'd gone at one another like wild animals. Beads of sweat trickled down their sticky skin. Q clawed the sheets as he pounded in and out of her from behind at feverish pace. The sound of the waves crashing underneath them intensified her pleasure.

Ahsim's long stroke and the feel of his balls slapping against her backside had her spewing words unknown to man. He was showing her pussy no mercy and she loved it. His dick game was hypnotic. Ahsim couldn't hold out any longer. It was time for him to cum. Grinding his hips, he hit Q with the death stroke causing both their bodies to shake uncontrollably. Q screamed out his name as he pulled out and squirted hot, creamy lava into the crack of her butt.

Spent, she lay flat on her stomach, panting heavily. Before heading for the shower Ahsim smacked her ass. The sight of it jiggling made his dick hard again but he contained his emotions and bathed instead. An hour later they both were dressed and standing on the sundeck. Nothing but aqua-blue water and nature surrounded them. The view was marvelous. Q was in her element, but there was still some unfinished business that needed to be handled.

After the trial had ended, Ahsim started coming to her with a bunch of suspicious questions. Q wasn't one to be questioned or quizzed. She'd hoped that he would back off, but his insistence to find out the truth was beginning to get the best of him. Q had planned on them taking a nice vacation before she ended things permanently, but unfortunately for Ahsim, things would have to end now. Q turned on the portable radio by the bed. The voice of her favorite female MC, Lil' Kim, filled the room. Q reached into her purse, pulled out a cigarette, and lit it. The first hit of nicotine sent a rush of energy through her veins.

"What you doing?" Ahsim watched as she blew smoke rings into the air. "I thought you didn't smoke."

"We all have our secrets," she smirked, placing on a pair of black gloves.

Suddenly, everything became clear. Q had been setting up the demise of her husband the entire time.

"Admit it. You were fuckin' Grip," he accused.

"Of course I was," she chuckled. "Now, you admit something for me. You were the one who gave the police Grip's ring, weren't you?"

"Yeah, I found it that night by the pool."

"I wish you wouldn't have done that." She shook her head. " 'Cause now I can't trust you."

"Just tell me. Why did you do it?"

"You still don't get it, do you?" she grinned. "I did it for the money. With Sean dead, I get everything: the houses, cars, jewelry, stocks and bonds, as well as his music. I'll be making money off of him until I die. All of it's mine now, plus I wanted to get rid of that sorry-ass, good-for-nothin' bastard that I called a husband. You see, Sean and Grip were already going at each other, so I used that to my advantage. I knew that Grip was gullible and that if I fucked him he'd go running and tell the world." She laughed sadistically. "I had that man wrapped around my finger. Anything I asked him to do, he did it; including killing my husband."

"But that doesn't make any sense. Why would he risk going to jail for you?" Ahsim quizzed, confused.

"That's the thing." Q took another pull from the cigarette. "Grip got smart on me. I don't know who got in his ear, but that night you caught me at the pool he decided to back out of our plan. So I had to think quickly. I arranged for our photo to be taken at the Loft that night. I knew that once Sean saw the photo he'd flip. Being humiliated was like death to him. He'd do anything to protect his rep, and I knew those idiots he hung with would amp him to do something drastic. And he did."

"So even though Grip backed out on you, in your own way you still had him kill Sean," Ahsim said, putting two and two together.

"Yep."

"And where do I fit into this whole scenario?"

"You," Q said, mashing the cigarette into the ashtray and approaching him, "were an added bonus." She licked his neck. "I didn't expect you to happen, and for a while there, I actually started to like you. But liking and loving someone is two different things. You see," she said, gazing into his eyes, "I'm in love with someone else."

Ahsim unconsciously reached for his gun, but quickly realized it wasn't on his hip.

"You lookin' for this?" Q placed the gun up to his head.

"Yo, Q, calm down. You making a big mistake. You don't want to do this," he said, panicked.

"See, that's where you're wrong. I have to do this. You almost ruined my plan, and now you know too much. I can't run the risk of you runnin' your mouth. I've come too far to go to jail now."

"I swear, I won't say nothing."

"You're right, you won't." She pulled the trigger without flinching.

The force of the shot sent Ahsim's body flying to the ground. Q gazed down at him. Ahsim's eyes were still open. It was almost as if he were staring at her. Q shrugged her arms and placed the gun in his hand. When the police came it would look like he'd committed suicide. Calmly, she stepped over him and grabbed her things. Her ride would be there any second. Q went back onto the sundeck. In the sky, a float plane began to descend. Once it landed, Q hopped over the railing and took the passenger's hand. Inside the plane, she buckled her seat belt and allowed the love of her life to kiss her cheek.

"Everything taken care of?"

"Yep, I'm all yours."

"Good." Roc kissed her hand.

"Where to?"

"I don't care where we go, as long as I'm there with you."

Trick, Don't Treat

Brenda Hampton

There wasn't a word in the English language that described my desires for handsome men. I didn't consider myself a sex addict, simply because I was somewhat particular about whom I allowed to dive into *my goods*. Working men were a bonus, and even those who hustled to get money weren't a problem for me. Since my job paid the bills, it wasn't that I *needed* a man's money, but it was always good to know that if I fell on hard times, the man in my life would have my back.

A few years ago, if anybody wanted to have the life of Rochel "Jakki" Thomas, I would have handed it over on a silver platter. One would say that I'd been to hell and back, but I guess I couldn't complain because I'd learned some valuable things along the way. The most important thing was that some men were dogs, but it takes a dog to know one. Players would come and go, but only a true player can overcome the setbacks. I wasn't married because I didn't want to be married. And, for the time being, the only things men were good for were performing oral sex and sticking their better-be-good muscle where it belongs.

I didn't always feel this way, and by all means, I consider myself a great catch: carmel silk skin, big bright eyes, a body like a professional trainer, and brains to go with it. A woman with class—I won't even go there because many women would beg to differ with me. To them, a ho would best describe me, but consider me a ho with a purpose. And under my delicate circumstances, a ho might not be a bad thing at all.

The make-me-melt-like-butter Parker Rhodes was the man who taught me my final lesson. He stood six foot two, was almost dark as midnight, and had a tight, muscular build comparable to a NFL running back. The waves in his coal black hair were never out of place, and his dark brown eyes could get him just about anything he wanted.

At first, Parker introduced me to an entirely different world. He had a rewarding career as an entrepreneur, was a Christian man (so he claimed), and flaunted lots of money. In addition to his extravagant lifestyle, Parker, I proudly profess, took good care of me. He'd stepped out of the box and done things for me that no other man had done. Cooked on a regular basis, sent roses to me at work, paid me touching compliments . . . all of which made me believe I'd finally met my match. In private, he called me by his last name, and his ability to make me ring out multiple orgasms made me crave him even more.

In public, though, I was Parker's friend. Sooner than later, I found out that Parker had an array of "friends." Friends who assisted him in keeping up his extravagant lifestyle by paying his bills. In actuality, the brotha was broke and didn't have a pot to piss in or a window to throw it out of. I made plans to work myself out of his life, but since the loving was so good to me, preparations took some time. That time was almost a year later, and by then, he had broken the bad news to me. He was engaged, and my booty call services were no longer needed. The traumatic news sent me plummeting to the floor; the dance floor, of course, as I hit the nearby lounges and nightclubs to shake away my pain.

I was definitely a great catch, and met many more men who saw in me what Parker had—nothing. And when I took a deeper look at myself, I realized that somewhere along the road of finding a partner for life, I'd been too damn nice to men. They always claimed to want good women, but what does being a good woman mean? To be obedient? Have dinner on the table when he comes home? Make sure the house is clean? What? Well, I've been there, done all of that before. And, frankly, I have no plans of being that woman again. As far as I'm concerned, this thirty-four-year-old is on her way to being the most confident, happy, and satisfied woman she's ever been. If anyone foresees a problem with the way I now choose to live my life, fuck 'em.

The Meeting Place

The long line at the local post office was ridiculous! I'd gotten up early to go just so I wouldn't have to wait. *So much for that,* I thought as I held number twenty-three in my hand; number two had just been called. I placed my four huge packages on the floor and folded my arms. The look of impatience was clearly visible on my face, but instead of tripping, I pulled a compact mirror from my purse and looked at it. My Nia Long short haircut was working for me, and I pressed my lips together to spread the MAC gloss I wore. Just as I was about to close my compact, the clear view of a mocha chocolate brotha was displayed. To get a better glimpse, I shifted the mirror. My eyes couldn't deny what they'd seen. *Nice,* I thought. *Very, very nice and workable.* As my pussy began to moisten, I knew I was on to something. This man hadn't even touched me yet but he was already feeling good to me. I quickly closed the compact, and just as I got ready to put it back into my purse, I heard a loud thud.

Like many of the other customers, I turned my head

and noticed the tall, dark, and handsome man as he bent over to pick up his package. My immediate thought was *clumsy fool*, but when his light brown eyes focused in my direction, I had a change of heart.

"Sorry about that," he politely said, as he eyeballed others in the facility as well. "It slipped."

Again, his eyes connected with mine and I smiled, giving him a slow blink and then turning around. The line started to move, but I was in deep thought, planning my next move. No doubt, he was gorgeous: casually dressed, nicely trimmed sideburns, and sexier than anything I'd seen in a long time. He kind of had that Reggie Bush thing going on, but not quite. I had already begun to think about my eventful afternoon, or possibly evening. His eye contact implied that he wanted me, too, and I wasn't about to let a man like him pass me by.

After standing and making several eye connections with Mr. Gorgeous, the clerk finally called my number. Dressed in my well-fitted, low-cut jeans and white body-hugging T-shirt, I headed to the counter. The clerk added postage and required payment.

"That'll be twenty-seven dollars and thirteen cents. We accept cash, check, credit, or debit," she said.

I searched my purse for my wallet and pretended it wasn't there. "What in the heck did I do with my wallet?" I patted my pockets and looked up to ponder. Many people waiting appeared to be very impatient with me, so I turned to the clerk and shrugged my shoulders. "I . . . I must have left my wallet in the car. I've stood in line for a long time and . . .

The clerk had no sympathy for me, as I figured she wouldn't. "Ma'am, I'll have to cancel your transaction. Whenever you find your wallet, you'll have to pull another number."

I let out a deep sigh, and clearly looked like a damsel in distress. Just seconds later, Mr. Sexy stepped up from behind me.

"How much did you say it was?" he asked the clerk.

"Twenty-seven dollars and thirteen cents," she snapped.

He handed the clerk his debit card.

"No . . . no, thanks," I said, using this opportunity to touch his hand. "I appreciate the offer, but my wallet has to be in my car."

"It's no big deal," he said. "Go check your car and I'll take care of this transaction for you."

"Are you sure? I . . . I hate to cause you any—"

"I'm positive," he said, and then took the receipt the clerk had given to him.

I touched his bicep and lightly squeezed. "Thanks. I'll be right back. You're a lifesaver."

I raced out the door, only to stand by my car for a few minutes. I then reached in my purse and pulled out my wallet that was surely already there. With the wallet in my hand, I went back inside and spotted the royal blue linen shirt that Mr. Sexy had on. He'd returned to the line and waited for his number to be called.

"I thought you'd take care of your transaction while taking care of mine," I said.

He smiled and displayed his full set of pearly whites. "No. I tried to, but was told that I'd have to wait like everyone else. It's no big deal, and my number is next anyway."

"Well, if you don't mind," I said, holding my debit card, "I'll pay for your package. It looks like mine might be a bit more expensive than yours, and if so, I'll mail the difference to you."

"Really, it's not a problem. I'm just glad you found your wallet."

"Me too," I laughed as the clerk called his number.

We went to the counter together, and the clerk tallied his package; it was only ten bucks plus change. We both handed the clerk our debit cards and she reached for mine. I smiled at her and took Mr. Sexy's debit card from his hand.

"Christopher A. Carter," I said, looking at his name and handing the card back to him. "Would you please write down your number—I mean, address—for me so I can mail your money to you?"

"No can do, but if you'd like to repay me, I might have another suggestion."

Either I had slightly peed on myself, or the moistness between my legs was picking up. I took the receipt and we stepped away from the counter.

"Repay you how?" I asked as we made our way through the exit doors.

"All I want is your phone number. Maybe I can call you later and we can hook up?"

I wasted no time in reaching in my purse for my business card. "Use the cell phone number. I'll be home after five and I look forward to hearing from you."

I walked away, and Christopher stood by the entrance while looking at my card. By the time I got to my Lexus, he was heading to his car. He glanced at me a few times and we both smiled as I drove off. Just to see what he was driving, I adjusted my rearview mirror and watched as he got into a Ford truck. I had hoped for a Mercedes, but since Fords were known for withstanding the test of time, it was all good. I had a feeling that this evening would be good as well, and had high hopes that a man as fine as he was wouldn't be capable of causing any major disappointments.

A Dazzling Dinner

Christopher presented me with something I hadn't had since Parker Rhodes and I had parted ways: a satisfying, eleven-inch muscle. We feasted upon each other while lying in a 69 position on my kitchen floor. Who would have expected it to come to this? Hmm . . . not me.

The night had started off a bit boring. Christopher arrived at seven o'clock, wearing the same royal blue shirt and black pants he'd had on at the post office. He carried a box of Godiva chocolates in his hand, and handed them to me as he made his entrance. My immediate thought was, *couldn't he have gone home first to change?* But I gathered myself and turned my thoughts to the golden box of goodies in his hand. While in my living room, we sat on the tan leather sectional and I dimmed the recessed lights to set the mood. Alicia Keys's latest hit was playing in the background, and the lit Villanova Candle Garden sitting on the table saturated the room with a vanilla fragrance. As I indulged myself with the chocolates, Christopher started to chat. He mentioned his occupation (manager at a nearby food joint), and talked about his two kids whom he adored so much. When I inquired about his babies' mama, he informed me that there were two.

"I get along with one of them, but the other, she's a real pain in the ass. She's a gold-digger, and she left me to be with a basketball player."

I wasn't the least bit interested in Christopher's private life, but only for the night, I decided to put my *real* thoughts aside. "It be like that sometimes, Christopher. I've been hurt too, but we move on and meet other interesting people, in the hopes that they'll be much different from the ones before."

"I agree," he said, turning to me. He reached for the chocolates, but I pulled the box away.

"Didn't you buy these for me?" I snapped, displaying a tiny grin on my face.

"Yes, but I was hoping to get at least one piece."

I wiggled my fingers over the chocolates and searched for one that probably had a yucky filling. I reached for it and placed the chocolate in Christopher's mouth.

"Mmm," he said, holding my fingers in his mouth. He laced the tips of my fingers with caramel chocolate and continued to suck them like a lollipop. Enjoying the feeling, I smiled, but soon retrieved my fingers.

"Can I offer you another one?" I asked.

He snickered and rested his arm on top of the couch. "No, thank you, but, uh, why don't you move a little closer. You have a lengthy gap between us, and I'd love to get a closer look at that pretty face while I'm speaking to you."

I moved closer and relaxed my legs on the couch. Since my silver silk robe had slid open, I pulled it over my legs to cover up. Christopher couldn't keep his wandering eyes off me, and when I noticed the increased movement in his pants, I decided our conversation was just about over.

"So, Rochel, I've shared some things about me, and I'd like to know more about you."

I shrugged. "Anything you want to know, just ask."

He lifted his hand and counted on his fingers. "First, are you involved with anyone? Do you have any children? What's your occupation? And, what do you like to do in your spare time?"

"I keep myself involved, I don't have any children, my job pays the bills, and in my spare time I like to fuck."

Christopher chuckled. I was sure only one of my responses had caught his attention. His brows went up and a more serious tone followed.

"Fuck? How often?"

I was blunt and to the point. "Daily."

"Are you serious? I mean, you don't look like the kind of woman who . . ."

"Who, what? Who likes to have sex, or who likes to have it daily?"

Christopher moved around a bit and I could tell my conversation was making him a bit uneasy. He quickly spoke up. "I mean, I hope you like to have sex, but there aren't too many women I know who like to have sex daily. Maybe men, but you rarely find a woman who wants it that often."

"Hmm," I said, uncrossing my legs and putting the almost empty box of chocolates on the table. I then returned to my position. "I'm a bit disappointed that you haven't run across women who enjoy sex daily. That says a lot about you because, if you're good, then she would want to have you every single day. Maybe for breakfast, lunch, and dinner. Is there a possibility that you're just not performing like you should?"

"Oh, I definitely know how to perform," he assured

me with a confident nod. His hand cuffed the growing hump between his legs. "It's just that some women can't handle what I got. You know what I mean?"

All this sex talk had me kind of hot and bothered. I reached over and lightly rubbed Christopher's waves. My voice softened. "I really don't know what you mean, but there's one thing I'm definitely sure of."

"What's that?"

I pulled my robe aside and let Christopher feast his eyes on my goods. "I'm awfully horny, Christopher. Can you take care of this little problem I've got stirring between my legs?"

No doubt, he loved my suggestion and didn't waste no time helping me with my "problem." He moved my robe further apart and dove into my wet spot with his fingers. As they rotated inside of me, my head fell backward and I sucked in my bottom lip.

"Damn, baby," he moaned. "That pussy feels off the chain. Lay back and let me feel the real deal."

I lay back, and with his other hand, Christopher reached for the belt on my robe and untied it. It slid wide open and his eyes examined my curvaceous, naked body. "You knew it was going down like this tonight, didn't you?" he said. "From the moment I saw you at the post office, you had plans for my ass, didn't you?"

I nodded as Christopher worked his thumb over my stimulated clit and finger-fucked me. I moaned out loudly with pure pleasure, and just as I was about to release my juices, Christopher eased his fingers out of me.

I squeezed my legs together and came up with the only word I could think of at the time: "Motherfucker!" Several deep breaths followed and my eyes shot daggers at him. "I hope you didn't come here to play games with me."

He ignored me, and with a satisfied grin on his face, he

stood up to remove his clothes. I was more than pleased by the size of his jumbo jack that was about to enter me, and I watched as he worked a condom on it. I had no intentions of letting him take control, so I sat up and ordered him to sit back on the couch. He did as I'd asked, and let one foot rest on the floor.

"Don't bite," he said. "And, don't choke yourself, either."

I hadn't planned on doing either, and even though his stiffness stood tall, his arrogance annoyed me. I reached for the lotion behind him and rubbed a generous portion of it on my hands. As they warmed, I placed one on Christopher's hardness and stroked him up and down. I tightened my grip over his head, giving him the feeling of a warm, tight pussy. He was tense, very tense, and couldn't bear to watch the pleasure I was giving him.

"Take it easy on me," he softly grunted. "That shit feels good . . . Real good."

I was well aware of how good my hands felt, and the tightening of his body confirmed it. Before he came, I started to work him with my mouth, and Christopher couldn't contain himself. He squeezed his fingers in my hair and I watched his sweaty six pack heave in and out while he took short breaths. At that moment, I released his goodness from my mouth and sat up.

"Hell, no!" he yelled, and grabbed his muscle. He quickly worked for the release he wanted and dropped his head back in relief.

"Okay," he said. "I deserved that, but let me make it up to you, all right?"

"Oh, you'd better be prepared to make it up to me. We got all night."

Christopher stood with excitement and removed his condom, only to retrieve another. "You're damn right we do," he said. "All night, and if you want it, all day to-morrow, too."

Now, that was my kind of man. I rested back on the couch and Christopher kneeled between my legs. He lifted my legs and locked them on his shoulders. He entered my wetness and a smile grew on his face.

"Wha . . . Where in the hell did you come from?" he asked while grinding inside of me. With every force, his ass tightened and I gripped his butt with pleasure. His package was touching all the right places, and with every swipe of my clit, I wanted to come. Christopher was talking too much though, and since I was so focused on how well his motion felt, I hadn't the time to respond. I did, however, offer him my "oos" and "ahhs" and when he touched the right spot, I couldn't contain myself.

"Right there, baby," I directed. "Keep forcing that dick in right there. The question is, where in the hell did you come from? This shit feels good . . . real good!"

"It gets even better," he boasted.

I'm sure it does, I thought, but kept the words to myself. It quickly got better, as Christopher backed out of me and pulled me to the floor. I wanted to feel him from my backside, so I positioned myself to do just that.

"G'on with your bad self, girl. Show me what ya working with."

I backed up my ass to Christopher and he separated my cheeks. His grip was tight, and as he massaged me, my gushy insides awaited him. He aimed at my hole and found his target. While doggy style, he worked me like a pro. His slaps against my backside made me come quickly, and just as I thought my outburst was over, he shook up things again. His pipe expanded inside of me and caused more juices to circulate. I dropped my head to pull my hair, and that's when he pulled out. He then turned onto his back and pulled me over his mouth to collect my overflow. My legs trembled, and all I could think about was how much I wanted this to be about business and not make it anything personal.

As I tried to regroup, I excused myself from Christopher to get some water.

"Don't take too long," he said. "You are coming back, aren't you?"

"Of course." I smiled and made my way to the kitchen.

I poured my water, and just as I was about to get some for Christopher, he came into the kitchen. Needless to say, that's how we wound up on the kitchen floor, feasting on each other for dinner. What an excellent meal it was, and as I was so sure the night wasn't over, I decided I would have to go back for seconds, maybe thirds.

Getting To Know Me

For the last two weeks, Christopher had been to my house every single day. Of course, sex was on the menu, and once it was over, we cuddled in each other's arms and fell asleep. Still, I knew minimal information about Christopher, but that's how I planned to keep it. I knew that this relationship wasn't going no further than the bedroom, and obviously, so did he. I was a dream come true to him; any woman who didn't delve into a man's personal life had to be right up his alley. He loved the fact that I didn't question him about his job, finances, children . . . or hadn't inquired about a relationship between us.

As for me, I loved the fact that he wasn't bothered by the numerous phone calls I received from other men. Or that I'd turned Michael away, when he'd shown up the other night unannounced. Christopher had played it cool, and even offered to leave so I could "handle my business."

Normally, when we spoke over the phone, our conversations were very brief. All I had to do was provide him with a time, and that was it. Either he was early or on time. Since he knew pussy was waiting for him, he was rarely ever a minute late.

After last night, though, things took a slight turn. I wanted to know a bit more about Christopher, and since I'd been dishing out the goods to him, I was curious to know if the brotha had my back. Again, that's just something I wanted to know.

Sex between us wrapped up hours before, and when morning came, I sat on the edge of my queen-sized bed taking a few puffs from a cigarette. I didn't smoke that often, but when I had something on my mind, the nicotine helped calm my nerves. Christopher was still resting, and as tender as my insides were, I should have been resting too. Instead, I was up getting my fix, thinking about my next move with a man who had become a true interruption in my life.

As I stared out the window, Christopher turned on his back and squinted from the reflection of the sun brightening the room. He slowly sat up on his elbows and glanced at me sitting on the edge of the bed.

"I didn't know you smoked," he said.

"Sometimes," I said, blowing the remainder of the smoke out of my mouth. I smashed the partially finished cigarette into an ashtray and turned to Christopher. "Especially when I'm worried about something."

Christopher pulled back the silk sheet and straddled me from behind. While naked, he wrapped his muscular arms around my body and pecked my neck. "What ails you? I hope I haven't done anything to upset you."

"No . . . nothing like that. I'm just having some financial difficulties right now. I was supposed to get a raise but that didn't come through. Then, I was promised a bonus and that didn't come through for me, either. My car payment is almost two months behind, and no matter what, I can't seem to keep up."

"Yeah," he said, releasing his arms from around me. "Keeping your finances in order can be a motherfucker. I know this place cost you a pretty penny, and driving a Lexus ain't cheap, either." Christopher got off the bed and lifted my chin to give me a kiss. "If I can do anything to help, just let me know. I'm getting ready to hit the shower. You wanna join me?"

I gazed at his nicely cut body and stood to remove my robe. He followed me to the standing glass shower, and once we entered, the warm water sprayed our bodies.

With a soapy sponge, I washed Christopher's body. He closed his eyes, and turned his back so I could finish up. I made it my business to thoroughly wash his body while he pressed his hands against the shower's wall. Obviously feeling good to him, he shook his head.

"I don't know why I can't get enough of you," he said. "I'm thinking about fucking you all the time, and believe it or not, I've never had this much sex with a woman before."

Christopher turned and looked down at my dripping wet, perky breasts. I stood five feet, five inches in front of him and wrapped my arms around him.

"I think a lot about you too, Christopher. But I prefer that we take this one day at a time."

He nodded and leaned down to kiss me. Afterward, he went for my right breast and cuffed it in his hand. He licked around my dark, healthy nipple, and then tightly plucked it with his lips. While gently massaging both of my breasts, he soon lowered one of his hands to moisten my slit.

"I thought you were supposed to wash me," I whimpered. "What about me?"

"Oh, I haven't forgotten about you. Never."

Christopher turned me around and pressed my back down to bend me over. He rubbed my back, and along with the warm water beating on it, the feeling was more than soothing. I felt his hardness poke against me, and as his thickness entered me, I reached my hand out to hold the towel rack. Things were about to get slippery and all I could do was hold on for dear life. I powerfully forced my ass against Christopher, and he expressed his joy of watching it jiggle. He continued to rub me all over, and by multi-tasking, he squeezed the soapy sponge over my back and dug deeper into me. His soapy hands washed my breasts and cleaned every other part of my body that he could reach. In a near panic from his touch, I slowed things down and turned to get on my knees. I backed Christopher against the tiled wall and opened my mouth to receive his package. With tightened jaws, I sucked with no regrets and stroked what had been so good to me for the past two weeks. The back of my throat was where Christopher wanted to be, and each time I put it there, he sighed with pleasure. He took deep breaths and I felt his juices rising. I focused on his head, and when his cum rushed to the top, I had myself one enjoyable moment. Christopher's legs weakened, and he pounded his fist against the wall, gritting his teeth. "What in the hell did I do to deserve this? You are amazing . . . downright amazing!"

I smiled and stood. Christopher rubbed his wet hands over my mouth, and, as the water had turned cold, we wrapped up with a long and satisfying kiss.

Nearly an hour later, Christopher was dressed and ready to go. It was Saturday, and even though he wasn't aware of it, I had shopping to do and dinner plans with

Michael. I walked Christopher to the door, and he took my hand and clinched it in his.

"I'll see you tomorrow," he said. "Call and let me know what time to come by. I know you have work on Monday, so I promise not to stay late."

"Oh, I'm sorry. But tomorrow is not going to be a good day for me. One of my friends is having a baby shower and I promised I would help her. I'll call you Monday . . . maybe Tuesday, okay?"

Christopher's head went back and his eyes widened. He looked shocked, as if he didn't believe me. He loosened his hand from mine and shrugged his shoulders. "All right, fine. Have fun and call me Monday or Tuesday."

"You're not upset with me, are you?"

"No. Why would I be upset with you? You have things to do and I understand that. Yes, I know there are other men occupying your time, and I assume, whether you're honest with me or not, that you have to make time for them, too."

"Does that bother you?" I pushed.

Christopher put his hands in his pockets and gave me a serious look. "I would be lying if I said that it didn't bother me. Not to the extent where it's going to interfere with us, because my main concern is about you and me. You're very private, and I don't want to scare you away by asking too many questions."

"From the beginning, I told you to ask me what you wanted to know. You haven't asked, so I haven't revealed much about me."

"Okay," he said. "Then, how do you feel about us? I mean, we seem to have a lot in common sexually, but can you see us dating each other or taking this relationship to the next level?"

"Possibly. But we still need to take it one day at a time. Jumping into a serious relationship is not something I want to do right now, but over time, I might feel differently."

"I don't have a problem with that. In the upcoming weeks, we'll try seeing each other outside of the bedroom and go from there."

"Sounds like a winner," I said, leaning forward to kiss him. He smiled and turned to the door. "Oh," I said, halting his steps. "I . . . There is something else I forgot to ask you."

"What's that?"

"Earlier, I mentioned my little problem and you said if I needed anything to ask. Well, if you could, uh, spot me three hundred dollars until next week, I would really appreciate it. I promise I'll give it back to you next week."

"I don't have three hundred dollars on me right now, so I'll have to go to the bank and get it." Christopher looked at his watch. "My bank closes in an hour, so I'll try to make it there before then. If not, I'll get it for you on Monday."

"Thank you," I said. "I really hate to bother you, but—"

"No problem. I'll get back with you today or Monday."

Christopher left and I headed out to enjoy my Saturday.

A Woman on a Mission

Since my departure from that slime bag Parker Rhodes, I'd never kept only one man in my possession. And even though I gave my time to many, I only involved myself sexually with one or two men at a time. My relationships never lasted more than six to eight months, and somewhere along the road, I always seemed to get bored. That's just how I wanted things, and thus far, I hadn't met any man who made me feel differently.

By noon, I was on my way to the park to see another one of my pussy-pokers, James. He was my nerd of the bunch; as smart as ever. He was a high school teacher, and treated me with much respect. I hated that our time was almost coming to an end, but that's just how it had to be. After four months together, he finally admitted to having a steady girlfriend whom he intended to make his wife. Ever since his confession, I'd been on a mission to end it, and rarely called him anymore.

As I closed the car door, from a distance I saw James sitting on a bench. He was casually dressed in khaki pants and a white polo shirt. His tinted glasses covered his grey eyes, and it was a pleasure to see that he'd gone all out to look well-groomed for me. I'd done the same for him; the black stretch mini-dress that I wore hugged my hips and criss-crossed over my breasts. James smiled at me with pure satisfaction on his face, and when the wind slightly blew the slit in my dress to the side, his eyes dropped to take a peek. Being a true lady, I kept on walking and allowed the man to see my hot pink lace boy shorts underneath. James stood up and reached out to me for a hug. We tightly embraced and he rubbed my back.

"Woman, I have truly missed you," he said, standing tall in front of me. He kissed my forehead and backed away from me to take a look. "You . . . you got it going on. Thanks for meeting me here. I hope it wasn't an inconvenience for you."

"Not at all," I said. I placed my purse on top of the bench and sat next to it. James sat as well, and seemed a bit nervous as he rubbed his hands together and looked down at his shiny loafers.

I reached over and touched his back. "Are you okay? It seems as if you have something heavy on your mind. Take a load off and tell me."

James swallowed hard and his voice cracked a bit as he spoke. "I'm okay, Rochel. It's just that this whole idea about getting married is starting to concern me. I do love my girl, but I've been thinking about you an awful lot. I miss being with you, and since you've distanced yourself, I feel as if I've lost something."

"I . . . I miss you too, James, but your proposal to another woman kind of rubbed me the wrong way. I don't like being the other woman, and I knew that if you'd have to choose, you'd choose her. I didn't want to put you under those conditions, so I've backed off."

"You've done more than just backed off." His voice

went to a higher pitch that made me uncomfortable. "I can't get you to return any of my phone calls, and even though I thought hard about telling you the truth, I never thought you'd remove yourself from my life as you did."

I didn't appreciate his tone, but I figured some type of explanation was needed on my part. I leaned back, placing the palms of my hands on the bench. My tone was soft, as an argument between us wasn't in my plans. "James, truly, I appreciated your honesty, but you gave me a choice. Like I said, I intend to back off and allow you some time to figure out who or what you really want. I've been very upfront with you about my relationships, and if you ruin a good thing for me, then you're doing yourself a great disservice. Let the truth be told, there's no way I can give you what the other woman does, and deep down, I think you know that."

He tightened his fist, and I could see how much he was struggling with his decision. "Yes, I know that you don't love me, but there's still something so damn intriguing about you. I don't know what it is, and believe this or not, it has nothing to do with your performance in the bedroom."

My brows instantly rose, as I didn't believe for one minute what he'd said. "Okay, so you like me . . . you like me a lot. What is it that you want from me? There's not too much I can offer a man who's about to get married, is there?"

James hesitated to answer. He massaged his hands together, then reached over to touch my thigh. "I want to spend time with you as often as I possibly can. I know it sounds crazy, but simply put . . . I want to have my cake and eat it too. Besides, you do and I've never questioned you about any of your relationships, even though I know they exist."

I quickly removed his hand. Another man trying to

have his cake and eat it too was a total turn off to me, especially a man who was so willing to admit it. I kept my cool and pretended as if his comment hadn't disturbed me. "Trust me, James, I have no problem with you having your cake and eating it too. I just wonder, though, what do you think is going to happen to me if or when you get married? Am I supposed to just vanish and ignore my feelings for you?"

James proudly pointed to his chest. "If or when I get married, nothing is going to change between us. If you decide to remove yourself from the equation, that's going to be your call. Still, I don't want that to happen, and my goal is to be with you for as long as you'll put up with me."

I'd heard enough from the educator, and stood up. As I reached for my purse, I cracked a tiny smile for James. "Give me some time to think about this, okay?"

His forehead showed wrinkles and eyelids looked heavy. "How much time do you need?"

I avoided eye contact and fumbled with my manicured nails. "A week . . . maybe two."

"Two weeks?" he shouted. "I—"

"Look," I said, holding my hand up to his chest, "I'm just not sure if I'm prepared to travel down this road with you and your future wife. I can't quite understand it; if you love her, and you want to marry her, then why do you need me?"

James reached up and straightened his glasses. He took a deep breath to calm himself. "I . . . I don't *need* anybody, Rochel. I *want* you and I *want* her. There's nothing wrong with a man wanting two women, is there?"

I shrugged my shoulders. "In this day and age, I guess not. But I need you to be as honest with her as you are with me. Have you spoken to her about your wants?"

"No."

"Why not?"

"Because she doesn't need to know how I truly feel."

I clutched my purse underneath my arm. James had said enough and it was time for me to go. "Thanks for being upfront and honest with me. Like I said, you'll hear from me soon."

I turned to leave and James reached for my hand. "Why are you rushing off so quickly? I hope you're not angry. I . . . I thought we could go to lunch and then go to my house and put my bed in motion."

I slightly chuckled at the thought, but kept my cool. "No, I'm not angry with you. Actually, I'm far from being angry. I just need some time to think about this, and the least you can do is allow me that. So, I'll have to take a rain check, okay?"

James frowned, shaking his head from side to side. He truly looked like a sad, lost puppy. "I guess I don't have much of a choice, do I?"

"I guess you don't," I said, leaning in to give him a tiny kiss. Surely, that perked him up, and just for the hell of it, I allowed his hands to roam over my butt. I knew he could feel my ass cheeks underneath my dress, and that aroused him even more.

"Come on, baby," he begged while stomping on the ground like a kid. "Please let me take you back to my place. I promise I'll be good to you . . . real good to you."

I backed away from James and wiped my lips. He had some of the prettiest grey eyes, and they always made my heart melt. Not today, though.

"I'll call you," I whispered. "And when we make up for all of this lost time, I'm positive that you'll enjoy it."

James smiled at the thought and nodded. Then he reached in his back pocket and pulled out his wallet. "How much did you say you needed for your car payment?"

"Four hundred and eighty dollars. Just round it off to five. You know I appreciate you giving this to me. I'd been so worked up about your news, I almost forgot I'd asked you for the money."

James handed the money over to me, and before I left, he gave me a lengthy kiss that I would soon forget.

Before my late dinner with Michael, I still had plenty of time to drop by the police station to see Lance, chat with Dwayne at the barbershop, and go to the mall to shop for shoes.

I stopped by the police station first, and as soon as I pulled up to park, I saw Lance sitting in his car with a lady-friend by his side. Just by the look on his face, I could tell she was one of his many girlfriends. She had a mean mug on; he hurried out of the car so I wouldn't overstep my boundaries.

"What's up?" he said, adjusting the policeman's cap on his head. "I didn't know you were going to stop by."

Giving my hips every swish that I could, I headed his way and swiped my bangs over to the side. "I was in the neighborhood and decided to stop by. Did I interrupt something?"

"Yeah, kind of, but, uh, where are you headed looking and smelling good?"

As soon as Lance spilled those words from his mouth, the overly thick woman jumped out of the car. "Who in the hell is this?" she snapped while rolling her neck around.

I knew Lance all too well; therefore, I figured he had this situation under control. "Baby, calm down," he said, forming his mouth to lie. "She's Rodney's woman and she stopped by to pick up some money for him."

The lady folded her arms and pouted. "Then, why are you out here complementing her on how good she looks and smells?"

"Because I like to pay women compliments, especially when they deserve them. Now, g'on and get back in the car. There's no need for you to be jumping out like a pit bull getting ready to bite."

I wanted to burst out laughing, but I held my composure. I looked at Lance and held out my hand. "Would you just give me the money? Rodney's been waiting all day, and I don't want to keep him waiting a moment longer."

Lance quickly reached into his pocket and pulled out his wallet. He was well aware of the routine, and the last thing he needed was for me to start running off at the mouth. After his woman got back into the police car, he followed me to my car. He opened the door for me, and once I got inside, he handed the cash to me.

"Thanks for not saying anything," he whispered. "I really need to get rid of my headache, but it's going to take some time."

My eyes widened and I cracked up inside. All I could do was whisper back at him, "Take all the time you need, Lance. You know that your women have never been a problem for me."

"So you say," he said, unconvinced, "If not, then why haven't you been calling me? I haven't dove into that pussy for quite some time, and Daddy's been anxious to smack it up and rub it down."

I put on my million-dollar smile to match Lance's. "When Daddy gets his women under control, he knows how to reach me. In the meantime, I'm not trying to get bit by your pit bull, so I must go."

Lance laughed and tapped the hood of my car. "Get out of here, woman. You gon' get me in trouble, and if you stay a minute longer, I might have to jump your bones on that back seat."

I chuckled at his bullshit ways and put my car in reverse. "I'll call you later," I mouthed just as his woman opened the door to hear our conversation. Surely, I wasn't about to argue with her over a man who, according to him, was separated from his wife and had seven children spread out in the city and counties of St. Louis. Even so, I clearly understood how anxious the woman was to protect *her* man, because Lance was quite a charmer and definitely knew how to make a woman feel wanted. He was a master at manipulating and could easily coax a woman out of her panties. It helped that he resembled Denzel in *Training Day*, but when it came to delivering in the bedroom, Lance was no prize. He failed miserably at pleasing me; he thought he was God's gift to this earth. *What a joke*, I thought while waving and driving away.

My last stop was to visit Dwayne, who worked at a barbershop not too far from the police station. Dwayne was not my type at all, but a thug could always, someway or somehow, have his way with women. It took a few months for me to connect with him, but when I did, I found out some interesting things. He was hard on the outside, but soft as butter on the inside. He'd spent a couple of years in prison, but assured me that his life was back on the right track. I didn't believe him one bit; cutting hair at a barbershop did not account for the extravagant lifestyle he lived. He was the most materialistic man I'd ever dated, but the good thing about him was that he wanted his women to look good as well. Whenever he saw me, which hadn't been that often lately, he always greeted me with the most pleasant smile that displayed his grille. He knew how much I hated his sagging pants, so he reached down to pull them up.

"What's poppin', baby girl?"

"Nothing much," I said, walking up to his workstation and giving him a hug. "I just stopped by to see you, that's all."

"Well, it's about damn time!" he yelled, obviously wanting to bring attention to himself. "Nigga thought you was on some kind of trippin' game or somethin'."

I pointed to myself and ignored his annoying behavior. "Tripping? Why would I be tripping with you?"

"You know how y'all women are. That PMS shit be having y'all buggin'." He stared me down and sucked his teeth. One of the fellows gripped Dwayne's hand, agreeing with his comment about women.

I crossed my arms and tooted my lips. "So, I guess you're a comedian now, huh? If you think so, don't quit your day job because being a comedian won't pay your bills. This job probably doesn't, either, especially since every time I come in here, you're the only one without any customers. You ever think about going back to school?"

"*Damn*," the brothas rang out and laughed. Dwayne looked insulted, but as usual, he had brought it on himself.

He reached for my arm and squeezed it. "Come on and bring your li'l feisty ass in the back with me. You need a whuppin', girl, and it's about high time you got one."

"Spank me good," I said, tugging my arm away from his grip. I knew he was all talk and no action, so I followed him to the backroom. Before I could say anything, he pushed me against the filthy white wall and placed his hand between my legs.

"What's up with my pussy, ma? You been leaving a nigga high and dry, and I need to know what's up with that. Somebody else been shaking you down or what? If so, holla at your boy and tell me what the fuck is up."

Always displeased about Dwayne's aggression and ghettofied ways, I shoved him backward and straightened my dress. I darted my finger in his direction and took charge of the situation. "Look, the only reason I stopped by was to say hello. We're not about to shake up anything in this filthy room, so you can forget about that. When you make plans to step up your game with me, then maybe I'll start coming around a bit more. As for me being with someone else, don't fool yourself, Dwayne. What you do, I can do better."

He stepped backward and placed his hands in the front pockets of his sagging jeans. His inquisitive hazel eyes searched over me, as he circled his tongue on his lips to wet them. My body felt a tingle, and it was hard for me not to appreciate the dark chocolate stallion that stood before me.

"I doubt that you got game like me, but it's whatever you say. You be driving a hard fuckin' bargain." He paused and removed his hands from his pockets to crack his knuckles. "What the fuck up with you, ma? Why you always turning a nigga on and off? Sometimes, I can't tell if yo' ass feelin' me or not."

I moved forward and placed my hand on the one thing about Dwayne that had potential. I massaged his dick and placed my lips closely to his ear. "Don't you ever think I'm not feeling you, boo, because I am. I feel every inch of you, but when you step to me, all I ask is that you come like you have some sense. Save all the tough talk and knuckle cracking for your other women. And, when you're ready to put a belt on those pants, get a decent job, and find something other than a toothpick to dangle from your mouth, a real woman will be waiting right here for you. Until then, I need a loan; a big one that ranks in the thousands. Will you be able to handle it or not?"

Dwayne squeezed my wrist and tossed it away from his hardness.

"You good, Rochel, but you ain't that good. Pussy don't motivate or inspire me to up my money, and even though I've dished it out to you in the past, you ain't got shit coming. I know when a bitch ain't feelin' me, and it would be wise for you to get the hell out of here before I find a motive to do something I may someday regret."

Dwayne and I stared each other down. Our eyes were in a deadlock. When he leaned forward to kiss me, I held up my hand. "I love the way you come at women, Dwayne, and your disrespect obviously allows you to have a lot of them. Unfortunately, though, not this, as you put it, bitch. It was fun while it lasted, I don't think it would be *wise* for us to see each other again. I don't take threats lightly, and I know when my time in a relationship is up."

He backed away from me and held out his hands in defeat. "Kiss my ass," he offered. I rolled my eyes and made my way up front to exit. I heard him spew some other harsh words, but was thankful that our connection had only been about the money.

I spent the rest of my day at the mall buying shoes, shoes, and more shoes. I was a shoe fanatic and all of the new styles had me going crazy. By day's end, I had forked out over seven hundred bucks for shoes, and purchased several purses that matched. Since I had plans to see Michael that night, I was sure he'd help me with my losses. And, since Christopher hadn't called to inform me about the three hundred bucks I'd asked him for earlier, I certainly knew what time it was with him. I laughed at the thought during dinner. Michael asked what was so funny.

"Nothing," I said, picking through my Cobb salad. "I was just thinking about something someone said to me at work, that's all."

"Well, tell me. I might want to laugh too."

I looked at Michael, and even though he was still attractive to me, I was getting bored. I'd met him more than six months ago, and just like Christopher, things had started off cool. I bumped into Michael at a gas station, and had joked with him about resembling Brian McKnight. That night, we hooked up and we'd been kicking it ever since. His sex was nowhere near as satisfying as Christopher's, but, just like the others, it served its purpose and just had to do. When I asked Michael to loan me money, he did. Afterward, he felt as if he owned me, even though I purposely took my time paying the money back. He'd done some nice things for me: dinners, plays, movies, other loans . . . but, unfortunately, he had a wife. He treated her like shit, so I treated him like shit. I dealt with him whenever I wanted to, and this relationship was always on my time, not his.

Michael tapped his knuckle on the table to get my attention. When I looked up at him, he sighed deeply. "Rochel, are you even listening to me tonight? If your mind is somewhere else, then maybe we should call it a night. Besides, you haven't told me about your new boyfriend, and I was surprised to run into him the other night."

I shrugged my shoulders and my pitch got higher. "I'm not sure why you were so surprised, Michael. You have a wife, and who I fuck is none of your business."

He snapped right back. "It is my business, and thanks for letting me know that you're fucking him. I guess I'm all played out, huh?"

I was happy to see him on the defensive. "I wouldn't say all that, but this controlling thing with you has no place in our relationship. The fact is, you're married and you have no say-so about what I do or who I see. You and I fuck each other, and every now and then we put sex aside to do other things. Unless you're willing to divorce your wife, this kind of conversation between us shouldn't exist. Personally, I don't want to hear anymore of your gripes, and quite frankly, your gripes don't mean a damn thing to me."

Michael rubbed his goatee and wiped his mouth with a napkin. He stood up and leaned over me. "I don't know what the hell has gotten into you, but I'm going home to spend some time with my wife. If or when you get an itch that needs to be scratched, give me a call. Until then, dinner is on you tonight. With your big mouth, you've embarrassed the both of us. The least you can do is pick up the tab."

Michael walked off and nearly every eye in the restaurant was on me. I loved to upset Michael, and to me, married men were some of the weakest men to deal with. They always felt as if they were the big players, but in actuality, to keep a woman like me they were playing themselves. Didn't he know that? I shook my head from the thought and dove into my salad to finish it.

As soon as I wrapped up dinner, I paid the thirty-six-dollar bill and left. I headed to my car and called Michael. I needed him to repay me for my shopping spree today, and leaving me at the restaurant definitely wasn't cool. On the first ring, he answered.

"What?" he said angrily.

"Ah, baby, come on," I softly coaxed him. "Don't even be like that. You're snapping at me like a vicious dog and you know how I get sometimes."

"Yes, I know how you get. But I'll be damned if I'm going to put up with your attitude, Rochel."

He was playing the tough role, which always turned me on. "You're right," I said. "You shouldn't have to put up with my attitude. I'm sorry for my actions, but I'm bothered by your controlling ways. A married man shouldn't be that way, should he?"

"Married or not, I do have true feelings for you. I can't do much about my situation right now, but you better believe that I'll be doing something about it soon. As soon as my children get older, I'm walking away from my marriage."

I tooted my lips and got into my car. I softened my voice even more, ignoring what he'd implied. "Baby, before you got all upset with me and left, I wanted to ask you for some money. I barely had enough to pay for dinner and my car payment is slightly behind. I know you're angry with me, but can I get a loan? Like last time, I promise to give it back."

He grunted, but managed not to raise his voice. "Like last time, you still owe me five hundred dollars. You know I'll give it to you, but I do want my money back. I don't want to hear that 'then give my pussy back' bull you women be talking, and I know that's what you're thinking."

I laughed, as Michael was beginning to know me all too well. And even though getting my pussy back wasn't going to do me any good, as long as I was dishing it out, Michael wasn't getting a dime of his money back.

"You're hilarious," I said. "I'm leaving the parking lot, and that itch you mentioned is starting to take place. Are you nearby so you can scratch it?"

"I can't wait. If you look in your rearview mirror, you'll see that I'm on your trail right now."

I glanced in my rearview mirror and saw Michael's steel gray Jaguar behind me.

"I thought you were going home to your wife. Did you stay in the parking lot and wait for me?"

"Yes, and my wife doesn't know how to take me into fantasy land like you do. And, if you thought I was going to allow that sweet piece of ass to get away from me tonight, you're crazy. That mini-dress is hugging you in all the right places, and it's either a hotel or your place. You make the call."

Poor Wifey, I thought. Even if she did know how to take him to fantasy land, he'd still find an excuse for cheating on her. I had him on my good side, and if I wanted to keep him there, my attitude had to stop. I planted a smile on my face and swallowed hard. "Let's go to a hotel. I don't want any interruptions tonight, especially since I plan to show my appreciation for the eight hundred dollars you're going to loan me. That won't be a problem, will it?"

"Like I said, as long as I get it back. And just in case you got other plans, you might have to put in a little extra work tonight. I need to make sure I'm getting my money's worth."

My stomach turned in knots, but I was willing to do what I had to do. "You always do get your money's worth, don't you? Even when you don't offer me a dime, I never leave you hanging, do I?"

Michael laughed loudly, then spoke with a serious tone. "Naw, baby. I know you're good to me. And please don't take my comment the wrong way. Just pay me back whenever you can."

"You know I will," I said, looking in my rearview mirror with a welcoming smile on my face.

Michael winked and blew me a kiss. "I know you don't believe this, and since you tooted your lips when I mentioned my wife, I doubt that you will believe me. But, if I weren't married, things would be different for us. I'm working on ending my marriage, and not solely because of you, but because I'm just not happy."

"So, you saw me tooting my lips, huh?"

"Yeah, I stayed in the parking lot and watched you. You're something else, Rochel, but I like that toughness about you. It turns me on and I love a woman who takes charge."

"That's good to know. Now, how about I turn into the

Marriott down the road? You're tying up my phone line, and someone is trying to reach me on the other end. See you soon."

Michael hung up and I clicked over to answer the other call. It was Christopher.

"Hey," he said. "I tried to reach you at home, but you weren't there. I didn't make it to the bank in time, so I'll bring your package to you on Monday."

"Thanks for calling, and I'll see you Tuesday. I forgot that I'm working late on Monday, but as soon as I leave work on Tuesday, I'll call you."

"All right. Have a good weekend and be safe."

"You too," I said, and hung up.

"The bank was closed" my ass, and hadn't he displayed a debit card at the post office? I guess the ATM was closed, too. I smelled a rat and he would soon get caught in a trap. I put my thoughts aside about Christopher and made my way to the hotel to entertain Michael.

Getting To Know Him

Tuesday was a very stressful day at work, and I couldn't wait to get home and relax. I had invited Christopher over, and yesterday, he had called and suggested bringing dinner. I definitely hadn't planned on going home to cook, and since he offered to bring Chinese, I was all for it. I rushed home, showered, and changed into my navy blue silk gown with slits on the sides. Even though it was very sexy, I had made up my mind that sex wasn't on the agenda tonight. Christopher had been getting enough freebies, and now he had to show me that he was worth my time.

At about five minutes to six, he showed up with a huge brown paper bag that carried the aroma of scrumptious fried rice. I invited him into the kitchen, where I had already set the table with fine china, chilled wine, and two tall lit candles. He smiled, appreciating my efforts, and set the bag on the table.

"Come give me a hug," he said, looking very delightful in his jeans and Bob Marley T-shirt. He kissed my forehead and held my chin before placing a soft kiss on my lips. "You're so pretty. Has anybody ever told you that you look . . ."

I finished his sentence. "Like Nia Long? It's only my haircut. And, that would be her back-in-the-day haircut."

"Possibly," he said. "Still, you know you got it going on, right?"

"I try. And for the record, I only involve myself with men who got something intriguing going on, too."

Christopher didn't comment and removed the boxes from the bag.

"Shrimp fried rice, no onion and extra egg. Half order of Pork Egg Foo Young, with extra gravy. Right?" he said.

"That's right. And . . ."

"Oops, I almost forgot. Two egg rolls."

"Correct." I smiled and took a seat at the table as Christopher insisted on preparing our plates.

"Are you going to eat all of this?" he asked. "This is a lot of food."

"You don't have to pile everything on my plate. Just a little bit of this and that will do just fine."

Christopher proportioned my food and fixed his plate as well. I poured two glasses of wine and we started to eat.

At first, things were quiet. I had intended to ask him about the money, but he brought it up before I did.

"Hey, listen. I haven't forgotten about your money, but my son got sick and his mother didn't have any money to get his prescription. When I took the money to her, she talked about him needing new shoes and his lunch money for school. I haven't been current on my child support, so I had to kick her out more than expected. Can I give the three hundred dollars to you sometime next week?"

"You know what, I forgot to tell you that I borrowed the money from someone else. *He* gave it to me Saturday night . . . no, Sunday, and I made plans to pay him back when I get paid on Friday. Thanks, though, and . . . Where did you get this Chinese food from? This is really, really good."

"From a Chinese restaurant close by my job. I can't remember the name of it, but I've been hooked on this place for a long time. Getting back to the money, I'm sorry. If I had it to loan, no doubt, I would have given it to you."

I glared at Christopher through the burning candles and cut my eyes. He couldn't even look up at me. Before I could say another word, the doorbell rang. Christopher looked up.

"Are you expecting someone?"

"No, I'm not."

I stood and headed for the door. I asked who it was, and couldn't believe that Michael had the nerve to show up again. As soon as I pulled the door open, he frowned.

"I see that you have company, but we need to talk," he snapped.

"Yes, I do have company, Michael, and if you want to talk, I'll be able to in about an hour or so. You can come back then."

He darted his finger at the ground. "No, we need to talk right now. My wife found out some shit about us, and she threatened to come over here. I don't know how she knows where you live, but she does."

Since Michael looked so pathetic, and Christopher couldn't get his lies together, I invited Michael in. He followed me to the kitchen and looked surprised to see the cozy atmosphere. Christopher quickly stood up and looked irritated.

"Am I out of here or what? It seems as if every time I'm over here, this man shows up. Maybe you need to work this—"

I threw back my hand and silenced him. "Christopher, please have a seat. Michael is a friend of mine, and since his wife is having some concerns about our relationship, he wants to talk. In the meantime, I haven't asked you to leave, but if you're that eager, you can always find the door."

Christopher looked at Michael and returned to his seat. I invited Michael to take a seat as well. He eased into a chair and I placed a plate in front of him.

"There's plenty of food here; something told me to order extras," I said, snapping my finger. "Would you like some Egg Foo Young, rice, or an egg roll? Everything is really good, trust me." Before Christopher could gripe about purchasing the food, I looked over at him. "You don't mind, do you? Besides, this is a great opportunity for us to get better acquainted with each other. Who knows what the night has in store for . . . us?"

I knew exactly where both of their minds had gone, and since I was enraged with my visitors, I decided to have some fun.

"Hey," Christopher said, opening his hands and looking at Michael. "Feel free to help yourself."

As if I were feeding a stray dog, I slapped an Egg Foo Young patty on Michael's plate and covered it with rice. After I poured his wine, he looked at me like I'd gone crazy.

"Listen," he said. "I'll just come back later. This ain't cool and I'm not in the mood for games."

I laid down my fork and huffed. "Michael, you came here and said it was imperative that you speak to me about your wife. What is it that you want me to know, and what shall I tell her if she happens to stop by?"

Christopher added his two cents. "Just tell her you don't know him, and that you've never seen him a day in your life. That's all she wants to hear anyway."

I turned my attention to Christopher. "So, is that what you would want me to tell your wife if she shows up?"

"I'm not married, but I suspect that Michael would want you to say something like that."

I held my wine glass and twirled it around. "You suspect, huh? Well, let me tell you what I suspect. I suspect that you're a married man, too. And, the only reason that you're dealing with me is because I don't ask questions, and I continuously make myself available to you. According to you, I was the perfect catch, and God, where did a woman like me come from? Just like Michael, you were so lucky to find me, right?"

Christopher dropped his fork and angrily looked across the table at me. "I don't know where all of this is coming from, and if I were married, how could I be spending all of this time with you? You're crazy for thinking that, but it doesn't surprise me, since you're use to dealing with married men."

I didn't even bother to look over at Michael, who I knew was indulged with the heated conversation striking up between me and Christopher. For now, he seemed to be a good target.

"Christopher, cut the crap. The first day I saw you at the post office, I opened my compact mirror and searched you up and down. I saw the glistening wedding band on your finger, and after you dropped your package, it suddenly disappeared. By the time you made it to the counter, the ring was history. And just to be sure that my eyes hadn't played tricks on me, the first night that you slept in my house, I searched your pants. I saw your ring, and with diamonds like that, how dare you fuck and suck me the way you do? Your wife would be devastated, wouldn't she?"

Christopher didn't have much to say. All he could do

was take a deep and hard swallow. Michael stood up and put his hands in his pockets.

"I . . . I'm leaving," he said. "Uh, I really need you to—"

"If the wife stops by, you need me to keep my mouth shut, right? You didn't say that the other night, and if or when your wife arrives, I will tell her what I wish to tell her. It all depends on my mood, and since you're so damn unhappy with her, my coming forth might do you a tremendous favor."

Michael didn't say one word, and when Christopher stood and reached for his keys on the counter, they both headed for the door. I followed and got a whiff of Christopher's panty-dropping cologne and an eyeful of his nail-gripping ass in his jeans. Maybe I had been too hard on him; at this point, one last night of passion wasn't going to hurt. Michael left, and as Christopher moved forward, I reached for his arm.

"Good night, Michael," I said, and got no response as he abruptly got in his car and left. Christopher held the door and waited for me to speak.

"Look," I said. "All you had to do was be honest with me about your situation and none of this would have occurred. I don't like liars, and as open as I was with you about my relationships, you could have been the same. If you're unhappy at home, that's your problem. It has nothing to do with me, unless you're foolish enough to get caught. Michael is history because he got caught. You're history, too, because I don't appreciate a man who lies to me. However, I was hoping that you'd stay for a few hours, and end this with me on a good note—if you know what I mean."

Christopher stared at me without cracking one smile or saying a word. He hesitantly walked back inside and tossed his keys in a chair. *The power of pussy is unbelievable*, I thought, as I pulled the silk nightgown over my head. He reached for my body, and I grabbed at his belt buckle. His eyes dropped to my lips, and as we intensely kissed, he rushed out of his clothes. He picked me up to straddle his hips and gazed into my eyes.

"I . . . I don't want to end this," he said. "I should have been honest with you about my wife, but when I saw you, I had to have you. I wasn't sure how you would feel about me being married, so I did what I had to do."

I placed my fingers on Christopher's lips to shush him. "Like I said before, one day at a time, Christopher. Now, fuck me like you'll never see me again, and I promise to do the same."

Wasting no time, while still holding me, Christopher focused in on my breasts and sucked them. He held my butt cheeks in his hands and inched his fingers over to my slit to wet me. I was beyond drenched, and anxious to get this piece of a damn good dick for the last time. I almost cried from the thought, but at that point, it was just how it had to be.

As Christopher hardened, he laid me back on the floor and smiled as he lustfully admired my body. He reached for his pants and pulled out his wallet. When it came out, so did his wedding band. It quickly spun around before landing flat on the hardwood floor. We both glanced at his ring, and Christopher shrugged it off as he removed the condom from his wallet. He put on the condom and found the spot *he* wanted, remaining there for the rest of the night.

Doomsday

I sat on my couch smoking a cigarette and thought deeply about the last year of my life. It had been every bit of interesting, and out of all the men I'd been with, the memory of Christopher stuck with me the most. Surprisingly for me, it was hard to let him go, but I always had a difficult time letting go of something so good. Greed, I guess, but the money I'd been paid was worth more to me than anything.

When the doorbell rang, I stood up and pulled down my fitted T-shirt to cover my midriff. I rubbed my hands on my thighs and was a bit nervous about meeting with her. When I opened the door, she cracked a tiny smile, but had a saddened look on her pretty face. I invited her in, and after we both took a seat on the couch, I opened the huge envelope in front of me. I took a deep breath and asked the Caucasian woman, "Are you positive you want to see this?"

She nodded and tightly squeezed her eyes before opening them again. Her hands trembled as I gave her the pictures and tapes of me and Christopher. "The pictures are just of him in my bed, but the tapes reveal much more than that. They're not going to be easy to look at, and it might be more than what you asked for."

Mrs. Carter nodded again, and slowly flipped through the naked pictures of Christopher lying in my bed. Tears formed in her eyes, and she lowered the pictures to her lap while offering me a comment. "He . . . he was supposed to be out of town on business," she yelled, then swallowed hard. She rubbed her hand across her forehead before she continued to look at the rest of the pictures. "I don't understand how he could do this to me . . . to us. We just had a baby and—"

I reached for the Kleenex box on my table and gave it to her. "I'm sorry. I understand what you're going through, but you asked for my assistance because you wanted to know."

She wiped her tears and looked at me as if I were the enemy. "How often did you have sex with him?"

I sighed, and for whatever reason, shamefully dropped my head and softly spoke. "Almost daily." I lifted my head and did my best to put her at ease, turning the anger back at him. That started with me having no regrets about enjoying sex with her husband, and encouraging her to follow through with her plans. "The tapes will tell you everything you want to know. They're going to be very difficult to watch, but please remember that you paid me to do a job and I had to do it well. Meeting him at the post office that day was your idea, and I don't want you to have any regrets for wanting to know the truth. Use the truth to your advantage, and don't allow this to happen to you again. If you do, it would be a true waste of twenty-five thousand dollars, and I hope you know what steps to take in order to get your money back from him. Please, use my information to your advantage and never look back."

Mrs. Carter slowly nodded and reached in her purse for an envelope. She handed it to me, and when I opened it, I saw that the money was there. Our business was finished, and even though I felt deeply sorry for her, I couldn't take any chances of Christopher showing up and my cover being blown. I stood and so did she. We shook hands, and I wished Mrs. Carter well. If anything, I knew how difficult it would be for her to leave a man like Christopher, but after seeing the tapes, hopefully, it would make her decision easier.

After she left, I headed to my next appointment with Michael's wife. Six months of my services had cost her a pretty penny. The money didn't seem to bother her one bit; to her, it was so very worth it. She couldn't wait to show her lawyer the information I provided.

"So, were you able to get more information like I asked?" she said, sitting across the table from me.

"I have more pictures for you and a taped conversation where Michael threatens to get rid of you if you fail to divorce him. He doesn't seem like the kind of man who would go to that extreme, but I guess you know him better than I do."

She snapped and darted her finger at me. "You're right, you don't know him as well as I do. I don't trust him as far as I can see him and I truly believe he's capable of doing anything. Now, give me what you have and let me hurry up and pay you so I can get out of here. In the meantime, you'd better promise me that you will never see Michael again and you won't tell anyone that I paid you for these services."

I folded my arms, rather disturbed by Sharon's behavior. "What in the hell would make you think I'm interested in pursuing a relationship with Michael? In case you forgot, I'm in the business of tricking, not treating. Michael is not the kind of man I would ever seriously involve myself with, and frankly, I'm surprised that a woman of your stature would go this far in dealing with her husband. You seem to have a lot going for you, and chasing after a man doesn't suit you."

Sharon put her hand on her forehead and rubbed away the pressure. "You know what . . . you're right. It's just that Michael and I have been together for almost thirty years. He's cheated before, but this is the first time he's ever mentioned divorcing me. When I look at the pictures and the tapes, I see how excited he is about you and it angers me. I used to make him feel that way and it's been such a long time since I've had that kind of impact on him. So, forgive me for my attitude, but I will make him pay for what he's done and make him pay in a way that only satisfies me."

"Please, don't share with me what you intend to do about your husband. I don't want to know what your plans are and you'd better be very careful about what you say and who you say it to. Like I tell all of my clients, I only provide you with the information you asked me for. Whatever happens after that is up to you."

Sharon took a sip from her ice water and slid an envelope across the table. "Tell me something," she said. "How do you not get attached to the men you're paid to see? Have you ever had feelings for any of them?"

"Getting attached to dog-ass men isn't in my vocabulary. Now, there are times that I feel sexually satisfied by them, but in your case, and for the record, Michael didn't move me in such a way. Still, if he had, I've learned to put business before pleasure. My business with Michael is finished and it doesn't bother me in no way to move on without him."

I picked up the envelope and tucked it underneath my arm. Again, I wished Sharon all the best, and left having no regrets.

Later that day, I met with James's soon-to-be wife, Lance's wife of ten years, and Dwayne's long-time girlfriend, all of whom had paid for my services too. Out of the five women I'd met, only one seemed confident that it was over. That was Michael's wife, and she was confident that her attorney would make Michael pay. I didn't doubt her one bit, and her cutthroat attitude meant major trouble for him.

The other women had tears flowing and somehow felt as if they were exempt from this kind of foolishness ever happening to them. I could see the anger in their eyes, and surprisingly, some of that anger was directed toward me. A part of me understood why, but it didn't necessarily take a woman as pretty, sophisticated, or sexy as me to lure these men in as I had. They were all game for whatever, and throughout the many dark and secretive days and nights that we crept, none of these women seemed to matter to their men.

My bags were already packed, and after almost a year, I was ready to leave my so-called happy home. Thing was, it wasn't really my home, and if Michael, Christopher, Lance, Dwayne, or James had inquired about me a bit more, they would have known so. Furniture was only in the bedroom, the living room and kitchen. The rest of my 4000-square-foot house was empty, including every single closet. I never mentioned a family, and "my house" didn't display pictures of anyone. After day one, none of them wanted to get to know me. My occupation didn't matter much, and telling them that it paid the bills seemed to be good enough. It was definitely good enough for me, and I was looking forward to my rewarding career. I knew it would earn me more money than I ever thought possible, so I guess being classified as an undercover ho/detective wasn't so bad after all.

It's Not Over . . . Yet

What can I say, other than my life was great. The money I'd made allowed me to travel to many places I'd dreamed of going, and I was finally able to purchase a place I could truly call home. I had plans of going back to work soon; finding more women who were willing to put their men on blast wasn't going to be difficult at all. I already had women contacting me about settling a score with their significant others, and as I reviewed some of the letters I'd received, one of them caught me by surprise. Through the letter, I could feel this particular woman's pain. Like some of the others, she'd been lied to, cheated on, and was willing to do anything to bring down her man. More than anything, she was ready to kill, and the man who had pushed her to this conclusion was Parker Rhodes.

I hadn't seen Parker in years, and the sight of his name made me uneasy. I remembered when I wanted to kill his ass too for the hurt he'd caused me, so I definitely understood what the woman in the letter was feeling. I'd figured that by now he'd changed his attitude toward women, and it was disappointing to know that he hadn't changed one bit. I was skeptical about doing anything and my involvement could very well mean serious trouble for me. Still, I wanted to see what end result the woman was looking for and how she intended to use me for help. With that in mind, I finished my hot black coffee, then called her, using my middle name, Jakki.

"May I speak to Vivica?" I asked.

"Who's calling?"

"Jakki."

"Jakki who?"

"Jakki who has your letter in her hand and wants to speak to you about Parker."

She paused. "Oh . . . oh, okay. Hold on."

I was left on hold for a few minutes, and then Vivica got back on the phone. "Jakki, I don't want to talk too much over the phone. Are you able to help me or not?"

"Your letter didn't specify how you wanted my help. Are you married and need evidence for your divorce? Are you just a girlfriend who wants evidence that her man is cheating? Are you a fiancé who isn't sure she can trust the man she intends to marry . . . What? What's your purpose?"

"I . . . I'm a woman who wants her man wiped off the face of the earth."

"Unfortunately, I don't do that kind of work. You may have to get a hit man for that."

She laughed. "I see. But, if it's not any trouble, can we meet somewhere and talk?"

"Sure. But first, how did you hear about me?"

"My friend, Sharon, gave me your card. She said you only worked with referrals and praised you for helping with her divorce from Michael."

"Yes, I did help her in a major way. Are you married to

the man you mentioned in the letter, Parker . . . Parker Rhodes?"

"Yes, I am Mrs. Rhodes. My husband is an asshole, and I'd like to see that he gets exactly what Michael got."

My throat ached a bit, as I hadn't known definitely that Parker had gone through with the marriage that basically ended our relationship. I was eager to meet this woman, even if I wouldn't be able to assist her in the way she wanted.

"Where would you like to meet?" I asked.

"I'm at work right now. Why don't you come to my office?"

"I can meet you around noon. Is that okay?"

"Absolutely."

Vivica gave me directions to her office, and I left an hour early so I could be on time.

When I arrived at the Wilshire Building in downtown St. Louis, Vivica's secretary asked me to have a seat in the lobby. I waited and paged through a *Business Matters* magazine until she came to get me. I was a bit nervous about meeting her, and even though I had dressed my best, I couldn't deny that meeting the woman married to Parker bothered me.

Vivica came out, and, mildly put, she was drop-dead gorgeous. Not as pretty as me, but some would beg to differ. She reminded me of Gabrielle Union and her strut was quite the same. While looking me over, she reached out her hand. "Nice to meet you, Jakki. Come on back to my office so we can talk."

Our high heels clicked loudly on the hardwood floors as we made our way to her office. The entire place was quite impressive. When we reached her contemporary-designed office, she asked me to have a seat in a circular tan leather chair. I couldn't help but notice the loving pictures of her and Parker on her desk and wall. The one that ate at me the most was a wedding picture she had smack on her desk. They looked so happy together. I reached for it to take a closer look.

"Of course, that's the scumbag I mentioned in my letter. Those days are long gone and I need to hurry up and do something about him."

I placed the picture back on her desk and crossed my legs. "Again, I'm not sure what you want from me, and if you'd be more specific, I can let you know if I'll be able to assist."

She held out her hand and touched her fingers one by one. "I want pictures, I want tapes, and I want evidence in his own words of what a liar and deceiver he truly is. I want all of the evidence you can gather, and when I take him to court, I want his head on a silver platter."

"I can get all of that for you, but my fees are very . . ."

"I don't give a damn about your fees. Whatever they are, if you give me what I want, you'll be paid in full."

"So, you don't mind if getting what you want means me having sex with your husband, do you? You'll have to remember that I'm in the business of tricking, not necessarily treating. I only treat when I have to."

"I don't want that to be your only source of connecting with him, but if you've got to use what you got, then do it. As I said, I want to use his own words against him. Anything you can get for me will make my case much easier."

From what I remembered about Parker, he was broke as hell. He pretended to have money, and often used the women in his life to get it. To me, she didn't stand to gain anything from a divorce but her sanity.

"How much is your husband worth, Vivica? Is this going to be worth it to you, if he has no money?"

"My husband won the lottery last year and there's plenty of his money left to go around. I'm afraid that his will leaves me out, and I don't stand to gain anything if he divorces me. Our marriage is rocky, and I expect for Parker to leave me for one of his tricks any day now. So you can understand why I don't want to be left without, and for me, this is an urgent matter."

I was shocked that a man like Parker could be lucky enough to win the lottery. I wanted to tell his wife that I also shared a hatred for him, but I wasn't comfortable letting her know who I was. However, if I could play a part in bringing him down, I was all for it and anxious to get this show on the road.

"At your convenience, I need pictures of Park . . . your husband, and if you could share with me his frequent hangouts that would be great. I need information about where he works, any girlfriends he might have that you know of, and information about his family."

Vivica pulled out a thick folder and gave it to me. "Most of the information you need is there. If you need anything else, let me know."

I glanced at the information, some of which I'd already known. I stood up and reached out my hand. "Vivica, I'm going to follow your husband around for a week, just to get a feel for the kind of man he is. I will then require half of my money up front, and you won't be asked to pay the rest until I'm done. I'm sure that I'll be able to get you everything you need."

"I hope so."

I smiled and left Vivica's office on a serious high.

Two Steps Forward and Three Steps Back

The following week, I followed Parker nearly every place he went. I was saddened about his continued disrespect of women, all of which made me more eager to nail his ass. I was surprised by the rise of my past feelings for him; it was hard not to feel attracted to a man I once loved more than life itself. His new-found money allowed him to clean up even more. It was like seeing 50 Cent on the cover of *GQ*. He seemed confident, and had an attitude as if he thought the world were his. The new women in his life were younger, stylish, and seemed to cater to his needs. I wasn't sure how he'd respond to me coming back into his life, but I was willing to take a chance.

Parker was no longer employed, and the easiest way to catch up with him was at the casino. He went there on a daily basis, sometimes to entertain his women, and other times to gamble.

On Friday, I slid into my white Baby Phat sweat suit and raked my short, layered hair. My bangs swerved on my forehead and my makeup was perfect. Parker loved a woman with class, but he also wanted one who could dress down and still look at her best. I tucked $1,000 in my purse and headed for the casino to meet my man.

As soon as I arrived, I spotted Parker at a blackjack table with a hundred-dollar minimum. Several people surrounded him, just to see if he could somehow beat the dealer. From a distance, I watched him give a little and gain a little. He seemed to break even, and when some of the onlookers walked away, I made my move.

"Long time, no see," I said, putting $500 on the table so the dealer could exchange my money for chips. Parker looked shocked to see me, and hadn't yet said a word. His eyes searched me over, and it was almost as if I could tell what he was thinking. Memories of our heated sexual encounters had obviously been in his thoughts, and being as close to him as I was, my thoughts were on the same page. He turned his head to the dealer and tapped the table with two chips.

"Good to see you, Rochel. It's been a long time."

The dealer gave my chips to me and I put one on the table. Parker laid down three chips. The dealer turned over a twenty for me and an eighteen for Parker, then revealed a nineteen that made me a winner. He swiped up Parker's chips and dropped one in my direction. I smiled, but Parker didn't say a word.

Almost ten hands later, I was up by nearly two grand, all of which I'd gained from Parker's losses. Instead of making him feel more like a loser, I stood up and decided to call it quits.

"You leaving already?" he said. "When you're winning, that's the best time to stay."

"I like to quit when I'm ahead. You should, too."

"Nah, I'm gon' stay and try to get some of my money back. Why don't you get yourself a drink and sit down with me."

I agreed, and after ordering my drink, I sat next to him.

Things quickly got interesting, and the more money Parker started to win, the bigger the smile on his face. He was up by thousands of dollars when he finally decided to call it quits.

"Are you here by yourself or with friends?" he asked.

"I was supposed to meet one of my girlfriends here, but she called and cancelled."

Parker walked up to the cashier to exchange his chips for money. I followed. "Do you have any plans for the rest of the night?" he asked.

"No, not really. I was on my way back home. Do you have something in mind?"

"Why don't you come upstairs to my suite with me? Of course, we haven't seen each other in a long time, and it'll be good to kind of . . . catch up."

I knew that the only way I could get any evidence for Vivica was to take Parker back to my place, where the cameras and tape recorders were. I did have a pocket tape recorder in my purse, but I wasn't sure about using it just yet. I was positive Parker would mention our past relationship and that would indeed mess up everything.

"I would love to catch up on old times, Parker, but I prefer that we go to my place. Hotel rooms aren't the appropriate place for people who want to talk; rather, I see them as places where people are encouraged to have sex."

"Well, then, maybe I should make myself a bit clearer. We've had sex plenty of times before and it would be nice if we could go down that road again. Seeing each other wasn't just a coincidence, was it? Who knows if we'll ever see each other again?"

I didn't want to send the wrong message to Parker and turn him off completely, so instead of going back to my place, we took the elevators up to his suite. On the elevator, Parker continued to look me over. He leaned against the glass mirrors and folded his arms.

"You are still one sexy-ass woman. I've thought a lot about you, Rochel, and I often wondered what happened to you."

I didn't say a word, and when the elevators opened to the tenth floor, we headed for his suite. The last time Parker had seen me, I was an emotional woman who looked as if I'd suffered a major breakdown. I'd nearly begged him not to leave me, and I remembered how turned off he was by my actions. Today, I showed confidence and looked like a woman who had recovered well from his disrespect. I intended to maintain my composure, but when we stepped inside and he removed his shirt, his nicely cut muscular frame was hard to ignore. I took a quick glance, and then turned my head to compliment the suite.

"This is really a nice suite. How can you afford something like this?"

Parker stepped up to me and touched my chin with his finger. "Last year, I came across good fortune. I'm able to purchase just about anything I want, and as always, I'm capable of having any woman that I want."

"Is that right?" I said, removing his hand from my face. "You'd just better hope that whatever woman you want, she wants you too."

I stepped away from him and sat on the mahogany leather sectional that was in the middle of the beige carpeted floor. Parker leaned over me and wasted no time in letting me know the reason I was there.

"Let's go to the bedroom. You remember how I like to spread out and get comfortable, don't you?"

"I remember a lot about you, Parker, but getting comfortable isn't one of them."

Parker leaned in and sucked my lips. His kisses were still on point, and I couldn't help but go for a little extra action. I lifted my hand to his muscle and stroked it to get a rise. I could feel it harden through his jeans, and when I lowered his zipper over the hump, he smiled.

"I see you still got that magic potion to make me rise. I knew you weren't capable of letting me down."

I lightly pushed Parker back and stood up, making my way to the bedroom. I wasted no time removing my clothes and lying on the king-sized bed that was covered in mahogany and gold satin sheets.

"Do me a favor," I said as Parker licked his lips, observing my naked body. "Let's stop talking about the past. I don't have good memories about us then, and I'm willing to only think about what you're capable of laying into me right now. If you take me back down memory lane again, I think it's best that I go."

"You won't hear me breathe another word about it." He took off his clothes and got in bed with me. It felt so awkward having him next to me; never did I imagine traveling down this road again. As I was deep in thought, Parker lowered his hand and separated my thighs. He touched around my goods before easing his fingers deep within me. I sighed and widened my legs so he could go further. Multi-tasking, he covered my left breast with his mouth and tickled my nipple with his tongue. His foreplay felt good, and I knew that the only way for me to get wrapped up was to get caught up in my thoughts about him. When he lay on top and entered me, I couldn't help the way I felt. He was the only man capable of making me come twice in a row. He was the only man who made me clinch the sheets and scream his name. And, he was the only man who knew how to hit my hot spot and yearn for so much more than I knew he could give. I couldn't help the way I felt and how dare I think I was strong enough to survive the punishment he was giving me.

"I miss this pussy," he whispered in my ear while stroking me. "I wanted to call and tell you how big a mistake I'd made ending our relationship but . . . but you got your number changed and disappeared."

I didn't say anything until Parker slammed into a spot that made me yell something. "I . . . I was angry with you. I never wanted to see or hear from you again."

Parker pulled me to the edge of the bed, and with one of my legs on the floor, he plunged into my backside.

"I never found a woman who could replace you. I've searched for so long, and you have no idea how I'm feeling right now."

I was feeling pretty darn good too, but I couldn't let Parker know it. Our connection was unbelievable and I knew it would be a true setback for me if I continued to see him. For now, though, today was what it was and Vivica's request had to be put on hold.

Back In Love Again

It didn't take long for me to fall for Parker again. Since our night at the hotel, I'd seen him almost every single day. We often made love, and Parker showered me with expensive gifts that he wished he could have given to me in the past. He seemed to be a changed man, and as I continued to keep my eyes on him, he started to cut off the relationships with his other women. That was a surprise to me, and when I asked him about his other women, he insisted that he wanted to make things right with me.

"I know I messed up in the past, Rochel, but I really want us to consider a future together."

"What about your wife? What are you planning to do about her? I doubt that you're going to drop all of your women for me and I'd be fooling myself if I take your word for it."

"I will and I've already started to do so. My word is bond. My wife and I haven't been getting along for months, and I'm planning to end my marriage soon. Once that's over, you and me can go on and do whatever."

Parker's news sounded like music to my ears, but I

knew he was a man who couldn't be trusted. I was worried about being betrayed by him, but a huge part of me felt as if our time to be together had finally come.

I got out of bed and slid into my robe. I felt so afraid of this relationship with him, and didn't understand how or why I'd let myself get back into this situation. I went to the kitchen, and before making breakfast, I turned my head to the hidden camera that was planted in a picture on the wall. The night before, it had taped us having dinner and fucking each other's brains out on the table and floor. The cameras throughout my house displayed the same, but I'd gotten to the point where I tried to avoid being in front of them. Parker had said many negative things about his wife and their relationship, and even went to the extreme of wishing she were dead. I hadn't gotten any of his words on tape, and I wasn't sure if I could go through with the setup.

After breakfast, Parker got ready to go and stood in the doorway with me wrapped in his arms.

"Let's take a trip together," he said. "Anywhere you'd like to go, just let me know and I'll take care of everything."

"Anywhere in the world?" I smiled.

"Anywhere. Just as long as we're together."

"Okay, I'll let you know soon."

Parker kissed the tip of my nose and jetted.

I got dressed and left to give Vivica an update on what was going on. She was at her office, and made me wait nearly an hour before seeing her.

"Sorry it took me so long, Jakki, but I was in a meeting. Please, sit down."

I took a seat, feeling guilty for behaving as I had. Parker had no doubt weakened me and I hoped she wouldn't be able to see through me. I reached in my purse and passed the tiny camcorder to her so she could see the action between us. For nearly twenty minutes, she reviewed the tapes and seemed to pick up an attitude. Several times, she shifted in her seat and swallowed hard. At one point, she tooted her lips and her eyes rolled to the back of her head.

"I can't believe him. You would have thought he'd known you for years. I knew he was a cheater, but going down on you like that is ridiculous. And who gave you the authorization to return the favor? I'm at least pleased to see that you had sense enough to put a condom on him."

"Look, you told me to do what was necessary. It was difficult for me to get Parker into my bedroom, but he easily got comfortable. I had to do everything or anything to make him feel that way."

She ignored me and looked at the camcorder again. "The two of you really appear to enjoy yourselves. If you're faking, then maybe you should be starring in movies."

"I'm used to performing quite well, Vivica, and Parker doesn't make me respond any differently than any other man I've been with."

She huffed and shook her head from side to side. "How much longer is this going to take? I need more from you. Where are my tapes at?"

"I'm working on giving you more, but Parker said he was going out of town for two weeks. Of course, I won't be able to see him for a while, but as soon as he gets back in town, I'll call him."

"Don't forget. If you can wrap this up within the month, I'll throw in an extra ten grand. It seems as if he's adjusting to you quite well, so whatever you're doing, please keep it up. Like I said, the tapes on the camcorder are fine, but I want him to get caught up by his words."

"I promise I'll get that for you soon."

"Has he said anything negative about me yet? I know he's said something, other than he's married to a witch."

"As a matter of fact, he said that he was married to a real bitch. One that he was ready to divorce, and couldn't wait to do so. I couldn't get that on tape because we were in his car. The next time we're together, I'll talk about you and get more from him."

I stood up and walked to the door. As usual, Vivica eyeballed me like she had a serious problem.

"Jakki," she said.

"Yes."

"I hope I can trust you. I know how charming Parker can be and you'd be a fool to let him work his magic on you. Whatever you do, don't fall for the bullshit, all right? If you do, I'll make both you and him pay."

"Vivica, must I remind you that your husband is no different from any other man on my client list? He may very well have you worked over, but the buck stops here. I have a job to do, and since my job pays very well, I'm focused as ever. So, there's no need for you to worry about me. The only worry that you should have is pertaining to your husband and what you intend to do about him."

She looked as if she didn't believe me, and I wasn't sure if she did. I was nervous during our meeting and I knew that she'd read more into those tapes. My connection with Parker couldn't be denied, and even she could see that. I tried like hell not to express my true emotions, but each time his dick went inside of me, it was hard for my feelings not to show. I honestly had no idea how I would continue with this charade, but I needed more time than she was willing to give me. Her attitude was working my nerves, too, and I was starting to dislike her more and more each time we met.

A Slap Back to Reality

Parker said that we could go any place in the world I wanted, and since I had already taken those trips myself, I simply chose the Bahamas. I wanted to stay at the Atlantis Hotel, particularly the suite that cost $25,000 per night, overlooking the entire Bahamas and Paradise Island. Parker made that possible, and I had one of the best times of my life. We went sightseeing during the day, and had many romantic candle-lit dinners in the evenings. I wasn't looking forward to returning home. I could stay in a place like this with Parker Rhodes forever. I fell asleep thinking about my feelings for him, unsure about what to do with my situation.

I woke up around two o'clock in the morning, and noticed that Parker wasn't there. I wasn't sure where to look for him, but I put on my clothes to go find him. I searched nearly the entire hotel, from the swimming pools to the casino. I was sure I'd find him there, but there was no sign of him. Afraid that something had happened, I went to the front of the hotel and looked for him by some of the yachts and timeshares that were nearby. I had no luck, and decided to head back to the room, in case he had returned.

Just as I made my way to the elevator, I heard loud giggling near an inside staircase. I walked over to it and got the shock of my life. Parker had one of the casino waitresses pinned against the wall, while lifting her short skirt and touching her all over her body. He pecked down her neck and tickled her waistline to make her laugh. Obviously, they'd known each other for a while. They both appeared to be tipsy and didn't see me as I stared at them through the tiny glass. A few minutes later, they rushed up the stairs and I heard another door close. I followed behind them, only to see them making out in front of a hotel room they eventually entered. My chest heaved in and out. I wanted to storm through the door and confront Parker about what I'd seen. I wanted to kill him for continuously being the man he was. How dare I fall for his nonsense again? I should have known that a man of his caliber would never change, nor was I the woman who could make him do so. He was set in his ways, and like it or not, I had a choice to make.

Instead of throwing a fit, I calmed myself and went back to our suite. I removed my clothes and got right back into bed. My stomach turned in knots as I waited for him to come in, which was almost forty-five minutes later.

"Baby," he said, sliding the cover off me. "Wake up, I got something for you."

I slowly cracked my eyes and stretched out my arms. "What time is it?" I yawned.

"Early. I just got back from the casino and won some money. Look what I got for you."

I sat up in bed and Parker handed over a tiny black

velvet box. When I opened it, there was a three-carat diamond ring inside. I was puzzled, but more so in disbelief by his actions.

"What . . ."

"Put it on," he insisted. "As soon as my divorce is final, I want you to marry me. Will you marry me?"

I was stunned by the man who sat on the bed with me, versus the one I'd just seen having a shindig on the stairs. What in the hell was his motive, and how could he turn himself on and off like this? Simply put, this motherfucker was crazy and the only thing I could do was continue to play his game with him. At this point, I wanted him wiped off the face of the earth, just as Vivica had mentioned.

I touched the side of his face. "I . . . I don't know what to say, Parker. I love you, but I'm not sure if I can agree to this with you still being married. Let's wait until your divorce is final."

Parker took the ring from the box and held my finger. "I'll wait, but in the meantime, I don't see any harm in you wearing my ring. Just wear it for me, all right? It'll give me hope that we'll soon be together as husband and wife."

I looked into his eyes and couldn't believe how he lied and played his games with such a straight face. He seemed so sincere, and if I hadn't just seen him in action, I would have fallen for it. When he leaned forward to kiss me, I touched his chest to stop him.

"Parker, I'm really tired. I'm starting to feel ill, and I hate to cut our vacation short, but I'm getting homesick. Can we go back home tomorrow?"

He looked confused and did his best to show concern. "What's the matter? How sick are you?"

"I want my own bed, and for the last two days, I've

been feeling nauseated. I don't want to ruin our vacation, but I'm really ready to go."

"Okay, well, I have some unfinished business to take care of. I'll make sure you get home tomorrow, but I won't be leaving for at least another week."

I nodded, sure that Parker's business had everything to do with the woman he had been with.

The next day, I wasted no time packing my belonging and getting the hell out of the Bahamas. Parker went to the airport with me and pretended to be so disappointed that I was leaving. Again, with a straight face he told me how much he loved me, and said he'd hurry back. I wanted to throw up, and did just that when I made it home. I was so miserable, and the thought of seeing Parker with that woman and his ability to get me back in the palm of his hand made me ill. I had to quickly get myself together, and being without him for the next week gave me enough time to do it.

The Thrill Is Gone

A week away from Parker did me justice. I had time to focus on the real reason he was back in my life, and that was all about the money. I was ready to put this mess behind me and give Vivica all the evidence she needed to seek her revenge.

Parker called and asked me to pick him up from the airport. Surely, I didn't mind, and when I saw him, I didn't have that spark in my eye like I used to. His presence didn't make my pussy thump and that was a cue that I was already getting over him. He was casually dressed in blue jeans that hung over his leather sandals, and a black wife beater. A silver chain hung from his neck and his coal black waves shined. I saw one chick tap her friend to share how fine he was, and he, of course, loved the attention. He smiled and the woman walked up to him. They conversed, and when she squeezed his bicep, his pearly whites were on display. That is, until he saw me. I made my way to baggage claim so he could see me.

"Hey, baby," he said. "I'm glad you're on time. As soon

as I find my luggage, we can get the hell out of here, all right?"

I smiled at him and at the woman who remained by his side.

"Nice meeting you," she said. "Maybe I'll see you around."

All Parker did was nod. Once he found his luggage, he slipped two bags over his shoulder and grabbed another in his hand.

"Would you like some help with that?" I asked, not intending to lift a finger.

"Nah, I got it."

Good, I thought.

Parker put his luggage in my trunk, and when I asked where he wanted me to drop him off, he suggested going straight to my house.

"Why are you taking your things to my place? Wouldn't you prefer to go home?"

"I'm going home, but not until later tonight. I missed you and I want to spend some time with you before I go home and face the Grinch. I know she'll be upset because I haven't called her in two weeks, and I'm not up for arguing with her tonight."

We got in the car, but I didn't respond to his comment until we made it to the highway.

"Parker, does your relationship with your wife worry you? I mean, aren't you afraid that she might do something to you?"

"Do something like what? Kill me?"

"Yes, kill you or kill me for that matter."

"I'm not worried about her doing anything like that. She might be stupid, but she ain't that stupid. Besides, if anything happens to me, she'll be one broke-ass woman—in jail."

"What about if you divorce her? Won't you have to pay her alimony?"

"I won't have to pay her anything. She signed a prenuptial agreement and the only way she stands to gain any money is if she can prove infidelity on my part. That's very difficult for her to do and I'm good at watching my back."

Parker's cell phone rang and he looked at it clipped to his jeans. "Damn," he said. "Speak of the devil."

"Aren't you going to answer it?"

"Do you mind? I just want to let her know that I'm back in town."

"Sure, no problem."

"Hello," he said, then paused. I could hear Vivica's loud voice coming through the phone. Parker smiled as if he got a kick out of her being angry. "Are you finished?" he said. She went on and on, but he soon cut her off. "Listen, if you would shut your mouth for a minute, I'll be happy to tell you where I was. Since you can't stop yakking, fuck it, Viv, you don't deserve to know. I gotta take care of some business and I may be able to see you tonight. If not tonight, then tomorrow. Gotta go."

Parker hung up at looked at me. "So, are you glad to see me?"

"Delighted."

"Then why doesn't it seem like it? You didn't give me a kiss at the airport, nor did you give me a hug. I guess you're going to make it up to me when we get to your place."

I provided him with a fake smile. "I didn't mean any harm. I have a lot on my mind and we need to talk about some things."

He nodded. I tapped my fingertips on the steering wheel and thought, *If he cares so much, he would ask about my nausea. Doesn't want to know because he obviously doesn't care.*

As soon as we got to my place, Parker took off his clothes and got into bed. He stressed how tired he was, but not tired enough to forgo sex. I had no intentions of letting him touch me, and decided to break my fabricated news to him while sitting on the edge of the bed.

"Parker I . . . I've been seeing someone else. The reason I can't marry you is because I'm confused about what to do. I love you, but I'm in love with him, too. While we were on vacation, I really started to miss him. I wanted to get home and see him and now . . . since you proposed, I don't know what to do."

Parker had a blank expression on his face. It was obvious that no woman had ever come to him with this kind of news, and how dare I tell him he was competing for my love?

"I . . . I don't know what to say, baby. I thought this was about me and you? I've been making preparations to leave my wife and I spent a fortune on the ring I gave you. Don't you know how much I love you? Don't you know I'll do anything in the world for you? How can you sit there and tell me about your feelings for another man? You should have said something about this sooner. Why allow me to fall for you again when you've been involved with someone else?" He paused to catch his breath. "I . . . I feel like such a fool."

Parker threw the cover back to get out of bed.

"Please, don't go," I said. "Just give me some time, okay? We don't have to rush into anything right now, do we?"

"So, I guess you want me to sit around and let you keep on fucking this other fool, huh? I can't do that,

Rochel, and you're way out of line for thinking I would even consider it."

"Look how long I've shared you, Parker. This relationship has never been about us, and I've been very patient with your situation. All I'm asking is for you to do the same for me."

Parker looked disgusted. In an effort to get him to see things my way, I straddled his lap and placed my arms on his shoulders.

"Come on, Parker. Work with me this time, okay? I know it won't be easy, but who knows how this will all turn out."

He looked away, but I turned his head and kissed him. He accepted my kiss, and when I started to undo my blouse, he reached around my back and unsnapped my bra. My perky breasts aimed straight at him and he leaned in to kiss them.

"Mmm," he said. "There's no way I'm going to share you. What will I have to do to get this other man out of your life?"

"Just keep on being you. Thus far, you've been doing a good job at making me forget about him. Eventually, I will."

Parker wanted to know more about my other companion, but I wouldn't give up anything. I quickly changed the subject and shared with him how much I wanted him to fuck me. He had no problem doing that. This time, though, I felt nothing for him and was thrilled that the fire burning between my legs was no longer there.

Cold Busted

Vivica had been ringing my phone like crazy. I didn't like her tone, so I waited to call her back on my time. She seemed so anxious to stick it to Parker that I often wondered why she hadn't just taken matters into her own hands. There was no doubt that I didn't like the bitch, but since our goal was the same, I dealt with the situation as best as I could. I called her back and told her we could meet at Forest Park.

While I sat on a bench, Vivica pulled her BMW in front of me and got out. There was no smile on her face as she immediately handed a letter-sized envelope to me.

"You need to tell me what's up with this shit right now!" she yelled.

Vivica stood over me as I calmly opened the envelope. Inside were pictures of Parker and me on vacation. We looked so happy together, and I didn't quite know how to defend myself after telling Vivica I wouldn't be able to see him for two weeks.

"Where did you get these from?"

"That doesn't matter!" she yelled. "What in the hell is going on with you and Parker?"

I laid the pictures on my lap and laughed. "This is . . . crazy. Are you telling me that you've hired a private detective to watch another private detective? How desperate are you?"

"I wasn't sure if I could trust you. Obviously, my suspicions were correct. I should have known that Parker would persuade you to join his circle of love, but based on the high recommendation from Sharon, I seriously thought you'd be able to handle the job."

I stood up and refused to let her get the best of our conversation. "Look, calm down, all right? I know it looks as if I lied to you, but I don't like to share my every move with my clients. At the last minute, Parker asked me to join him out of town. I did, and not only was he working me over in the Bahamas, but he also met another woman while there. I have evidence of that, if you'd like to have it. So, if you think I went to the Bahamas to have a funky good time with Parker, you're wrong again. The next time you accuse me of not handling my business with your husband, this deal is over."

Vivica folded her arms and tapped her foot on the ground. "Jakki, you're good, but you forgot one thing—pictures don't lie. From the beginning, I knew there was something up with you and Parker. There was something so authentic about the two of you, and after searching a little deeper, I found it."

Vivica opened her purse and pulled out two pictures. She gave them to me. "Honestly, how long have you known Parker?"

The pictures were of him and me back in the day. We were hugging in one picture and pecking lips in another.

"There are more of those around, and I'd like to know

why the hell you insisted on wasting my money and time."

I crumbled the pictures in my hand. "I didn't want you to know that Parker and I had a previous relationship. Our time together was rough and it was very similar to yours. Thank God I never married him, but when I got your letter, I couldn't resist an opportunity to seek revenge. So, yes, this is definitely about the money for me, but it's also about seeking revenge. Bottom line, you're not the only one who wants to see Parker get what he deserves."

Vivica laughed. "Do you really expect me to believe that? If anything, this gave you an opportunity, Rochel, not Jakki, to sink your claws into my husband once again. Well, for the record, you've been replaced. Your services are no longer needed, and if you ever come near me or Parker again, you'll regret it."

Vivica got back in her car and left. She had my blood boiling and I wasn't one to take threats lightly. Since I wasn't going to get paid for all the work I'd done, I at least had to come up with a different plan. I didn't think she would like it, but this wasn't about Parker anymore; it was about her.

Payback, then Layback

Hanging out with Parker was . . . fun. According to me, I'd ended my relationship with the other man and Parker now had me all to himself. He was extremely delighted about that—so delighted that divorce papers were on the way to being served to his wife.

We sat at dinner and clinked our glasses together.

"Here's to our future," he said.

"I'll drink to that. And then some."

We sipped our wine and gazed at each other from across the table. "I can't believe this is finally happening," Parker said. "After all these years, we are finally going to be together."

"I hope so, Parker. Do you think your wife is going to fight the divorce? If she does, that could mean trouble for our future."

"Yeah, I've been thinking about that too. What you don't know is I've offered to pay her off. The last time I spoke to her, she said she'd consider it."

"Was the price right?"

"I offered her one million dollars and I couldn't come

any more correct than that. She's all about the money, so I doubt that she'll put up a fuss. Besides, her love for me ain't that strong where she'll say to hell with the money. Trust me."

Parker knew his wife better than I, so for his sake, I hoped he was right. We finished up dinner and headed for Parker's Hummer so we could leave. As soon as he opened the door for me, Vivica appeared out of nowhere. She shook the papers in her hand and shoved Parker in his chest.

"You couldn't wait, could you?" she yelled. "I asked you to wait until I made my decision."

"I'm sorry, Viv, but I didn't want to wait. Why don't you just sign the papers so this fucked-up marriage can be over with?"

She gritted her teeth. "Not a chance in hell, you bastard! A million dollars is not enough after what you put me through, and I will delay this shit for as long as I can." She turned to me and we stood face to face. "I warned you, didn't I? It's on, bitch, I swear to you it's on!"

She smacked the shit out of me, and when Parker jumped between us, she turned and ran away. I held my cheek in disbelief and Parker stepped up to me. "Are you okay? Why didn't you tell me she'd spoken to you before?"

"Because I didn't want you to know that she'd threatened me. You said that I didn't have to worry about her so I felt as if you had everything under control."

I entered the car on the passengers side and Parker closed the door. As soon as he got in, he tore into me. "You should have told me, Rochel. She may not do anything to me, but now that she knows we're seeing each other, I don't know where she'll turn her anger. I cannot allow her to get any evidence against me, and we might have to keep things on the down low until our divorce wraps up." He turned my face and looked at the swelling underneath my eye. "Does it hurt?"

"No, not really. I'm sure an ice pack will do the job. And I agree about us chilling out on seeing each other. I'm game for however you want to handle this."

Parker pulled off and when we got back to my place, instead of coming inside, he dropped me off and left. I was glad about that, because the so-in-love attitude I had to keep up was working my nerves. Truth be told, I hated Parker for the man he was. I hated everything about him and my negative feelings increased with each moment we spent together.

For the next few weeks, I talked to Parker almost every day. We hadn't seen each other, though, and for now, that was how he wanted it. I continued to follow his every move, and he was back to visiting his other women and spending numerous hours at the casino. I figured Vivica had another private detective on the case, and at the rate Parker was going, it wouldn't be hard for her to get the information she needed. Hell, if she could get pictures of me and Parker in the Bahamas, why didn't she take the evidence she had and present it to her lawyer? The shit just didn't make sense to me. Why the hell wasn't it adding up?

I sat outside of the casino, looking at Parker through a pair of binoculars. He had just gotten out of his Hummer and was entering the casino with a woman. He already had another woman entertaining him in another room, and having two women at the same hotel at once had become a habit. This was nothing new for Parker; "risky" was his middle name.

I had seen him before with this woman, and after I snapped a picture of the two of them, they went inside.

While looking through the binoculars, I followed them up the escalators and assumed they were headed to his suite. I then got caught off guard when my binoculars connected with someone else watching them. A man with a swollen face looked at me and I looked at him. I pulled the binoculars away from my face and noticed him abruptly walking away. I was dying to know who had hired him and why he'd been watching me. I hurried out of my car and ran toward him. While turning to look behind him, he kept moving forward. I was on his trail, and when the elevator wouldn't open fast enough, he went for the stairs. I followed, and that's where I caught up with him.

"Stop, please," I yelled. "Ca . . . can we talk?"

He removed his dark glasses. "Ma'am, I don't know you. I don't know what you'd like to talk about—"

I reached for the tall black man's trench coat and pulled on it from behind.

"Please," I said. "Tell me why you're following me. If you don't wish to talk here, please give me your card so I can contact you later. This is so important, and whatever you're being paid, I'll double it."

Surely, that got his attention and he handed over his card. I thanked him and he rushed off.

I lay across the chaise in my bedroom and held the business card in my hand. The man I'd seen earlier, Terrance, was on his way to see me. He claimed to have valuable information for me and I couldn't wait for him to come. When it came to a private investigator, I knew offering more money was the key to getting information. This situation had become even more personal to me, and I agreed to lay plenty of money on the table. When Terrance got there, I learned so much more about the woman who had hired me to do her dirty work.

"So, you're telling me that Vivica already knew about my past relationship with Parker?"

Terrence nodded. "Yes. She used you because Parker always compared her to you. She knew how he felt about you and how much he regretted marrying her. I'd been following you for a while and when I found out what kind of business you were in, she took that opportunity to go after you."

"That bitch," I said, slamming my hand on the table. I felt like a fool. I should have known better than to trust her and involve myself in such a way.

"Well, now you know. I don't know what her plans are for either of you, and all I've been asked to do is keep my eye on the two of you. She's obsessed with bringing down Parker, but I think she might be attempting to bring you down, too. Make sure you watch your back."

The information Terrence gave me was extremely helpful. I gave him some cash and promised him even more.

"All you have to do is disappear for a while and drop yourself from the case. I'm sure you know Mr. Rhodes is loaded with money and I could possibly gain a whole lot of it, if this thing goes according to my plan. You'll earn a substantial amount of it if you do as I ask."

Terrence's choice was easy. He turned over most of the evidence he had and told me his phone would be disconnected. He also gave me a timeline, which gave me three weeks to wrap it up. He said he'd been in contact with me then.

I was on Parker like white on rice. Literally. I convinced him that I was miserable without him and was anxious for his marriage to be over. We started to see each other again on a daily basis, and he broke the news to me about Vivica agreeing to their divorce. I figured her options had run out on her, and with Terrence no longer willing to participate anymore, the million that Parker had offered her started to look better by the day.

"So, when are we going to do this marriage thing?" Parker asked, kissing the ring on my finger as we sat at the museum.

"Soon. I was hoping that we could possibly celebrate this Friday at your favorite little suite at the casino, get married sometime next week, and take off for our honeymoon following that."

"You got this thing all worked out, don't you?"

"I've waited a long time for this, Parker. You just don't know how happy you've made me."

"I do my best."

I laid my head on Parker's shoulder and licked my ice cream. "Baby, I know you've offered to give Vivica a million dollars for not fighting the divorce, but I'm concerned about our future. That's a lot of money to give away and I hope that it doesn't leave us without."

"First of all, I'm not going to give Vivica a million dollars. I got plans for her, and you need not to worry about our future. Vivica will not be a part of it."

I pulled away from Parker. "Are you planning to do something to her? I don't like for you to talk that—"

He kissed my forehead. "Don't worry about it. All you need to worry about is us getting married and figure out where we're going to go on our honeymoon."

I smiled and lifted my cone for Parker to lick my ice cream.

"I love you," I said.

"I love you too."

Doomsday . . . Again

Friday couldn't have come soon enough. Parker started the day off with having dozens and dozens of red roses sent to my house, and attached was a card that implied his anxiousness for us to be together that night. I slid into a black-and-white fitted dress that had white ruffles at the top and a slim black fit at the bottom. My curves were in full effect, and as I stepped in my three-inch heels, I looked and felt like a million dollars.

At the hotel, I slid the key in the door and the green light came on. When I opened walked in, I saw Parker standing by the tall glass windows, looking out. He looked dynamic in a black single-breasted suit and silk black shirt underneath. His shirt was opened and revealed his chest that I admired so much. I had a moment of lust for him, and when his eyes connected with mine, my heart dropped. I took in a deep breath and focused on my purpose.

"Hey, baby." He smiled with a glass of iced Vodka in his hand. He set the glass on a table and stepped up to me. "You look sexy as ever. I can't wait for you to be my wife and I wish like hell I would have made that happen a long time ago."

I placed my arms on his shoulders. "I've always told you to stop referring to the past. This is now and the future is what we have to look forward to."

Parker agreed and escorted me to a nearby table he had prepared for us. It was beautifully set with fine china, candles, and wine. The steaks, string beans, and potatoes looked delicious and a full belly is what I needed to calm my nerves. Parker poured our wine, and when his phone rang, he said it was business and stepped away to take the call. By the time he'd returned, I had already bitten into my steak and had finished my second glass of wine.

"What took you so long?" I asked.

"I've been buying up a lot of rental property and one of the guys I have working on them for me got some issues. I apologize, but I needed to take care of that."

"I see. I didn't know you were investing your money in buying property. When we get married, I have a lot of ideas about investing money, too, but now is not the time for us to talk about it."

"I agree," he said, taking a seat. "All I want to talk about is what I'll have to do, as a husband, to keep you happy for the rest of your life."

"That's easy. Just keep on being you. You know . . . there was a time I never thought you'd change. I thought you'd be a womanizer forever and I'm so grateful that you've decided to change your life around for me. I love who you've become, Parker, and I'm glad that I'm the woman who's responsible for this change in you."

Parker couldn't say a word. He knew that he was still a dog-ass fool, and for him to sit there and not man up to what he truly was was gut wrenching. I didn't expect him to come clean because he was such a coward. And it bothered me that he thought I was even a bigger fool than he was. Did he think I was that stupid and couldn't see him for the man he was? I admitted to falling for his mess before, but now, my eyes were wide open and I could see the person . . . animal he'd become.

"What's on your mind, baby?" he asked. "You seem awfully quiet tonight."

I picked at my string beans with a fork and looked down at my plate. "I don't know, Parker. I have to be completely honest with you about my feelings. For you to treat your wife as you have, I'm concerned about you treating me the same way. I don't know much about your relationship with her, but I can't help feel as if I can't trust you. You've hurt me before and—"

Parker got up and came to my side of the table. He kneeled in front of me and took my hands. "I know how hard it is for you to trust me, but you can. My word is bond. I married Vivica because she was pregnant. Let me correct myself: she told me she was pregnant. I later found out she lied about the baby and our marriage had been on a down slope ever since. I never loved her like I loved you. Like I said, I tried to tell you how I felt, but I couldn't find you. Eventually, I stuck with my decision and it was a decision that brought nothing but misery to me."

Parker's words were on point. It was like he had a twin brother, one who was kneeling before me and being the loving man I always dreamed he could be. But then there was the one who was a bold-faced liar who had to have his women and totally disrespect his wife. This seemed so easy for him to do—almost too easy, and was quite scary. I knew what kind of man I was dealing with so his comments were falling on deaf ears.

"Just don't hurt me," I said, staring deeply into his eyes. For whatever reason, I wanted to let him off the hook. "If you have any doubts whatsoever about us being married, just say so. We can always be friends, Parker, and you wouldn't be committed to me in any way."

Parker got angry and slammed his fist on the table. "Damn it, Rochel! How can I prove myself to you? It's as if you're looking for an excuse not to marry me, and if you're still in love with that other—"

I touched his fist to calm him. "No, this has nothing to do with him, Parker. I just want you to be sure about this, that's all. Are you sure?"

"I'm very sure," he said. His eyes began to water. "I'm more sure about this than I have ever been about anything in my entire life. That says a lot."

We finished dinner, and while cuddling each other on the floor, we danced. I wished like hell that the feelings he had for me were real, as well as the feelings I had for him. I guessed that if I could be as fake as I was, then he could, too. Sadly, for both of us, our time was soon coming to an end.

I changed into my silky popping-peach negligee and waited for Parker to come out of the bathroom. I heard him on the phone again, and when he came out, he still had on his clothes.

"Rochel, I'm really sorry about this. I gotta go see about the property I mentioned to you earlier. Just that fast, some fool done set my shit on fire. Give me about an hour or two and I'll be right back."

I didn't really know what Parker was up to, but his excuse smelled like a big fat alley rat. "Would you like for me to go with you?"

"Nah, stay right here. It shouldn't take long and I will rush back as soon as I can."

I encouraged Parker to take his time, and as soon as he left, I cracked the door and watched him walk down the hall. Several times, he turned to watch his back, and when he didn't see anyone behind him, he pulled out a card and entered another room down the hall. I pretty much had this thing all figured out, and closed the door.

Nearly an hour-and-a-half later, there was a knock at the door. I figured it was Parker, but when I opened the door, Vivica stood on the other side. She rushed the door so I wouldn't close it and came inside.

"Where is he?" she yelled, looking very unstable and out of control. I remained calm, and still in my negligee, I walked over to the bar and poured myself a drink.

"Would you like something to drink?" I asked.

She snapped. "Bitch, don't be nice to me. Just tell me where I can find my husband."

"If you've been keeping a close eye on him like you have, then you should know where to find him." I took a sip from the glass of iced cognac and gave my body a shake. "Whew, this is too strong. But, the stronger, the better, right?"

Vivica walked up to me and snatched the glass away from my lips. She pointed her finger at me and left no breathing room between us.

"You listen to me and listen to me good. Parker and I are never going to get a divorce and if he's telling you that we are, you're a fool for believing him. For the record, we reconciled our differences, and I'm surprised to see that he's still creeping with you."

I chuckled and shoved Vivica away from me before taking my place on the couch. I crossed my legs and re-laxed. "You know what, Vivica? Women like you make me so damn sick. You go around making threats to other women, trying to protect a man like Parker who could care less about you or me. All you're doing is making a big fool out of yourself, and at the end of the day, Parker is still going to be the ho who he truly is."

"And what are you going to be? The ho who tried to destroy his marriage? You can say whatever you'd like, but I already know how much you love Parker and your willingness to do anything for him. You're dying for me to divorce him, just so you can pick up where you left off. It ain't happening, honey, and I'd rather see him dead than see him with you. Now, where is he?"

This dingbat just wasn't getting the picture. I reached for my purse and pulled out my cigarettes. I tapped one from the package and lit it. "Would you like one?" I asked.

My calmness angered her and she plopped down on the other side of the couch, threatening not to leave until she saw Parker. I looked at my watch. "I'm expecting him in any minute now. We'll both get a chance to confront him together."

She loved that idea, and with her being "the wife" I expected for Parker to sing a new tune. I heard whistling on the other side of the door, and it soon came open. Immediately, Parker's eyes zoned in on me and Vivica sitting on the couch. She rushed off the couch and ran up to him, swinging.

"I thought this bullshit was over!" she yelled. "Why'd you lie to me, huh?"

He grabbed her arms and pushed her backward. "Calm the fuck down! What the hell are you doing here? Didn't I tell you I needed some time to deal with Rochel?"

I laughed to myself. I guessed dealing with me meant marrying me. "This kind of atmosphere doesn't look like you're dealing with your situation," Vivica said. "With her sitting over there half naked, it looks to me like one romantic hellava night."

"Tell 'im, girl," I shouted and continued to work my cigarette. "After all, you've seen it with your own eyes."

Parker turned his head and let out a soft chuckle. He slid his hands into his pockets and sighed. Vivica pushed the side of his face and demanded an explanation. "Tell me, Parker. Is it going to be her or me? Now is the time for you to put up or shut up."

He pushed her back on the couch and she had one dramatic fall. He dared her to get back up and his tone was enough to keep her in place. He looked over at me, then back at her.

"Let's clear up something." He put his hands back in his pockets, presenting himself to be almost professorial. "Did either of you bitches think that you could fool me? From the beginning, I knew about the setup. My wife hired you as a pawn to trap me, not knowing that you were my ex. I hope that you were able to get enough pictures of us and taping me, Rochel, was quite impressive. It's too bad, though, that this plan has faltered. It's over, ladies, and unfortunately, the times that we all had together must come to an end."

Parker strutted to the door, and when he opened it, in walked Terrence. He reached down inside of his pants and pulled out a 9 mm. They came closer to us and Terrence wiggled the gun around in his hand.

"Which one of these bitches would you like for me to pop first?"

Vivica covered her mouth and tears flowed from her eyes. "Terrence, how could you lie to me? Didn't I pay you enough money? I will give you more, just don't do this, please!"

I was nervous as hell, but did my best not to show it. Vivica was bringing too much attention to herself, and she would definitely get popped before I would. Terrence laughed and moved over close to Parker.

"She's making too much noise. Let me hear her squeal first, and then I'll handle the other one."

Parker slid his arm around Terrence's waist and kissed him on the lips. "Do whatever you want to, baby. You know I got your back."

He touched Terrence's ass, and Vivica's and my expressions were frozen in time. I couldn't believe Parker was on the down low, but for a man to have sex with as many women as he had, and to hate women as much as he did, the proof was in the pudding. Their actions disturbed Vivica so much that she hurried off the couch and caught Terrence off guard. She swung her Coach bag across his hand and knocked the gun away from him. We all rushed for the gun, and as fast as I scrambled across the floor to get it, it wound up in her hands. She yelled for everyone to back away and threatened to shoot.

"Back up!" she ordered again. "Rochel, get the phone and hurry up and call the police."

For me, calling the police wasn't going to suffice. I stood still and Vivica looked at me like I was crazy. "Bitch, did you hear what I said?"

"I heard you, but—"

Terrence thought Vivica was distracted, so he moved forward. She pulled the trigger and his body flew backward onto the floor. Her hands trembled and she started crying hysterically.

"I . . . I'm sorry," she said, covering her mouth. "What have I done? God, what have I done!"

Parker held up his hands and tried to calm her. "Baby, it's okay. Give me the gun and let's get out of here. Let's go home—"

I knew what he was up to and yelled loudly for Vivica to shoot him. Instead, she dropped to the floor and rocked back and forth on her knees while sobbing.

"Shoot him!" I yelled as Parker kept moving in her direction. I knew if he got the gun he'd kill us both.

She tearfully lifted the shaking gun and aimed it at me, then him.

"Don't either of you move. Please don't make me do this," she sobbed. "Please don't take another step."

Parker stopped dead in his tracks and tried his best to work her over. "Viv, baby, I'm sorry. I hate like hell that our marriage has come to this, but you left me no other choice. You wouldn't stop throwing this bitch up in my face and I got tired of you complaining about a woman that I never, ever loved. Unfortunately, I found comfort with Terrence. He was the only person I could turn to, and if you want me to get help, I promise you I'll do it. I'll do it because . . ."

I could see that Parker's efforts were working, and Vivica stared at him without blinking an eye. She wanted every word that he said to be true, and he was so good at convincing women to see things his way. I hurried to her side and yelled at her again.

"Pull the damn trigger," I said with a strained voice. "Now, you stupid—"

Parker dove forward and I snatched the gun from her hand. "Trick or treat, you asshole," I said and shot off two bullets to his chest, not waiting around to see his body drop.

My Life Will Never Be the Same

I sat in a lawn chair on the beach with my two-piece bikini on and let the sun caramelize my body. I was so glad that it was all over with and the man I once knew as Parker Rhodes was in hell. After I left the hotel room that day, Vivica came after me. She didn't know what we'd do with two murders on our hands, and I encouraged her to calm down and not to worry. The ball was definitely in our court and I was the one sitting on all of the evidence. Parker and Terrence's incident looked like a wife gone mad about her husband's secret life, and I convinced Vivica to go to the police and say it was done in self-defense. She spent a few days in jail, but with the help of her lawyer, she was cleared of all charges.

She basically felt as if she owed me her life, and once again, I was paid dearly for the services I provided. I never thought I could go to the extent of shooting anyone, but killing Parker Rhodes gave me much pleasure.

I had no regrets, but wasn't sure if I had the guts to ever kill again.

The sun was baking my body, so I sat up and looked for the tanning lotion I'd placed by my side. I didn't see it, but was interrupted by a tall, dark, and handsome man who stood close by with the lotion in his hand.

"Were you looking for this?" he asked.

"As a matter of fact, I was."

The man kneeled down beside me in the sand. "My name is Marcus. Do you mind if I put some of this on you?"

I revealed my back to him by bending slightly over. "That would be nice. Thanks."

Marcus squeezed the tanning lotion on his hands and massaged it into my back. I closed my eyes and looked over to the left, then to the right. When I opened my eyes, they connected with Marcus's wife, whom I had met only a few days ago. She was clearly in disguise, so I asked if he wanted something to drink from the coconut bar and excused myself from the relaxing massage he was giving me. As he got comfortable in the chair beside mine, I went to the bar to order our drinks. Marcus's wife stood next to me and whispered as softly as she could, without displaying anger.

"I want you to make him regret every—"

I quickly cut her off and winked. "Don't worry. I love my job and take it very seriously. I'll be in touch soon."

The bartender handed me our drinks and I displayed a wide grin while making my way back to Marcus. His lustful eyes already said what the day and night had in store for us, and I was enthused about the money that would soon reach my pockets. But, no matter how excited I was about the money, nothing entertained me more than the game itself, the electrifying sex that came with it, and the thrill of watching all of the men like Marcus tumble down. It was a feeling like no other, and yet again, I was so ready to roll up my sleeves, or pull up my dress, and get to work.

Breaking Down A
Brickhouse

Edd McNair

"Niecy, you need to stop talking like that," Janelle said to her sister over the phone. She was going through it with her man and Janelle couldn't understand why.

"I'm tired of this, Janelle. I am tired. This nigga has put his hands on me and scared my kids for the last time, the *last time*," she cried.

"He just came home and fucked you up and left? Come on, Niecy," she said, knowing there was more.

"I'm tired of his kids, tired of my kids; I'm pregnant again and all this nigga do is run the street and run hoes, beat my ass, and use me. But I got a trick for his ass tonight; I got a trick for everybody!"

"We both know Poppa don't roll like that. He take care of you good, and yeah, he run hard, but you know the life and he just opened the club. He told me how you jumped on him, wylin' out, kicking holes in the wall, and breaking shit. Drinking like you lost your mind. You been acting real fucked up lately, not the big sister I know, that taught me how to get down. Now you all depressed and shit, letting yourself go, and how you get pregnant again if you tired of him?" I asked, waiting for a harsh comeback.

"Can't explain it Janelle. I can't in God's name . . . I can't explain nothing in my life."

"Why?" Janelle asked.

"I'm telling you, I don't know why!" Niecy cried.

" 'Bye, girl, you fucked up. I'm going to the grand opening of 'Reign,' your man's club. You supposed to be celebrating with him and you home playing. Love you, girl, but you got to get it together. I ain't never seen you act like this."

"Because you don't hear me when I say I'm tired," Niecy snapped.

"Well, get some rest, I know those kids sleep. I'll call you when we leave the club. Hollah," Janelle said and hung up.

Janelle had never heard her sister like that. It was like she didn't know her, listening to her talk. Over the years, she'd learned so much from her sister. First she learned what to do, now in the last year, she was learning what not to do, but every time that Saturday night played in her head, she would shake, cry, and wake up screaming.

She remembers her last conversation with Niecy that Saturday night. It's been almost a year and it still plays in her head like it was yesterday. She always starts crying when she pictures her sister at 3:15 AM that early Sunday morning, and he goes into a deep stare. The same stare that met her sister's eyes that night.

It was the grand opening of Reign, the newest club in Tidewater, located in Virginia Beach. It had taken a lot of money to get Reign open, and even bigger connections. The grand opening was beautiful; the club held about

900 guests and they had about 400 that night. It was off the chain.

We weren't surprised, because the guest list extended to most of the biggest moneymakers in the Hampton Roads. From local store owners to elite beauty and barber shops, as well as other well-known guests and business owners that held status in Hampton Roads area. A few of the other club owners had stopped in to see what Poppa had put together. He had two performances that night, one hip-hop and one R&B. Poppa had set that up with the CEO of Money Island, Big Sherm, and Straight Dough Entertainment owner, Dough. Many egos and much money packed the club. Poppa was running around on cloud nine, but at the same time stressed out. His stress jumped two notches when he saw his cousin come through the door followed by eight more niggas: two dressed in black, and two of them wearing long platinum chains that read "LEP."

The night was going well and every time Janelle looked at her sister's man, she wondered why she wasn't here sharing this moment with them. Janelle sat in VIP with her girls Reece, Lowe, and Danyelle. Even though her man was a silent partner in the club, she sat back and played her position. Poppa had them; they never had a problem being taken care of. Wherever they went, niggas always showed love, offering to buy drinks and breakfast.

She looked at her phone to check the time and saw she had three missed calls. Then she saw the text message: Don't do it like me Janelle, do it right. Appreciate life. Love you!

What? she thought. *It's 1:45 and she still up acting crazy.* She looked around the club for Poppa. He was standing on the wall talking to Dundee, chilling. Poppa wasn't the prettiest nigga, but his style and swagger showed he was *that* nigga. The $340 Red Monkey jeans and the $380 matching hoodie, white T-shirt hanging out, and new Tims, no jewels, still sent an aura of money. Her sister had her mind gone, she had Janelle scared. As the club faded out, she saw Poppa stare at his phone. A disturbing expression came across his face. He began searching the club, and Janelle's eyes met his as he searched VIP. He came right over to her.

"Stick around so you can roll to my house, your sister acting . . ." he said, and began to stumble over his words as if searching for something to say but in a nice way.

"Say it, cause I know," she said.

"Ignorant as fuck, crazy, depressing, sick, I don't know, I don't know her," he said. "But I want you to come by and check on her."

"I'll roll with you. I came here with Danyelle; she'll be all right getting home," Janelle added.

Poppa paid his security and waitresses, then counted money from the door, the bar, and the separate VIP bar. He paid his bartenders and locked up the club. He and Janelle jumped in his 2007 champagne-colored Tahoe and headed to the home he shared with Niecy in Alexandria, on the new side of Virginia Beach.

"Did you call her?" Janelle asked.

"Yeah! She didn't answer. I know she ain't asleep 'cause she just texted me a little while before two o'clock, talking about 'bye, I need to be alone, I don't need no family, I'll be better off by myself, her and the kids going to a better place."

"I called too, no answer," she said. Janelle was scared now; Niecy was being real crazy. They pulled in front of the four bedroom ranch-style home. The house looked dark as they walked inside. There was no sign of Niecy. Janelle stood in the great room as Poppa hit the light. She glanced at the kitchen as he made his way down the hallway. He reached for the bedroom door on the left and opened it. He heard water running in the bathroom opposite the bedroom.

"Is she here?" Janelle yelled .

"Niecy, Niecy!" Poppa screamed out as he walked into the bathroom and hit the light switch.

"Aah! No!" Janelle heard him yell in a pitch that was so stabbing, she closed her eyes and began to pray.

"Uugh!" Poppa cried as he quickly turned off the water and fell to his knees to lift both of his kids' limp bodies from the steaming hot water. He scalded his arms in the process, yelling in agony as he held his kids. He never heard the bedroom door open, but Janelle did. She watched as Niecy walked across the hall to the bathroom door. That's when he saw her raise the .32 Beretta.

"Do you feel my pain now, motherfucker? Do you feel my pain?" she said in a deep voice that was far from the normal. Poppa was really surprised when he looked up at her and she pulled the trigger twice, shooting him in the head. He fell over, allowing their kids to slide back into the water.

"Nieecccy!" Janelle yelled as she grabbed her face and began shaking uncontrollably as the tears began to pour. She was hurt and scared. She could barely catch her breath when she turned to look at Niecy.

"I'm so tired, Janelle. I'm so tired. My kids are gone to glory, they happy. I'm happy now, Janelle." As she put the .32 in her mouth, she stared into her sister's eyes. Tears began to roll down her cheeks. She no longer saw the gun; all she saw was the hurt and confusion in her sister's eyes.

"Please, Niecy, don't do this! I love you! I can't live like this, I need my sister, I need my sister," she said through tears and stutters. "Please don't Niecy, don't do this to—"

BOOM! Niecy had put the barrel in her mouth and

used her thumb to push the trigger. Janelle saw the smoke from the gun and watched helplessly as the force from the blow knocked out her sister's teeth. She saw pieces of the back of Niecy's head hit the wall as her lifeless body crumbled. Janelle fell to her knees and passed out.

When her eyes opened seven hours later, she was laying in Virgina Beach General Hospital with her body shaking from the anxiety attack. She was staring into space as if her mind had seen something it couldn't handle. After administering different medications, doctors came to the conclusion that she should be released into the care of Tidewater Psychiatric Institute. It would be months before she could even handle talking about the situation.

It wasn't until they rolled Poppa in her room four months later that she got the strength to move. She gave him a hug that felt like forever. Poppa had spent the last four months in Norfolk General Hospital. It was the only hospital that was equipped to treat his gunshot wounds. They both had a long cry, stared at each other, and hugged again. A rise of strength came in them both until she asked about the kids. Everyone she talked to, the doctors, nurses, and police had all had asked her what happened, but all she knew was that her sister had killed Poppa (so she had thought), and killed herself.

"What are you talking about, Janelle?" Poppa asked, confused that she of all people would be asking about the kids.

"How are the kids and who they with?" she asked again, wondering why he was looking at her so strangely.

"Do you remember what happened that night?" he asked reluctantly.

"I don't want to, Poppa, I don't want to remember,"

she said, getting frantic and shaking her head as the tears began to form. He rolled closer to her bed, took her hands, and held them tightly.

"Calm down, baby, calm down. I know what you feeling," he said as her therapist, doctors, and detectives looked on, all needing to know what was going on in her head.

"Tell me what you remember, Janelle. I tell you what I remember, then I'll tell you the facts," he said as his eyes filled with water. She began to slowly explain as she tried to remember that Saturday night after arriving at Poppa's house.

"We walked in the house, you walked in the bathroom and screamed. Niecy walked out from the room, said something, then shot you two times. Then she looked at me, put the gun in her mouth, and . . ." she said, breathing hard, "then shot herself!" she yelled as the picture slowly played in her head. "I couldn't stop crying and I was losing my breath. Then I must have passed out, because that's all I remember before this and being here. Talk to me, Poppa, please, I'm scared."

"When I walked in the bathroom . . ." he said with his head pointed down to his lap. Janelle listened quietly and stared at the bandages wrapped around Poppa's head. They'd had to perform a craniotomy on Poppa because the bullet had shattered his skull and caused swelling of the brain. One bullet was left lodged in the skull. The other bullet had hit his skull but exited through the temple, which sent Poppa into a coma. His recovery was slow coming, but it was a miracle he was even talking. He slowly put his words together, trying his hardest to remember this tragic incident.

"TreVonne and Azia were floating in a tub full of hot water with the water running," he said, squeezing her hands.

"Oh my God," she cried softly, trying to keep control.

"I reached in and scooped them both up as their skin slid off and my arms got burned to shit," he continued as he let her hands go and pulled up his sleeves, showing his disfigured forearms and hands.

"I'm sitting there over the tub with them in my arms, when I hear her behind me. I thought it was you, but when I looked up, I watched the woman I gave my heart to shoot me. Last thing I remember was that first shot." By now, Poppa had his face squinted up, trying to hold back from breaking down. "When I woke up a month later in Norfolk General Hospital after fighting hard for my life, I realized I couldn't feel my legs. The doctors said she shot me a second time. When I asked about my other kids and where they were, I had forgotten that I left Quin and Taye with her." Janelle's head dropped as he lifted his head and gripped the arm bars on his wheelchair. She began to rub her hands together. She was crying hard and the tears wouldn't stop.

"She smothered Taye and beat little Quin unconscious. He's living, but he's a vegetable." It was hard for Janelle to retain all this; she shook her hands and fanned her face as if she were hot, while gasping for air as tears covered her face. Poppa could do nothing to help her, he was doing all he could to hold it together. This was the only time he told this story and it was too painful. Never again, he thought. Never again.

Janelle began to calm down only because of the Percocet they gave her. She became calmer, but the pain inside was bad; it wouldn't stop. She sat looking at Poppa; he stared back at Janelle.

"What about your oldest boy?" Janelle asked as it came to her.

"He's all right. He was with his grandmother that weekend. She still got him."

Two Years Earlier

"Come on Niecy, let's be outta here," Janelle said, entering her sister's condo in Newpointe. "You know they tow quick as hell out here."

"Put this pass in the window so I can finish this el," Niecy said, handing Janelle a visitor's pass.

"Where Polo?" Janelle asked after coming back inside.

"Gone, carried his broke ass. Told that nigga he had to go. My rent is eight hundred fifty dollars and that nigga don't come with shit but dick and weed," Niecy said, handing Janelle the dutch. Janelle started laughing.

"Where he at? His mom's?"

"Probably. I'm twenty-six and I've done it all. And don't got time for games," Niecy said, standing up.

"You late on your rent again?"

"Yeah, I'll get it. Shit, I ain't worried, don't you." Niecy applied her MAC lip gloss.

"Girl, you better get it right. You can't lose your place or your car," Janelle said.

"Well, let's go see which one of these niggas in the club gonna pay this month's rent. And if he act right, I might let him pay next month's, too," she said sarcastically.

"I heard that, stepping out with a four hundred dollar Coogi dress on, I know those shoes two hundred dollars, smoking haze, got the condo right, and can't pay her rent. Do you got club money?" Janelle laughed as they headed out the door.

"Don't worry about it li'l sis. I've been holding my own shit down for how long?" Niecy asked.

Janelle said nothing.

"Excuse me?" Niecy said sarcastically.

"You good, my bad!" Janelle said.

"Naw, I ain't hear you. How long?"

"Fifteen girl, damn! Since you turned fifteen."

They hit the interstate toward the beach. As they exited onto Laskin Road, they saw the cars backed up trying to get into Encore's parking lot. Janelle hit seven on her speed dial.

"What up, J?" Lowe said. "We parked up the street by Wa-Wa. Danyelle right here with Reece."

"Y'all don't see me? I'm in the truck."

"Yeah, now I do."

"Y'all jump in here. I'm gonna valet, I ain't walking tonight," she said, stopping as Danyelle, Lowe, and Reece pushed in the Escalade.

"What's the deal, girl? Niggas is in that bitch tonight," Reece said.

"We out to have a good time, ain't nobody studying these broke-ass niggas," Danyelle said.

"If you broke, carry your ass, nigga!" Niecy said, laughing. They all laughed as Janelle pulled up in front of the club and got out of the truck. All eyes hit each one as they stepped out. Janelle was tight with her fitting Frankie B black velvet pants and off-white button-down that stopped just past her waist. Her three top buttons were undone, allowing the pushup bra to do its job and fool everybody. She had swagger and her money showed. Danyelle was dressed cute in a silk chiffon flutter-print dress and red sandals. She knew nobody could fuck with her clothes because her shit came straight from the Miami boutique that her man Tiger owned. Reece looked like a million bucks in the short skirt and blouse she'd gotten from T.J. Maxx, and shoes she had picked up at Barefeet in Janaf Shopping Center. She was cheap, but she could put shit together and fuck with any bitch. But as they approached the door, all eyes fell on Lowe and Niecy. The had the same swagger, they both walked slow, and they put an extra twist in their hips. Lowe also wore a pushup bra to appear to have bigger breasts. When she stepped in her heels, her ass was so phat that it swayed. Girls envied her and niggas stared to get a mental picture to talk about it later. Lowe stood four foot eleven and wore a size 11/12. She was a dream to every nigga who crossed her path. She hung tight by Niecy, because even though she, Janelle, Danyelle, and Reece all came out of school together and were now in their early twenties, the objective was to be like Niecy, act like Niecy, and fuck niggas like Niecy. Niecy was three years older than they, but she had trained her sister to keep her shit tight and her friends followed suit.

Security checked their purses and opened the door. The owner, Jeezy, greeted each one, but he hugged Niecy real tight. "Your night ends with me," he whispered in her ear, setting up his ass for later.

"No, baby, your night ends with your wife," she whispered back as they continued to hold each other.

He looked at his security and signaled to let the other girls in for free, then he leaned back, leaving his hands on her waist as she pressed against him, her hands resting on his chest. She watched her crew enter the club and turned back to Jeezy.

"It's like that baby?" he asked, staring at her.

She shut her eyes for a second and opened them back up. She stared back at this nigga standing five foot five, medium build, rocking his Antik jeans, black Pradas, and eighty dollar T-shirt he'd picked up from C.R.E.A.M. that stopped at his waist, showing his $200 chain belt. His $25,000 Rolex was all the jewelry he needed and every bitch knew the cream-colored S550 sitting on twenty-twos in front belonged to him.

"Don't start, Jeezy, please," she said. They'd spent many late nights together, and she'd fallen for him, but she knew she was just a side thing and had started distancing herself. He looked out, but she felt she was too bad of a girl to play second.

"Have a good time, but you heard me, Niecy," he said, looking into her eyes. Her flawless brown skin, small shiny lips, and high cheekbones made her irresistible. The fact that she only stood five foot two and her ass was the phattest and softest he'd ever seen in his life, along with the gap that came from her slightly bowed legs, was killing him. She made not only him, but any nigga want to give her the world for just a night. Even though he'd fucked her several times he never got tired of her, and wanted her just as bad as the first time. He released his grip and got lost in a trance as he watched her ass jiggle with every step. He shook his head and walked back to his office.

Niecy walked over to VIP where her sister and friends were sitting. They had ordered drinks and stood looking over the dance floor. She had to get her head right, because Jeezy did to her what she did to him, but she knew wifey wasn't going anywhere.

"What he want, Niecy?" Janelle asked, seeing her sister spaced out sipping on her drink.

"You know, putting in his bid," she said as if it were nothing.

"He can bid over here, I'll eat his little ass up," Reece said, leaning back and thrusting her hips as if she were fucking. They all laughed, but they knew Reece was serious.

As 12:30 grew closer, Reece and Danyelle began to loosen up and started dancing. Cats began to stare and other girls danced with each other to shut them down, but when "Bust It Baby," came blasting through the loud speakers, the bitches began to go crazy, and Lowe stepped down and began to dance. As she swung her ass from side to side, holding her drink, she drew the attention of everybody near her. She began to move harder and her crew crowded around her.

"Go Lowe, go Lowe, go Lowe," they yelled to amp her up. Niggas began to move closer to see the VIP crew drawing all the attention, but cats stood their distance because they knew that stepping to these bitches meant they had to come correct. Then Big Rodney came through the crowd with three niggas from his team. He stepped into VIP, signaled for the waitress, and ordered two bottles of Moët and a round of drinks for his team. Not saying anything to the girls, they tried to push them out of VIP. Rodney knew of Janelle and her crew, and knew it wasn't happening. Other girls began to dance in front of them as they slowly began to take over VIP, until Danyelle looked at Janelle and smiled. Janelle got the waitress's attention and ordered three bottles of Moët and a bottle of Grey Goose. She could see Rodney catch an attitude, so she invited Twin, Fats, and Ashley to join her, as she took VIP back over. Twin was her girl from P-town. She had a twin sister and both these girls worked for Janelle. They moved weight, having most of downtown Portsmouth locked down from Effingham to Lincoln Park; these bitches slung hard. Hard all day. Ashley also worked for her, but Ashley lived in Newport News and she was the only girl Janelle knew who sold diesel. Fats worked for her man, Choice. Now, Choice was from Brooklyn. He had come to Virginia and locked shit down with cocaine and heroin, but Choice kept getting locked up because of his quick temper and his attitude toward Virginia cats. He was quick to go to a nigga ass and even quicker to bust his gun, which had earned him a name in the street. This time, he had to give the state of Virginia eighteen months. He expected Janelle to hold down his business in his absence and do her own shit. Things usually went smoothly, because he had quickly built a name for himself. Cats in the street knew he would not hesitate to go back to jail or step to a nigga's ass like it won't shit. As quick as he came home he would go back, so they stayed clear of him and never fucked with Janelle.

"Leave me alone, boy," Lowe yelled as one of Rodney's people kept trying to talk to her as she danced and drank.

"Leave her alone, Duke. Them bitches ain't all that, fuck them," the other dude said, touching his man.

"Bitch, ain't no bitches here. Carry yo' broke ass, bitch-ass niggas," Niecy said, squinching her face. "Looking like six niggas on one blunt," she added, laughing and giving Reece a pound, knowing she would join in. Breaking down niggas down was her specialty.

"Fuck you, ho," Rodney said, stepping closer to Niecy. "Better watch your mouth, bitch."

"Y'all mad because we shut y'all down. You need to just leave. We having a good time, and y'all fuckin' up the program. Because these bitches in the club know from your dirty old Tims that y'all broke. Y'all came from work to the club," Reece said, swinging her head and allowing her dreads to fling all over, showing attitude.

Before things got ugly, Jeezy saw what was going on and walked over. "Y'all okay, baby girl?" he asked Janelle.

"They being stupid," Niecy yelled.

"Yo, I need y'all cats to go over to the other VIP; this one's reserved. Thanks!" Jeezy said to Rodney and his crew.

"Fuck that, tell them hoes to move," Rodney said.

"What?" Jeezy questioned with an attitude. He was trying to keep these cats from being on Choice's list when he came home. Jeezy turned to the girls. "Calm down, it will be okay. Give it a sec," he said, walking away to the back.

He looked over the club and didn't see a crew that he

needed, so he waited. Thirty minutes later he got a call: "Yo, I'm pulling up, got my VIP?"

"Yeah," Jeezy replied, smiling. "How many?"

"Four."

"Meet you at the door," Jeezy said.

Fifteen minutes later Jeezy stood at the door, allowing Dundee and his Lake Edward team to slide into the club for free and without being searched. Dundee and his team came up wearing their LEP platinum chains, draped in black.

"What up, fam?" he asked Jeezy, giving him a hug and a pound.

"You know what it is? I was holding your VIP over there, but those cats hard-headed and wouldn't move, then they started beefing with my shorty and Choice's girl."

Dundee looked at his team and told them where their VIP spot was. "That's us," he said, pointing at Rodney and his team.

"What up, ma?" Tee said, getting close to Danyelle.

"What up, Tee?" she said.

"I still want you. Yo' man ain't fucked up yet?" he asked.

"Naw, fool. He acting right," she replied. Danyelle never fucked around her man was good to her. He had her caked up, he was caked up, and he showed her love like nobody had ever done. In return, she respected him to the utmost. Not to mention, he and his team had come up from Miami, hustled from Hampton to Richmond, and took murder as a game.

"Respect, girl, respect," Tee said, thinking Danyelle's man was Jamaican. "Did I sound like your man? *Respect gurrl?*" Tee added, laughing.

"He's not Jamaican, he's Trinidadian," she said with attitude.

"Girl, I don't give a fuck. Them niggas is all the same. You know where I'm from and he hit that Lake Edward yell 'Lelelelele.' " She looked at him in disgust before he leaned closer to her ear and added, "And can't nobody fuck with it, believe that," and kissed her cheek. She wiped it off, but she was all right with Tee, and she knew he ran with an unstoppable team: Lake Edward Posse, run by the infamous Dundee.

"Yo, my nigga, this us," Dundee said to Rodney and his team.

"Naw, my nigga. We got this," Rodney said. Before Dundee could react, Los walked up, followed by Nitty.

"You heard my man," he said, knocking the bucket of ice and champagne on the floor. Then Jah slapped two of their drinks out of their hands, and smacked Rodney unexpectedly as he tumbled out of VIP.

"Where is this going?" Dundee asked as he gripped the cocoa-colored gun, revealing the Coco-Bologrip, staring at this bitch-ass nigga team. They moved on and eased out the club, swearing revenge, looking sad.

Dundee grabbed the waitress and ordered five bottles of Dom, so everybody on his team could have a bottle. Then he ordered a bottle of Goose & Patron. As they drank, Jah eased over to Niecy. Los eased over to Lowe, and Dundee began talking to Janelle. Janelle tried to ignore him, but his swagger and the words he spoke had "baller" all over them. As they got drunk, they got funnier, and before long they were all having the time of their lives. Then Lowe and Niecy began to dance, and it had niggas mesmerized like they were dancers on a stage. Just to fuck with Janelle, Dundee pulled out $200 in fives and began tossing them at the girls until his crew yelled, "Make it rain on them hoes, make it rain Dun, make it rain." Dun, caught up in the moment and drunk, stood on the chair, pulled out a stack of twenties equal to two grand, and let it rain on Niecy and Lowe. The club went crazy. Bitches went crazy and Lowe stared at Dundee, knowing he was that nigga. She eased over in front of him, put her ass on him, and he rode her ass until his dick was rock hard. He stared at Janelle with thoughts of her being his bitch. She was too real. But he knew of Choice, and the thought of a New York nigga having anything he wanted was some bullshit. Dundee felt *he* was that nigga.

Lowe did a move where she bent over slightly and positioned his dick, which she felt through the jeans, right in the middle of her ass and pressed back. Dundee almost lost his balance, but his attention was now on Lowe. She threw her head back, stared at Dun, then continued to dance as she moved away and eased over to Niecy, just like Niecy had taught them: do something to make the nigga want you, and he'll come running like a little puppy. Dundee finished his bottle while glancing over the crowd. He saw Jeezy heading for his office with security around him, which meant he had the door money. Dundee walked over to Lowe and leaned down to whisper in her ear, "Gotta hollah at Jeezy and then we out." He walked away.

"What he say?" Danyelle asked.

"He wanna fuck," Reeci said. "I know he do."

"He gotta hollah at Jeezy, then we out."

"Out where? We came together." Danyelle said.

"We leave this bitch together," Janelle said, but Niecy and Reece didn't agree with that one, and Dundee had Lowe's mind in a blur.

Dundee walked to the back office. "What up, baby? I'm outta here. What you doin' after this?"

"Shakespeares!" Jeezy yelled.

A light went off in his head. *Hell yeah!* The after-hours club out Oceana sounded like a winner. "I don't know, cuz, I got to see what shorty gon' do," Dundee said with a smirk.

"Who?"

"Lowe, nigga! That bitch phat as shit."

"That she is, but she got two kids by my man, Stink."

"Stink from out Carriage Houses?" Dun asked.

"Yeah!"

"I heard that, but guess what?" Dundee said smiling.

"What's that, son?"

"That's your man and I ain't never fuck wit' him like that, but I'm gonna fuck the shit out of his baby momma. That's real talk," he said seriously.

"Do you, nigga. Stink been gone almost two years, pussy probably dripping and she broke," Jeezy said.

"With those kids," they said simultaneously and broke out laughing.

"Naw, man, check this, Janelle and Danyelle, they got dough and they shit straight, but yo' girl Niecy and especially Reece, money and more money, but Niecy so bad, she can get it and keep getting it.

"She crazy though," Dundee said.

"What you mean, I been hitting her for a minute," Jeezy said, laughing.

By this time they were standing at the open doorway leading back to the club, when Reece came by, headed to the ladies' room.

"Where you going? Come here," Jeezy said, smiling and easing back. She stumbled, but got her composure and stared at Jeezy. She wanted him to hollah, but remembered who he was fuckin' with.

"Where you know Janelle and Niecy from?" Dundee asked.

"Ingleside, why?"

"Because I like Janelle," Jeezy said. That wasn't what Reece wanted to hear. Janelle always caught attention. It wasn't that she was hatin', but sometimes she wished she would get the attention her friends got.

"We only fuck wit' hoes with class" Dundee said, testing Reece to see how she would react.

"I got class, nigga," Reeci said, getting mad.

"But not like them, they come from class," he said, trying not to laugh, but Jeezy couldn't hold it.

"That's what you think, nigga. You don't know them like I know them," Reece snapped, feeling shit on.

"So, what the deal then?" Jeezy asked, smiling at Dundee.

Finally, Reece talked and talked, releasing some of the tension she held inside toward her so-called friends.

"We all from Ingleside, but Janelle and Niecy moved out Lake Edwards when Janelle was nine, and Niecy was twelve or thirteen, but anyway, they went to live with their older sister because they momma had a nervous breakdown. She had like eight or nine kids. Four boys, three in the penitentiary and one gay as hell, living out Ocean View, dying of AIDS, just like they daddy. One got forty years for rape. Raped and sodomized this lady in the back of a newspaper truck. The other two was hustling and terrorizing Norfolk, until they got crazy time. The oldest sisters are like thirty-nine and forty. They took in Janelle, Niecy, and Naquel."

"Who?" Jeezy asked with a crazy expression.

"Niecy real name is Naquala, her twin was Naquel. Their momma started fuckin' them up, choking, beatings, burning them, and just doing crazy shit and then one day she broke down. Janelle, Naquel, and Naquala went to live with one sister out Lake Edwards, but after a year, it was said the sister's husband kept trying to fuck Naquel, so she sent her to the other sister, who still lived out Ingleside. They ate lunch and met up quite often;

Niecy said that Naquel kept saying he wouldn't stop and nobody believed her. She was trying to say the other sister's boyfriend was raping her, but anyway, three days later, Naquel supposedly killed herself with a shotgun in the house. Niecy went crazy and she always said that her sister's boyfriend killed her twin. And she ain't been the same since. She started fuckin' grown men at fifteen, probably had at least five abortions, and the one baby she did keep, she threw out with the trash," Reece said, laughing.

Jeezy and Dun looked at Reece like she was crazy.

"She had the baby for six months and decided she didn't want it. People were around, they watched her, then she told the judge she did it because she didn't want it no more."

"Where is the baby now?" Dundee asked.

"I don't know, noboby never ask or bring it up," she said.

"So you got all the class, now I see," Jeezy said, smiling.

"Yo, I'm out," Dundee said.

"Be safe, Dun," Jeezy said, and they guided Reece back to the club. She'd given them a lot to think about, but soon as he saw Niecy leaving the club, he watched her. Even intoxicated, that bitch's shit was tight as hell.

The valet pulled Janelle's truck up to the front. They piled in, but Dundee put his hands around the back of Lowe's neck and pulled her to him. "I got her," he said to her crew. Lowe looked at her crew hesistantly for a second, but then she saw the money green LS460 sitting on dubs with cream leather interior. The Lex was screaming with $15,000 rims.

This nigga got the new shit '08, Lowe thought as she gave her crew the signal that she'd be all right. *Bitches see me and niggas too,* she thought. *Now they know how they better come at a bitch.* The valet opened her door and she got in, letting the leather absorb her. Dundee slid the dude twenty dollars, as he turned and gave Jah and Los a pound. They were still around trying to hollah at Niecy and them.

Dundee got in his shit, feeling the vibe of onlookers peeking his swagger; looking, acting, and feeling like money. *That's me,* he thought as he glanced over at Lowe, *and I'm leaving with one of the baddest bitches in the club. Damn! I'm that niggah.* He pulled out onto Laskin Road, headed to the interstate.

The cream S550 turned into Newpointe Condos, and Jeezy dialed Niecy's number. "Hello, sweetie, bring the pass to the door."

"All right," she said, opening the door.

He jumped out, grabbed the pass, and threw it on the Benz. He walked inside the candle lit room. Niecy locked the door, and he turned to follow her to her bedroom. She reached over and lit the backwood filled with haze. Jeezy's eyes lit up as the aroma hit his nose. She handed it to him, and he took a long pull so the taste would sit on his tongue. Niecy hit the CD player, and Ginuwine came creeping through with "In Those Jeans."

She wore a short, wintergreen silk teddy that barely covered her ass. Jeezy thought she ain't have no panties until she took off the teddy, then he saw the top of the thong around her waist. That phat ass had eaten up the thong. His dick jumped at the thought of getting in her. She eased up against his body, then she pulled up his shirt and started sucking and biting his chest. She pulled open his pants and reached in to massage his dick. In seconds, the Pradas were off to the side along with the jeans and boxers. Jeezy sat on the bed with the lit backwood in his hand as Niecy bent over with her ass in the air, sucking his dick. He stared in the mirror at her ass and as her legs gapped open, all he saw was a thin string disappearing in a phat ass and pussy. He was so turned on, his body began to shake and he came.

Damn! This bitch turn me on like I never fucked before, he thought as he caught a feeling inside like he was ready to go again.

She climbed on the bed and brought her legs back wide. As she ran her fingers across her vagina, she stared at him with nothing but seduction in her eyes and said, "Please, Daddy, give it here, I've missed you so much." She reached out and gripped his dick, pulled it to her and forced it in. "Now get in there, give it here," she said sternly.

At that moment, Jeezy mind was gone. A much wetter, much warmer feeling began to massage his dick and it felt like heaven. He began to go hard, and the harder he went, the wetter she got. The gushing sounds of him going in and out turned them both on. He turned her over, and climbed on her ass. As he pounded and pounded, he got so excited he came again, never realizing she had begun to get dry. He got up and went into the bathroom. Minutes later, he was dressed and out the door.

Niecy lay in bed, crying. As she thought about what had just happened, a tear rolled out of the corner of her eye. "No matter what I do, no matter how hard I try, they never stay. They love the package 'til they get it," she sighed. "God, I want my own man, please give me my own. I'm so tired of being alone. You've taken so much from me, when are you gonna let some good come into my life?" She prayed.

She got up and went into the bathroom, got a rag, washed her face, then wiped her ass clean and jumped back into bed. She lay in the dark, staring at the clock; it read 4:20 AM. "Jeezy wasn't here an hour," she said in frustration. She was trying to doze off when she heard a knock at the door. She jumped up and threw on her silk nightie.

"Who is it?" she asked.

"Polo. Open the door," he said. She let him in, then walked to her room.

He sat on the couch and pulled out a syringe and a bag. He began to put his work together, and in a matter of minutes he was yelling at Niecy, who was in the back in her bedroom. She had crawled up in the bed. This was the very reason she had put him out; coming home late, wylin' out, and getting high. Polo had a tendency to catch her at her lowest points in her life. Like when thoughts of her baby came to mind, or when she thought about the abuse she suffered from her mom, or their dad being so high and drunk he'd fondle their brother's privates and do God-knows-what else when nobody was around. Thoughts of her sister boyfriend raping her twin and then killing her that continuously played in her mind, that she wished she could forget. *There was no way my twin could have taken the shotgun and pulled the trigger. I tried it,* she thought, crying, standing up and *I know she didn't, so I don't see why everybody else couldn't see it.*

She walked into the living room, dazed out, as if she were another person. Polo sat her down. He knew Niecy. He knew what was on her mind and knew she wanted to escape as she had done several times before. He took her arm and found her vein, then took the needle and began his task while talking to her. "You gonna be all right, baby. You are beautiful, you that woman. Nobody can fuck with Niecy," he said slowly. "Lay back, and let all those problems disappear. Let them go, Niecy, you deserve to get away." Polo laid her back as Niecy went to another world. Polo waited before he did his. He went over to Niecy and took out his dick. Pulling her mouth to it, he said, "Come on, baby, make me happy. You know that's why niggas talk to you, just to sex you up, but I love you," Polo said.

"You love me," she said slowly, slurring her words as she started sucking.

"You know I do, baby, I'm gonna be here always," he said, stroking her head.

"Okay," she said with a mouth full of dick. He pulled away and turned her over. He got on her and entered her from the back. That ass was so powerful, he came in a minute. He sat down and grabbed his work as he began to get the needle right. He reached over and guided the needle into his vein. When morning came, Niecy found Polo in the same spot, eyes wide open, naked, dick hard, dead from an overdose.

Niecy called Janelle and she arrived right after the ambulance and coroner arrived. She sat beside her weeping sister as they removed the body from the condo.

"What the hell, Niecy?"

"I didn't do shit," she explained.

"What you mean? I ain't no fool. Polo wasn't doing this shit by himself," Janelle said. "Don't lie to me, please, Niecy."

"Don't worry about me, I'll be okay."

"This ain't weed or coke. Y'all shooting up and that nigga dead. What you trying to do?" Janelle asked. "I know you been through a lot. So have I, but I still respect life. Don't you, Niecy?"

"To be honest, Janelle, I don't care. Our dad wasn't shit up until the day he killed himself, overdosed, whatever you call it. Our mom has serious issues. It's just you and me; and you have Choice, a New York nigga, girl, and he truly love you. And me, who I got? A handful of friends who want to fuck; niggas who got wives and girlfriends.

They come around for a couple of hours, then niggas ghost," she said in a very sad tone.

"You allow that, Niecy. You need to keep your legs closed, let niggas know there ain't no pussy there, unless they earn it. But you let niggas play you. You better than that, you fine as shit. I ain't saying that because you my sister, you got a lot to offer. You can't just keep giving of yourself and not getting nothing in return," Janelle said, sadly staring into her sister's watering eyes.

"My mind is cloudy and fucked up. I feel if I love a man hard enough, he will love me back."

"Not a nigga who already got a woman, especially a wife," Janelle said with a serious expression.

"I be feeling as if the walls are closing in. I let Polo talk me into trying different shit because I wanted . . . no, I needed to escape. Weed don't do shit, coke make me numb, ecstasy make me feel good, but I don't escape. I don't like getting piss drunk because it reminds me of momma and I can't remember shit, but when he gave me the heroin, I actually felt great. Better than sex, Janelle, and I didn't care about anything. Just for a little while, I forgot about everything."

"Fuck all that, you see where the fuck Polo at, you see what happened to him."

"And?" Niecy said, unconcerned.

"And? That's all you got to say."

"Polo had gone through hell, his life was fucked up. And now, Polo is at peace, Janelle, he found peace."

"You'll find peace if you get a job, keep your legs closed, and go to church! Try that and see what happen, because shit seem to be getting worse."

"It can't get no worse, Janelle," Niecy said, grabbing the pillow on the couch and balling up. Janelle's phone went off. The twins were calling to see her. If it were her money, she might have ignored it, but this was Choice's heroin money that had to be put up and never touched.

"What up?" she answered.

"You know what it is, baby, shit popping in Bad Newz," Ashley said.

"Heard that. Give me an hour and I'll see you."

"Waiting on you, girl, waiting on you," Ashley said, knowing that if Choice were home, he would make her ass move quickly knowing how that diesel moved. She would have been straight already. Ashley had lucked out, asking Janelle about dope when she was only moving crack. Janelle hollered at Choice and Ashley became the only one she fucked with who sold dope. Janelle could move the hard with ease, and she knew how crack moved, but that diesel was another story. The houses that were set up for the diesel were only open for a couple of hours, and they could make all their money before noon if the product was there. Ashley figured she would head to Norfolk so the wait wouldn't be too long.

"I'll be on your side, waiting on you," Ashley said nonchalantly.

"Bet," Janelle said and hung up.

"Bitch think she gonna rush me, better settle her ass down," she said, thinking out loud.

"Who dat? Ashley?" Niecy asked.

"Yeah. I gotta go, girl. Are you okay?" Janelle asked, concerned. She questioned if she should leave her sister alone after what she'd just been through, but she had to get this money.

"I'm good," Niecy said without moving. Janelle stood up and kissed her, then headed out the door.

For the next six months, things would keep falling into place for Janelle. All her business was good except for the few people she had off Newtown Road. She had a few girls whom she was teaching to get down, but every time they went to the block niggas would come and rob them, so she was taking a loss.

She began to let her status go to her head, forgetting that Choice had been gone for fourteen months and had a release date of May 17. His name wasn't ringing like it was before; out of sight, out of mind. Janelle felt she had product, and because she lived out Lake Edward, went to Bayside, and knew everybody, she had the right to pump anywhere off Newtown and Baker Roads.

One Wednesday night at Luxury Brown's, one of the hottest clubs in Virginia Beach, she ran into Toya and Tiffani. These two shorties were set to graduate in May, but in their family, money always came short. She saw potential in these two young ladies, but she saw them headed down the wrong road. Tiffani was a slim brown-skinned chick with long hair and a phat hip for her slim frame. Niggas were intrigued by her cuteness and wanted to lock her down; she reminded Janelle of Reece. Toya, on the other hand, was built like a little Niecy, slightly darker than Tiffani, slightly shorter, but her body was much more defined. She wore the cutest smile, which made her come off as if she were shy. It drove young niggas crazy, and made older men wish they were still in high school.

Janelle saw that their gear was off the chain. They kept fresh kicks, and she knew from experience that one of those little hustling niggas was on his way to pulling them into that street shit, strictly off of cars and change. She decided to step to them and let them know they needed to fuck with her and learn to get this money for themselves. She always said, "Fuck a niggah and that slick shit they have with them; nothing comes free." She ended up setting them up and giving them a half-ounce each. She showed them how to break it down, and where to set up shop in the back of Campus East: another set of rowhouses right next to Lake Edward. They listened and caught on fast. Sales came quickly, and money began rolling in for the young ladies. They were out in the hood walking around like they usually did, but they had a product and the fiends fucked with them because of their accessibility. But all the niggas who had left the block and was working from pagers and phones started to feel their pockets getting light.

One night, as they stood out on Campus Drive, a white Ford Expedition pulled up. Jah and Nitty jumped out and told them to empty their pockets, but the girls refused. Nitty caught Toya with a kidney shot and she fell to the ground, crying. He felt Tiffani's blows to his jaw and body. Standing six foot two, and weighing 280 pounds, he laughed before slamming her to the ground and emptying their pockets of their drugs and money. The girls weren't only physically hurt, but their pride was crushed. They instantly called Janelle.

"What up, Toya?" she said, laughing as she answered the phone. Toya was sniffing and could hardly get it out.

"What's wrong?" she asked harshly.

"They beat us up," Toya said before Tiffani took the phone.

"They robbed us, took your shit and your money," Tiffani yelled in the phone.

"Who?" Janelle yelled.

"That boy with the white Expedition and Nitty punk ass," Tiffani said.

Janelle was pushing the BMW X5 down Princess Anne Road at crazy speeds. She had just bailed Niecy out of jail for acting out and not fucking thinking, and she was done with all the bullshit going on. It seemed as if everything was falling, not coming together like it should.

"What's wrong, Janelle?" Niecy asked.

"I know niggas ain't fuck with your girls," Lowe said, surprised.

"Bitch-ass niggas robbed them," Janelle said, hyped with anger. "Jah and Nitty," she added as she turned on Wesleyan Drive, making the right on Baker, then the left on Baccalaureate.

Tiffani and Toya stood on the side, looking sad in their fresh gear. They'd gotten used to getting their own and were thankful to Janelle for showing them, but sad because they didn't want to disappoint her. She could see their eyes were red and glassy from crying.

"Stop that crying shit," Janelle said sternly.

"Naw, the niggas trying to fight us, punching and slamming us, that's what's up," Toya added, upset.

"Not because we got robbed," Tiffani added sadly.

"Bitch niggas need to get fucked up putting their hands on a girl," Niecy yelled as she got out the car. Tiffani and Toya noticed her big stomach, wondering what she was gonna do.

"Be careful, girl," Lowe said.

"You seven months pregnant girl, better sit yo' ass back in the car," Janelle said, "I just bailed your ass out of jail. You need to chill." She knew Niecy was still ready to go to a nigga's ass if she had to.

"Come on, let me drop y'all off. Tomorrow another day and I'll be out here with y'all tomorrow night, and then we'll see what type of heart niggas really got," Janelle said as they climbed in the back next to Lowe.

Janelle dropped off the girls. "Hit me tomorrow evening. Don't worry about it, it will come back to me. Believe it," she added as they stepped out of the burgundy X5. They pulled off and headed up Baker Road, toward New-pointe to Niecy's house.

"Now, what the fuck is wrong with your dumb ass,

Niecy? That nigga don't give a fuck about you. He done called you every name in the book when you told him you was pregnant by him four months ago, then he said it wasn't his and to stay the fuck away from him. You tried to fight him, until he went and put a restraining order out on you. Stay the fuck away from that nigga, Goddamn!" Janelle yelled.

"I ain't do nothing, I'm not wrong, Janelle," Niecy said, beginning to cry. Her hardness was gone.

"Kill that crying shit. You had no business fuckin' with that nigga wife. She ain't fuck you."

"So, I was—" Niecy began.

"So what!" Janelle said, slamming on brakes. "Leave that bitch alone and stay the fuck away from her," she said with mad head movement, trying to get her sister to see the seriousness of the situation.

Niecy had been going through hell trying to get Jeezy to accept responsibility of his baby that was on the way, but he didn't want to hear it. He cut Niecy off and changed his number. Niecy found out where his wife got her hair done and went to confront her.

"Excuse me, Shaquelle, my name . . ."

"I know who the fuck you are, bitch. And I know you aren't supposed to be near me or my husband," Shaquelle said sternly.

"This is Jeezy baby," Niecy said, rubbing her stomach with a slight smirk, trying to irritate Shaquelle

"And how do we know this?" Shaquelle asked. "When did you find the time to do all that?" she asked suspiciously.

"Nights when he closed the club, bitch," Niecy came back. She felt she owed her that.

"So you let him come by after he leave the club, fuck you, and leave. What type of bitch does that? There's a name for that: J-u-m-p off! Don't tell nobody else that," Shaquelle said sarcastically as she turned to leave. But when she turned, she was shocked as Niecy grabbed her hair and tried to pull her down. She went with the pull and turned into Niecy, coming with a right across Niecy's jaw, then a left uppercut. Niecy let go of her hair and tried to gain her composure, but Shaquelle kept the blows coming until she saw the opportunity to get Niecy's hair. She grabbed it as she threw blows on Niecy, yelling, "Stay the fuck away from me you stanking-ass, no-good bitch. I will beat that baby out yo' ass!"

Niecy fell to the ground, and Shaquelle didn't hesitate to kick her stomach repeatedly, until the girls from the beauty shop ran out and stopped her. Somebody had called the police, and when they arrived they arrested Niecy because she had come within 100 feet of Shaquelle. Niecy rode in the car crying, not because she was going to jail, because she had gotten her ass whipped. She knew Shaquelle couldn't have fucked with her if she weren't pregnant, but her stomach had held her back from doing her norm.

Janelle pulled up in front of her condo. Niecy got out and Janelle started to drive off without waiting for her to get into the house, then she stopped. She was mad as hell at Neicy for approaching Jeezy's wife while she was pregnant. "Hey," Janelle yelled out the window. "Stay the fuck in the house and don't go doing no dumb shit. I got you, you hear me?"

"Yeah!" Niecy said, holding her head down, still embarrassed. She lifted her head and watched Janelle's truck disappear.

"Bitches don't want me to get no drink tonight, they don't want me to have a good time, but that's a Goddamn lie," Janelle said, shaking her head. "I can't worry about this bullshit with my sister, but you better believe if I see that bitch, she will have to beat my ass. Now picture that."

"Girl, calm down. Where we going, anyway?" Lowe asked, ready to go somewhere.

"Granby Street, Club Dolce, Club Seven, Guadalajara, I don't care," Janelle said, hitting the interstate, headed downtown.

"So, what up, girl? A bitch got to pull you out the house," Janelle said.

"Girl, I be chilling wit' my man. That nigga be putting it down and he ain't stingy, either, got me and my kids straight," Lowe said, smiling.

Yeah, Janelle thought. She knew Dundee would hollah every time he saw her, and he'd been trying to fuck her for a long time, but she would never tell Lowe at this point. She was happy, and she felt nobody could touch Choice. He was nothing but truth, and she couldn't wait for him to touch ground.

"I know you all in love and shit, Lowe, but look at me," Janelle said seriously. She looked briefly in Lowe's eyes, then back to the road. "Dundee a wild boy. He a lot like Choice, a live wire. So be careful. Don't get caught," she added, knowing she should be listening to her own advice. "You met his man yet?"

"Who? Nitty, Los, or Jah? You know those his peoples, right?" Lowe said. She dreaded having this conversation, since the earlier incident had kicked off with Dundee's people running Janelle off the block.

"They work for him, I know. But those just his niggas, he get money with them. I mean his *peoples* people, Ponic and Rudy."

"Yeah, they be at the house playing Playstation and that X-Box shit."

"Now, if he call them niggas out, it's some shit. If them motherfuckers start doing that 'Lelelelele' shit." They both laughed at Janelle, imitating the Lake Edward niggas when they did their hollah. "That shit mean something."

"Yeah! They in the building or we got a problem, where y'all at," Lowe added, and they both laughed.

"Yo, be careful around them niggas, they some peoples nobody want to fuck with."

"I'm good, girl, I ain't in they business, and nobody involves me in shit. My Dundee got me straight. I know I ain't followed all the rules that I should have; lot of this shit I put together just to get dough, Janelle. Niggas using me like I'm a mule, for change and dick. This nigga come along and make me feel like I can miss a day of work, like he give a fuck, Janelle," Lowe said as if she were talking to a therapist, which was a release.

"Bitch, that nigga got you open off money and dick."

"And coke," Lowe said, hyped.

"What?" Janelle came to a stop as she reached the light.

"I like that shit, fam. For real. It make me feel good. Fuck weed, that smell linger on, boom, boom, I'm good," Lowe said, shaking her head.

"That's bullshit, you fuckin' up. I'ma cut all y'all bitches off. You coke, Niecy heroin and shit."

"Janelle, look at me, Niecy fuck with everything. If you didn't know, now you know, unless you want to play stupid. But we go back too far for dat."

"What you mean, Lowe, for real?" Janelle asked, stern and direct. Her attitude turned a little more serious.

"Please. Niecy been sniffing, smoking, popping ecstasy . . . shit, she been getting high as hell a long time. That's why I got the nerve to try X and the courage to sniff. Shit, it wasn't hurting her, but I can't fuck with no heroin. I seen The Wire and see what that shit do to people. You need to help her if she doing that."

"I'm gonna have to do something. I ain't know all that until Polo was found in her house, overdosed on that shit. I thought if he was doing she must have been, but she keep that shit from me. All I know is the smoking weed and drinking. All that other shit new to me. Now I understand those crazy-ass mood swings like she bipolar or some shit, now I see," Janelle said, more to herself than to Lowe.

Her mind was going a mile a minute; she couldn't believe what she'd heard. Shit was going too far, and she had to get her sister under control somehow. Niecy was all she had.

The following day, Janelle was on her way to Niecy's when she spotted the big white Expedition at E Outfitters *Niggas probably spending my money buying gear for the club,* Janelle thought. Anger rose in her as she thought about the thousand in cash, and the entire package. These niggas owed her two grand and they needed to see her. "I can't beat these niggas, but if I have to I will bust on these niggas," she said out loud, trying to convince herself. She checked her purse for the Glock 25 she'd gotten from her brother three years ago, He was a gay prostitute who lived and worked the streets of Ocean View. He had been beaten and raped so many times, he had gotten himself a gun. But when he was forced to use it, it disturbed him even more than he already was, so he passed it on to Janelle. He figured it was a ladies' gun and she may have needed one day. Janelle had taken it and put it away, but then felt a need to carry it once Choice had gotten locked up.

As she pulled up by the truck, she felt in control. Niggas knew Choice, and niggas knew fucking with her was like dealing with Choice, nobody wanted problems with her man. She exited the car, leaving the Glock on the seat. She felt maybe these niggas didn't know the product was hers and that Toya and Tiffani were her protégés.

She walked up as they exited the store. "What up, Janelle?" Los said, greeting Janelle with a smile. "You trying to find you something for the club? Because you know I got you."

"Naw, I'm okay!" she said, looking at Jah and Nitty.

"Leave her alone, Los, that's that nigga Choice girl," Nitty said, playing like he cared.

"That nigga been locked up for twenty years, I want to know is you ready to fuck?" Jah said, laughing as he walked to his truck.

"Naw, I ain't fucking nobody, but I ain't let nobody fuck me, either," Janelle said with mad attitude.

"Yo, Jah! This girl is really upset. She got a real attitude," Nitty said. "Why you mad Janelle, what's up?" Nitty asked seriously.

"Y'all got my shit. Y'all ran up on my girls, Toya and Tiffani. They roll with me and y'all got my shit the other night. How we gonna handle this? I need mine," she added, as if she were a gangster.

"My bad, we didn't . . ." Nitty started to apologize to Janelle because he had nothing against her. He really didn't know those were her youngens working the corner. But Jah cut him off.

"Hold up, Nitty. Janelle, because you cool and you from out the way, no, because you been living out the way for a minute, I'm gonna put you up on game, since you want to be gangsta and shit. One, if you got a problem with anybody and they got you like I got you," he said, pointing to himself, "you come up, pull out your burner, look me in my eyes, and tell me, 'empty your pockets, nigga, I need two grand.' If I don't pull out close to it, blow a motherfucker brains out. But don't step to niggas unless you ready."

"Come on, Jah," Los said, "Leave her alone, she just trying to get money." Los didn't hustle with LE niggas, even though he was from there and fucked with them. But he didn't hustle or fuck with them niggas on getting money. And he thought it was wrong that they stooped that low to rob those young girls.

"And two, those hoes ain't supposed to be out there. All the shit being sold out here come from two niggas and I ain't seen you spend money with neither one. So you carry that shit somewhere else. Go out North Ridge, Plaza, Twin Canal, I don't give a fuck, but if you or any other bitches walking these streets out here, you better be smoking or selling pussy. Now get the fuck out my face," he said, standing less than a foot from her so she wouldn't miss a word.

"Fuck that, you need to give me my money or your fat ass gonna pay. I mean that shit," she said, stepping closer to Jah.

"Don't get fucked up out here, girl. Now carry yo' ass," he said, mushing her on the side of her face, making her stumble.

"Yo, chill, son, you going too far," Los said, realizing things were getting out of hand.

"You don't put your hands on me, fuck that," Janelle screamed. He had chastised her like she was his child, like she wasn't shit to him. They got in the truck and turned up the new Plies about the same time Janelle reached her car. She jumped in with angry tears in her eyes. She looked over at the Glock 25 and jumped back out, as anger and revenge took over her thinking. She pointed and started busting the Expedition as it pulled off. The first two shots shattered the back and side windows. Three more shots whizzed by, one shattering the rearview mirror and exiting the front windshield.

"That bitch shooting," Nitty yelled as he pulled out the Desert Eagle .44-caliber.

"She is busting." Los laughed at this girl who was not playing.

"She just shooting. Fuck her, bet I get her ass," Jah said as he heard the sounds of the .44 set off the parking lot and send Janelle sprinting to her car for dear life.

"Yo, son, chill," Jah yelled at Nitty, laughing. "We beat hoes, we don't shoot them.

"Shit, if they shooting at me . . ."

Janelle never made it to Niecy's house. She went straight home, poured some Hennessey, and rolled a Dutch of cush. She downed the Henney straight and shook it off, poured another shot, and lit her el. As the Henney began to sneak up on her, her body relaxed, her nerves relaxed, and as she exhaled the smoke from the Dutch her body began to slow down. Another pull put her body in slow motion, which she felt as she reached for the ringing phone.

"Collect call from Virginia Beach Jail." She heard the recording say "Choice. Please press . . ."

She knew the routine and quickly pressed the necessary number to receive the call.

"What up, ma?" he asked. The sound of his voice instantly broke her down.

"They robbed me and tried to kill me," she cried. "They were shooting at me," she yelled, and cried harder.

His laid back attitude changed. All he could see was his girl handling that street shit and caught up in the bullshit. "Who the fuck tried to kill you?" he yelled so loud that other inmates could hear him over all the noise.

"Jah, Nitty, and Los. They tried to kill me," she screamed. Choice knew the names, but it wasn't adding up. Those niggas didn't know where they lived, so he knew they didn't run up in his house. Los he knew from fucking around in Norfolk and around Brambleton. They knew some of the same people in Norfolk and even cats from home. He didn't seem like that type of nigga to be fuckin' with the petty shit.

"Calm down and stop fuckin' crying. Tell me everything because shit don't sound right."

"What you mean it don't sound right?" Janelle asked loudly, confused.

"Yo, ma! Watch your tone. Don't forget who the fuck you talking to." Janelle got quiet.

"Did you hear me?" he asked with force.

"Yeah, I heard you," she said softly.

"Now, first thing, you say Los robbed you and bucked on you?" he asked as if he still couldn't believe it.

"Los was wit' Jah and Nitty."

"They all just came up on you and robbed you?" he asked with sarcasm in his voice.

"No, they . . ."

"You fucking up, Janelle, don't make me fuck you up, Janelle."

"Stop fussing at me, you confusing me," she said, whimpering.

"You get confused in court when you making sure you don't say the wrong thing to a judge; this is me. Now tell me everything before I make some calls."

She knew she had fucked up. She wasn't supposed to have put her girls out there. She had to choose her words carefully. "These young girls out the way asked me to do something, and they been beggin' for a while so I did something for them on the front. They went to work back Campus East. Last night, Jah and Nitty caught them and robbed them for one thousand dollars and that."

"How much was that?" he asked.

"Another thousand," she said. "I go to Subway and who I see coming out of E Outfitters? Jah, Nitty, and Los. I go up to them and ask for my shit."

"Now what did Los do?" he asked directly.

"Told them to leave me alone and kept going to the truck," she answered.

"What did Nitty do?"

"He said I was Choice girl, they better chill." Choice smiled at the mention of his name. While he was locked up, that showed power and recognition.

"And what did Jah do?"

"He fussed me out, cussed me out, then slapped my face and grabbed me by my hair and shoved me. I fell and scraped my hands and leg. I just lost it. I ran to the car and got the thing and let off at his truck, until that boy Nitty leaned out and shot at me with a real loud gun." She got quiet and silence rested in the line.

"They had no reason to shoot at you or put they hands on you. For that, I'll see those niggas. But you, you shouldn't had nobody, nowhere doing shit. You should have approached them niggas under no circumstances. And fuck is you out there shooting up shit for, you could have got fucked up, right in here with me, or even shot and killed." The thought fucked him up, made him choke. "Look, we got plenty dough put up? Right?"

"Yeah! Your shit, my shit weak," she said.

" 'Cause you fuck it up. Yo, I need you to chill, lay low. Really lay low. This is too much, while I'm locked. Terminate your shit, my shit, I got thirteen weeks. We'll get it cracking then. Time up, baby, tomorrow!"

"Tomorrow call early, Choice. I miss you so much. I love you," she said.

"I know, ma, I know. Don't forget what I said. All right? And don't tell nobody when I'm coming home, okay?"

"Yeah."

"One—" she heard him say, then the phone went dead.

Choice went back to his bunk. He lay back on the thin mattress and the piece of mush the city called a pillow. Things were rough, but keeping his head on the inside was what made things easy. Now he had this to deal with. It was hard keeping his head, but he tried to relax. He closed his eyes, but all he could picture was Jah touching Janelle and Nitty shooting at her. He came to the conclusion that his being locked up had contributed to their decision, but niggas must have lost their minds thinking he ain't coming home. He smiled at the thought of killing three more cats. He thought back to the murder he did out Norview when he left the dude in the wet grass. Then there was the cat he shot as he exited his car coming from the club and the shorty who was with him at the wrong place, wrong time. Then the cat he stabbed because he started wylin' over his girl. Three murders in Virginia and he'd been living there for two years. Shit was hot for him, but it was getting ready to get a lot hotter.

"Where are you?" Danyelle asked.

"Why, girl? Handling my business," Janelle answered.

"I was gonna tell you meet me down at Waterside to go to Joe's Crab Shack for some lunch, but I see you on that bullshit. I ain't begging a bitch to spend my money."

"Yo' treat, girl? Know what, I got something I got to do. I'll catch ya later. I know that ain't that nigga," Janelle said, surprised at the sight of the cream S550, pulling all her attention.

"What is it?" Danyelle said.

"Jeezy car. Shit up here at the nail shop or the barbershop," she said, making the U-turn.

"What you gonna do?" Danyelle asked. "Leave it alone, Janelle. Choice told you to lay low."

"Fuck Choice. Nigga can't tell me shit, his peoples ain't get fucked up. Mine did." The rage built up in Janelle. Her sister had taken a beating. "I ain't pregnant, bitch. Fuck me up, please fuck me up."

"I'm on my way. Don't do shit, you can't beat Jeezy."

"I don't know who driving. If it's Jeezy, I'm gonna shoot him, because it's his fault. If it's his wife, I wanna see if this bitch really got skills," Janelle added.

"She ain't fighting you Janelle."

"Bitch ain't got no choice."

Janelle parked and waited. When she saw Jeezy come out of the barbershop, she hopped out of the car with her gun in her purse. "Jeezy, what up?" she said, gritting real hard.

"Don't get simple like that look on your face. Get in the car," he said with no smile. He could see the anger in her eyes as he opened the driver side door.

"I ain't got shit to talk about. You and yo' bitch fucked up."

"Don't get loud out here. I ain't those niggas you been playing bang-bang with. Now get in the fuckin car, and say all you got to say."

They sat in the car and stared at each other. Janelle was mad as shit at him, his wife, and whoever else she could blame for her sister's shit.

"Look, Janelle, we go way back, girl! I fucks with Choice, baby! You know I got your back always, and I got Niecy back, no doubt! Look at me, Janelle," he said. "Me and Niecy been at this shit since I been getting money and you know that's a long time. She knew the deal, we talked many times. She was still doing her thing, too, so I'm still saying, I don't know about her seed. If it's me, she good, if it ain't me, she still good, 'cause I love her ass. She my girl, but I still got a wife and family and you know Janelle, I . . ."

"Can't leave them, that's how it usually fall. You need to get yo' shit straight with Niecy. You be fucking her up and she don't handle pressure well. When shit crazy, she get crazy."

"I know, I heard she be getting more than high, Janelle. No names, but somebody close told me, 'Watch yourself Jeezy, shorty a cokehead and she mix hard in her weed and she was with Polo when he overdosed.' 'She out there,' were the person's words. That's why I stepped back, but when she call or I see her, we got a connection. Plus, I know y'all, not just y'all, I remember y'all momma, Mrs. Brickhouse, and your brothers when y'all moved out Ingleside. Girl, don't forget I'm a Norfolk nigga first. Your brothers gave Ingleside the name and reputation that it had. Come out there and your ass was as good as got."

"You ain't know," Janelle said, smiling, thinking of the early part of her life, before her mom suffered an aneurism and later had a nervous breakdown.

"When I first started fucking with Niecy, it wasn't about the big ass, it was because I knew her and where she came from, and she knew me and she could talk to me. I know you upset about all this, but you and Niecy are different. You live two totally different lives, and how you live, you need to keep shit low. You heat yourself up, you heat up Choice. And I'm here to tell you, you are no good to my man hot! He hot enough. You on some ill shit right now, and you need to calm yo' ass down. You smart and on point for a female, but you wylin' with real niggas. Leave that to Choice," he said, looking in his rearview mirror at Danyelle and Lowe getting out of the new Jag that Tiger was driving. Tiger was wondering what was going on, but he knew it wasn't his battle so he

and his boy sat in the Jag and watched the bullshit un-
fold. "They playing gangster brother," Tiger said with his
gold fangs smiling.

"I play gangsta wit' that big ass. Shit, she phat," his
man said, showing all golds from top to bottom, express-
ing that he liked Lowe, who was hanging with them
when the situation with Janelle popped off.

"She is phat, man, but the other girl they hang wit', ass
is crazy like Pinky." They laughed at the comparison.

"So, what up, girl?" Danyelle asked, walking up to
Jeezy's car.

"We good, just talking," Janelle said.

"Well, if everything all right, let's go," Lowe said hur-
riedly.

"Y'all go ahead. I'm okay," Janelle said to her friends
before she felt Dundee's hand wrap around her neck and
pull her through the window. They were so into themselves, the girls never saw the black Magnum pull up
and Dundee jump out when he saw Janelle. He pushed
her back on Jeezy's car and pulled out his burner, putting
it to her lips. "Open your mouth or I will bust all your
teeth out," Dundee said, staring into Janelle's eyes. She
saw an outraged devil, and did as she was told. Dundee
shoved the gun in her mouth as Danyelle and Lowe
looked on, begging him to stop.

"You making my shit hot, little niggas can't get money
because you got my shit on fire. Listen to me, shorty, " he
said, positioning himself between Janelle's legs. "Stay
the fuck off my corners and blocks. Don't bring that shit
around here. I hope you understand, girl," he said, stepping off and placing his gun in his waist, still revealing
the Coco-Bolo grip. As he approached the car, he fixed
his eyes on Lowe and Danyelle helping Janelle.

"What the fuck wrong with that nigga?" Danyelle
asked.

"Fuck him, you don't put yo' hands on me. You gonna pay for that shit. Promise you that shit," she yelled with tears in her eyes.

"I hate his ass for that shit," Lowe yelled, holding Janelle. "He crazy, fuck him, I mean that sh . . ." was all she got out of her mouth before the open-hand slap made her see stars and black out for about two seconds. Then she felt pressure as she was gripped by the back of her neck and thrown in the black Magnum. People just stared at Janelle and Danyelle as they stood there, looking confused.

"Come on, Danyelle, I'm out," Tiger yelled.

"Hold on, girl," she said to Janelle with attitude, then walked over to Tiger. "Don't you see what my girl going through? And you ain't do shit," Danyelle said, coming out of character.

"Me? I don't know what she did and he must be fucking her, if he take her off like that. Not my problem. And if you don't get in, you'll be riding and living with your friend," he said, getting into the car and throwing it in gear. Danyelle waved at Janelle as Tiger drove off.

Jeezy stood staring at Janelle as she slowly walked to her truck. "What you gonna do, Janelle?" he asked, concerned.

"I'ma fuck the nigga up. I don't need nobody, *nobody*," she said to Jeezy with watery eyes.

"You need to leave it alone. I have no idea what you did, but its not good. And yo' girl need to peel back. Those are good words for ya," Jeezy said, getting into the Benz and pulling off.

Janelle drove back home thinking she should have never stopped. She got in all that bullshit, and now what? She picked up the phone and dialed Lowe, but there was no answer, so she dialed Danyelle.

"What up, J? You all right?" she said.

"What you doing, chilling?" Janelle said.

"Hell, naw! Been arguing with this nigga like he my daddy. This shit is getting on my muthafuckin' nerves," she responded with attitude.

"Where Tiger at?" Janelle asked.

"Gone with his man cross the water to fuck with them other Jamaicans and shit." Janelle finally smiled.

"You talk to Lowe?"

"Yeah, she fucked up!" Danyelle answered.

"What you mean?"

"She fucked up. That nigga fucked her up and told her not to fuck with you or he was gonna hang her."

"What?"

"Yeah, she scared as shit of that nigga. And she said, he ain't going nowhere. I told her to call the police."

"Naw, don't do that, he'll kill her before I can kill him. I'll hollah back, girl," Janelle said before hanging up. She began feeling worse; she couldn't believe all this shit was going down and Lowe was in a fucked-up situation.

Having to choose between her man or best friend was bad, but what really bothered her was that Dundee was making up her mind for her. She tried calling her again, still no answer. She arrived back at home and drowned the shot of Hennessey VSOP she hadn't finished earlier. She poured another shot then pulled her Dutch from the box and began to roll. Her hands shook and she didn't know why. When it finally came together, she lit it, took a long pull, and blew it out. Another long pull of the cush made dealing with everything a little easier. She turned the television on to BET and sat back with the Dutch in one hand and her drink in the other. Janelle wondered why she wasn't happy. She had a home, a man, cars, and money to do whatever, but she wasn't smiling inside. *Maybe I need Choice more than I thought*, she thought. She really missed him. She didn't have so much pressure on herself when he was home; he took charge like a real man, and made things happen. She could just chill. When he came home, shit was gonna be different, and he wouldn't leave her again. She began to fade out with thoughts of Choice. She grabbed her pillow, hugged it tight, pulled her feet up on the couch, and thought about Choice. Deep in her mind and heart, she thanked God for sparing her life and showing her that she needed her man not only for his love, but also his protection.

"Oh my God, nigga, what the fuck? Aah! Aah! That shit feel so good I'm about to cry. Please don't stop, Show," Niecy said as she placed her hand on the back of Show's head, leaning on her elbow, watching him eat her like she was his last meal. She was almost eight months and her stomach still wasn't that big. She was still smoking, drinking, and tooting, but shooting up was not in the picture for now. She hadn't seen Show in more than a year. He was one nigga from Norfolk who had made a lot of money, carried his ass to D.C., and started promoting clubs, gospel shows, and working with up-and-coming artists as their agent/manager. *This nigga had money and status, and here he is licking my pussy,* Niecy thought, but the thought of her fucking Twon just hours ago and that she probably had cum still draining made her wetter. Show sucked on her clit, trying to pull it off, then he came straight down and licked her ass. Niecy tightened up, but he forced his tongue deep into her ass as she plunged forward.

Smack! His hand came across her ass.

"I love this shit. Ain't noboby in the world this phat," he said, holding her ass in the palms of his hand, as he kept his face buried in her privates. He began licking her clit again, then he pushed two fingers inside of her and moved them around, pulling them in and out until her juices ran across her asshole. The coke they'd sniffed had her body screaming and it had Show freaky as shit. He sucked on her clit firmly, not hard, as he gently slid his finger in her ass. He brought his other hand over and slid two fingers inside her, gripping the ridges on the top part of her vagina and pulling her to him as he sucked harder. Niecy lifted her ass higher, spread her legs as wide as she could and screamed. Then she moaned as she pushed Show's head back and turned on her side, exhausted. But Show wasn't done; he had flown in just to freak and Niecy was his girl. They had a special friendship that nobody could ever explain. He turned her over by surprise and threw her legs up as he rubbed his dick across her vagina lips and across her ass. As he slid into her ass she said, "What the fuck?"

"Come on, Naquala. I'm in there."

"No, that shit hurt. Yo' finger okay, but naw," she said, pulling back.

"All right," he said, turning her over and sliding inside her from the back. He palmed her ass as he enjoyed the greatest feeling in the world. As she began to get into it, he got more excited and began to buck harder. Soon the rhythm got off and he slipped out, and as she lifted her ass wanting him, he came up and pushed his manhood into her ass. He grabbed her waist, a sharp pain shot through her body, and then she felt as if she was going to lose her bowels. She tried to get away but he had a tight hold on her, riding and still pumping, trying to stay inside. It was so uncomfortable, but she couldn't break his hold, so she fell on her stomach as tears formed in her eyes. But going flat down suddenly brought relief. He had slipped out and when he reached for his penis, her body lost control and she released her bowels and exhaled in relief, before she felt him push his dick through the bowels and back into her ass, bucking like a wild animal. The more she moved to get up, the more of a mess they made, especially when he wiped it on her and himself, then she heard him scream as she felt her ass fill up with warm juices. His body jumped uncontrollably for seconds before he collapsed on top of her. She lay there, disgusted with herself and with Show. She couldn't believe what had just happened.

"Goddamn! You's a stankin'-ass bitch," Show said, getting up and laughing.

"You are sick, for real," Niecy said seriously, going into the bathroom, turning on the hot shower, and jumping in. Show followed and they showered until the water turned cold. They dried off and went back to the bedroom, looking at each other as soon as the stench hit them. They balled up the sheets, pillowcases, towels, and comforter and tossed them in the garbage.

"You know I got to get up outta here, my driver be here in a few," Show said, getting dressed.

"I know the routine," Niecy said, unconcerned.

"When you due?" Show asked.

"Why, Show? That was some nasty, degrading shit you did. And I said no."

"Girl, I got problems, I'm nasty and freaky, but you know that and you are, too. But we going to hell with our secrets. All I ask is that you don't stop loving me," he said, smiling. He reached into his pocket, peeled off ten one hundreds and gave them to her. "That's for you to buy some new sheets and a comforter. And those are for little Showtime," he said, peeling off five more hundreds and making his exit.

"Love ya, Naquala, see ya soon."

"Talk to ya," she said, shutting the door. She walked to her room, pulled out her short, beige house dress and threw it on. Big as it was, it still clung to her ass, moving with her every step. Even pregnant, she was desirable and she knew it. But inside she felt like nothing, that nobody truly cared and if it weren't for her phat ass and big breasts, she wouldn't get any attention at all. *Fuck the world*, she thought. "I will be all right," she said to herself.

Awhile later, she exited her '95 Honda Civic, getting ready to go in Walmart and rubbed her stomach. "If life don't get better, you'll leave here with me. I'll never leave you to deal with this cruel world. You hear me, Naquel? I'll never leave you here unprotected," Niecy said out loud as if somebody were with her. She continued to talk to herself as she pushed her cart through Walmart. She could feel the eyes on her from men, she caught the glances of couples who tried not to look, but even pregnant she was fine as shit. Not to mention her breasts had grown tremendously and were sitting up, and the full, one-piece dress did little to hide her stomach. Nothing could hide her ass and the movement under the skimpy material that rested and swayed with her every step.

She felt as if the aisles were closing in; she knew it was time to get what she came in for and be out. She grabbed a bag that contained a flat sheet, fitted sheet, and two pillow cases. "Eighty-nine dollars, shit must be good, eighty-nine dollars in Walmart, got to be good, oh yeah! Martha Stewart shit," she said out loud, tossing it in the basket.

"Can I help you make up yo' bed?" an unfamiliar voice said.

She turned to see a little-ass man standing about five foot two with a toothpick hanging out his mouth. He smiled, showing a shiny gold tooth on the left side.

"You don't see this?" Niecy said, rubbing her stomach.

"Naw, I see it and I don't care. I'll be that baby daddy," he said, holding his hands up, showing his oily blue pants and light blue shirt.

"How you gonna be my baby daddy, fuck you got nigga?" Niecy said, surprising the dude. Her pleasant demeanor had changed.

"I gots plenty, baby. I gets mine," the dude said, proudly patting his pocket.

"Nigga if you got more than me, I'll give you mine. Now run yo' shit, nigga, pull it out," she said loudly.

He stared at her and stuck his hand in his pocket, but hesitated.

"Just what I thought, fool. And you talk about changing my sheets, sexing me up," Niecy said, moving closer to the dude, pushing her basket. He looked at her cautiously. "Show me your dick," she said. He looked at her as if she'd lost her mind. "Show me your dick, mechanic. Now you acting like you scared," she said loudly when he turned his back and walked away. "Show me something, fool." She was breathing hard, leaning on the cart. People were staring as the dude hurried away. Her anger began to subside and she took deep breaths as she guided the basket down the aisle of comforters. "Why you snapping, girl? That shit came from nowhere, you need to calm down. Niggas was just talking. He wanted to fuck. He wanted to rape you. He wanted to fuck you and hurt you. He wanted to love you! He wanted to love you, hah hah hah hah hah hah hah." She heard the laughs and covered her ears and closed her eyes and then there was silence. She opened her eyes and things were regular.

"Thirty-nine dollars, probably ain't shit. Sixty-nine dollars, getting better, oh! That shit pretty as can be," she said, picking up a multicolored comforter that could be flipped over to a cream. "One hundred thirty-nine dollars and all they give you is two pillow covers and a sham. This will work," she said, throwing it in the basket.

"Damn, did you see that?"

"She bad as shit, damn."

Niecy heard the two men, then she saw them walk by three times just to admire, but didn't have the courage to say anything. Niecy was making her way to the register when she walked past the infant section. She felt a pain in her heart; she had ignored the fact that she was carrying a baby. She was still living life, doing what she wanted, except fucking on a regular basis. Before, she changed niggas like she changed drawers and she did that twice a day, but since her pregnancy, it had been twice a month. Until Show had shown up unannounced talking about "let's party," he hadn't seen her in over a year, but that's how they got down. When they saw each other, they fucked, it had been like that for more than five years and hadn't changed. And Twon was that young boy out the way who called every blue moon to see if he could come by. That had been going on for about two years and through her pregnancy. Before, he had to catch her, but these days she was wanting and waiting on that call.

"I need to snap out of this shit and get what the hell I came in here for," she said out loud.

"How much longer you got?" a voice said.

She said nothing, then turned to see who was talking.

"How far along are you?" the pleasant man said.

"Eight months," she said real short.

"You don't even look that. Like my mom and aunties say, you carrying yo' baby in yo' butt," he smiled, pointing. "Must be a girl or something like that."

"That last comment you could have kept to yourself," she said sarcastically.

"Have you ever heard that before?"

"Yeah," she said, bored.

"Why you acting like that? Like I'm foul, but to be for real, I saw you and thought you were . . . my bad, reminded me of . . ." He shook his head with a confused look. "But you take it easy and tell your girls that ain't seeded up right now to come out to Club Shadows. I got it on Thursdays and it's off the chain," he said, handing her a flyer.

"Why you let me run you off? Like you scared," she said seductively, ready to pull her prey in and attack.

He leaned toward her, close to the side of her face, so only she could hear. "I'm mad cool, but my attitude subject to change real fast. And you will get the hell slapped out 'cha, before I even think. You'll make a nigga go to jail for destroying a pregnant woman."

She stared into his bright eyes, long eyelashes, and dark skin. He wasn't that fine, but the six foot two frame, short cut, large build, and his straight forwardness made her feel that he was in power. She wasn't able to respond before he stared in her face with a puzzled look, shook his head, and walked away. At this point, she was confused. This nigga could smother her with a hug and it did something to her, but she swore she wouldn't add anyone else to her team until after she had her baby. Niecy got her items and headed out the door, and as the man punched her ticket and examined her bags, she saw the guy outside. When she walked to her car, she heard somebody say 'Naquel.' She tried to block it out, but she heard it again. She kept going, and when she reached her car, the gentleman was standing there. He looked into her eyes and with a sad and scared expression, he parted his lips and softly said, "Is your name Naquel?" She stared at him.

"I'm sorry, but you got me really fucked up right now. You look like this girl."

"What was her name?" she asked in a dazed state.

"Naquel."

"My name Naquala. I had a twin named Naquel," she said, trying not to get emotional, but that's what came whenever she mentioned her sister.

"Oh my God, I don't believe this," Poppa said. "It's been a long time, but never would I forget Naquel. Y'all were from Ingleside, right?"

"Yeah," she answered, wondering how much he knew about Naquel and her life.

"Let's go get something to eat and talk. I don't do too much driving, my els ain't right, so I'm with you."

"What's your name?" she asked.

"Poppa," he answered.

"Tell me some more before you go jumping in my car."

"I know your whole family from Ingleside: your brothers who's locked, your brother who think he a girl, your sister . . . She held me down, her letters of encouragement, before I knew what it was." He held his head down. "I never thought I would meet anybody to replace her, and I never did. But I met a young lady, we fell in love, had three boys, then she died giving birth to Taye, my youngest boy, three years ago."

"How old are you?" she asked.

"Thirty, and you are twenty-six, and both your birthday is September twenty-ninth and you have a younger sister, Janelle, and her birthday is September thirteenth. My memory is still good. Now can we roll?" he said, opening her car door.

"Flyin' Fishbone, I always wanted to try that."

"I'm with it. I'm rolling with you," Poppa answered. They rolled down the Boulevard in deep conversation and Niecy began to let her guard down a little. Talking to Poppa was like talking to a long-time friend, someone who really understood where she came from. After dinner she drove him back to his truck, he gave her his number, and told her to call him anytime, he was always available and didn't want to lose touch. After spending hours talking to Poppa, she felt alone again driving down the Boulevard heading home. As she turned into New Pointe, something hit her and she began to cry. She didn't know why but she couldn't stop. She parked the car and leaned back in the seat. "Maybe I shouldn't but Goddamn!" she yelled, pulling a small package from her purse. Dipping her fingernail inside the pack, she pulled a little out and brought it to her left nostril, then she hit the right and leaned back. She reached for her phone, and scrolled down to Poppa's number, and pressed send.

"Who this?" he answered.

"Naquala," she answered. It was what he'd been calling her all night and she kinda liked him calling her by her real name. He seemed different and laid back. He looked good, too, and the cologne he wore was still in her nose.

"So you want me over there with you?"

"Yes," she said, knowing she should have said no.

"All right, and relax yourself, I want you to know coming in the door, I don't want to fuck. I ain't pressed. That ain't what I need in my life, nor do I want that. I need you as my friend."

"Love you already, hurry up," she said, smiling. "816 Crows Nest Court, downstairs on the right. See ya! And hurry up."

Twenty mintues later she heard the knock at the door. She grabbed the pass and gave it to Poppa before he came in.

"They tow quick out here," he said, coming back in.

"Long as you know," she answered him, locking the door.

"Hold up, that's the kitchen and those are the bedrooms, mine over there, company over there. Get what you want 'cause I waits on no one," she said, sitting down and hitting the remote. Poppa sat down, kicked off his Tims, and relaxed. They talked until the wee hours and he fell asleep on her couch, with her on the love seat.

Janelle woke to the special tone of her phone. It was set to the date to remind her that Choice was getting out. They had talked like lovers for the last two weeks. Before, it had been all street shit, but they were back to the "I can't wait . . ." He showed no emotion except when they talked of their lives coming together. All the other things like niggas getting him, and Dundee threatening Janelle, and putting his hands on her never made him flip. He seemed to have found peace, as if he found a stronger force to help him deal with all negative things.

Janelle stood in front of the jail waiting for Choice. She wondered what was taking so long as she pranced around anxiously in her black PZI jeans and top, with her fresh new white, black, and gray Jordans. Her shirt hugged her breasts, but stopped at her waist barely; you still could catch a glimpse of her stomach, but her jeans showed her every curve, which made the solid 140 look inviting. The athletic look and cute face was what kept niggas coming at her, and she looked so cute in her clothes.

"Yeah, that's what I'm saying, ma! Looking like money," Choice said, walking toward Janelle. She blushed, ran over to her man, and jumped in his arms. He had put on fifteen to twenty pounds, and she was feeling him. She squeezed like she was never going to let go.

"Let's be out, get the fuck outta here," he said.

"Believe that shit," she said, walking back to her truck and smiling.

"Did you stop when I said stop or did you off the rest of that shit?"

"I off it. Twin and them called, my girl cross the water, everything gone, yo' money stacked. Fats and yo' other peoples, told them you was on hold."

"You should have said we stop like I told you. That's why you be getting in shit," he screamed on her. "The smallest thing can get us fucked up, you and me. Gotta listen to me, for real, ma."

"So, you don't appreciate what the fuck I did?" she asked with attitude.

"No, ma, I didn't say that. Whether I came home to money or my shit, I would have been all right. Coming home to you make me happy. So stop being fuckin' smart and listen," he said with attitude. "I don't need us both fucked up."

"Don't worry about me, I'm good. You weren't worried when you were on the come up. You won't worried when you had me and Reece running to Brooklyn bringing your shit back. That's when your ass should have been worried. Huh! Who was your down-ass bitch when you just had to make that sale to Dre and Dex? And your life, niggah, your life was in those niggas hands; who saved ya? Who dropped those bodies? Two to the head, just like you showed me," she said, looking at him. He opened the door and waited for the garage to open. He was tired of hearing her mouth. Things weren't like this when he left and this wasn't no shit he was coming home to. She got out and closed the garage.

"Nigga, I got my shit covered," she said, opening the door to their four-bedroom condo in Witchduck Lakes.

"What the fuck did you fuck up in the last few months? Shoot-outs and nobody dead, trouble, ready to shoot Jeezy, trouble, and over your trifling-ass sister?" he said. She came charging at him and he grabbed her arms. "Fuck is wrong with you?"

"Don't say shit about my sister. Don't you ever call her that again," she said, gritting her teeth.

"After what you did, letting your niggas get her fucked and doing God-knows-what.

"I ain't do shit, get it right. She's a grown-ass woman with her own mind and capable of making her own decisions," he said.

"If she fucked up, motherfucker, you let it happen, you knew what those niggas was about."

"Blaming people for yo' shit and y'all fucked-up ways, straight hood bitches," he said, snatching off his shirt and kicking off his boots. When he unbuckled his belt to take off his pants, she rushed him as his pants hit his ankles. They fell over and her punches started coming. He grabbed her and pinned her down on her stomach, and as she struggled to get up, her ass grinded against his dick and he instantly got hard. He turned her over and slapped her. "Calm your ass down, before I break your damn jaw," he said, opening her jeans and snatching them off along with her panties. He looked down at her neatly shaven womanhood, and leaned forward, spreading her legs, guiding himself into her. She was snug; he was forceful and didn't give a fuck. She grunted as he pushed deeper into her. He held it in and grinded a minute on her clit, enjoying the feeling of his woman. He allowed her juices to flow as he began to move in and out, and in minutes they could hear the squishing sounds of him going in and out. She dug her nails into his back as he began to pound in and out of her. She felt his body tense and he grunted as he let out a long-waiting nut. He got up and kicked off his pants, then picked Janelle up off the floor and took her to their first floor master bedroom.

He laid her on the bed, and before she knew it he was inside of her again, banging hard for minutes until he exploded and collapsed. He rolled over and put his arms around her as she snuggled her ass up against him. He kissed her cheeks as he squeezed her.

"I'm gonna end up killing you, man," she said.

"As long as I die first, because I can't live without my better half. If something was to happen to you, whoa!" he said, and squeezed her.

"I feel you, baby. I feel you," she said, turning toward him and kissing his lips.

"So what's up for today?" she asked.

"This right here. We gonna chill out like this, and in a little bit, get up and order some Chinese rice and chicken wings, then regroup, then fuck the night away."

"That's what it is," she said, agreeing.

"Tomorrow, New York. Brooklyn, baby," he said, closing his eyes.

"For how long?" she asked, not surprised.

"Until I call you and let you know that you and Reece need to get on that Chinese bus."

"When we start that again?"

"We just did. Couple times, then I got my peoples, but we got running around to do when you come up, you'll be up there for a couple days before you come back. Relax, don't I always make shit fall in place? Even in my absence, I take care of you, true?" he said.

"True," she said, cuddled under him, and closed her eyes.

Poppa sat watching one of his favorite shows, *Law and Order: Criminal Intent*. It was toward the end when Niecy started talking. "Hold up, give me a sec," Poppa said, holding up his finger. Niecy stared at her new friend patiently. She was due any day now and she was hot as hell. Poppa had spent some part of his day with her al-most every day since they'd met more than two months ago. She thought he was gonna fall prey to her phat ass and large breasts, but he never made that attempt. He had issues he was dealing with. He had lost his kid's mother to childbirth, then had fought against the grand-parents in a two-year custody battle because they said he was a ruthless and dangerous person who sold drugs. After it was over, he was down $60,000 but he walked out a proud single parent and took his kids home. One year later he was doing a five-year bid. The kids went to live with the grandparents. They talked shit about him until the first of the month came and he had somebody drop off $1,500 to the grandparents. That $1,500 was there every month for sixty months. When he came home, he got his kids back. And he been trying to make up, but he still wasn't over the death of his babies' momma.

"God damn! That shit was good," he said before turn-ing the bottle of Remy Martin up to his head. "Damn, that's good, too!" he said, setting down the bottle and laughing.

This pussy good, too, nigga if you want some, Niecy thought, and began laughing at her inside joke.

"Fuck did you want disturbing me and my show?"

"I want some ice cream and something sweet," she said, knowing his response.

"Fuck that, you should have called me before I came over. I ain't going nowhere," he said, seriously turning his attention back to the TV.

"What do you want from me? Why do you do what you do?" she asked, referring to the other room she'd turned into a baby room with Poppa's help. Poppa had made her go the doctor, because she hadn't been, and made her promise to stop fucking with drugs and alcohol, at least until she had the baby. He bought everything from the crib to the car seat. Janelle had come by and wondered who he was, and was happy her sister had found somebody who cared and wasn't just trying to fuck her.

"I feel like I been knowing you forever. I come over and you don't expect shit of me. You don't worry me, I just feel relaxed. I don't want it to change."

"But you treat me like your cousin or something."

"Because we close like that. And I also feel that me and Naquel had something. Something I really enjoyed. I could express myself and tell her anything. She would do the same and our bond became strong like family."

"That was then, when you were younger and had young ideas and a young mind, but now you a grown-ass man, with new grown-up things on your mind. So the talks are different and feelings, too."

"You right, but we still wear scars of yesterday. You feel me? Sometimes those scars are hard to rebound from, it make you who you are," he said, turning the Remy up again, and staring straight ahead at the the TV, but not seeing it.

"I realize you got many scars and you've shared quite a few with me, but what haven't you shared? You still into girls, right? Ain't nothing got you that fucked up, do it? Or is it because I'm pregnant? You looking at me like I'm a fucked-up person," she said, holding her head down.

"First of all, I still love y'all bitches. Things can't get that bad. Second, pregnant pussy is the best pussy, but I try not to look at you that way. I'm gonna be straight. My life was hell when I lived out Ingleside. I mean fucked up. I stayed to myself and was a quiet nigga, keeping my tears inside. One day I saw your sister. I had always known her to be quiet and only fuck with you and your brother, the gay boy. I'm coming home from the store and she walk past me, crying. I keep walking, then something hit me. I turned around and ran up on her.

"I asked her was there anything I can do. She said 'kill my moms.' That blew my mind, because I wished the same thing. We walked back to the store, and I brought her a soda and a honeybun." He paused, smiling.

"Hostess, with the thick icing," Niecy added as her eyes began to water.

"We talked for hours and every day after that we talked and kept each other minds sane. We never overstepped the line because we needed each other as friends. It wasn't until I got locked up that I realized I wanted to see her and hold her. Especially after we started writing each other and I found out so much more was going on that she couldn't look me in my face and tell me. It fucked me up that I couldn't protect her," he said with a very disturbed look on his face.

"I thought she was keeping a diary, writing her problems away," Niecy said.

"Naw, I was her diary, her release. I read your life, her life, yo' brother life and Janelle life every day." She looked at him, confused. "Naquala, I know about your older brother coming home from jail and raping her and your brother. That's why he got that forty years. I remember she said your mom used to come and finger y'all stuff to see if you been fucking and if y'all stink. If she smelled something, she would beat the shit out of y'all. I was fucked up when she wrote me and told me about your moms making y'all hold her down, and she burned her with the iron because she had on a wrinkled shirt."

"That shit was fucked up," Niecy said with a straight face and squinched lips. Anytime that crossed her mind, she realized how much she hated her mom.

"I remember when they took y'all from her and put

y'all in foster care for a month, until Brenda said y'all could live with her. She wrote me while sitting in Norfolk General waiting on you. That was the last straw, when she jumped on you and beat you like you were a woman in the street."

"She beat the shit out of me. I was twelve and she walked in like, 'Bitch, you think you grown,' and started swinging, I couldn't do shit, but scream, and then all of a sudden shit went dark. I woke up and found out she had grabbed a hammer and bust me in my head three times. Would have killed me if my brother didn't come in. All the man across the street said was, 'You better watch Naquala.' She went off," she cried, shaking her head, still confused more than ten years later. "Know what, Poppa? What hurt even worse was to find out my brother saved my life and got sent to a boys' home til he was eighteen."

"No, your brother got sent away because your mom and your older brother fucked him up. Your mom beating him senseless and your brother fucking him and making him suck dick and dress up like a girl. And your mother knew about it."

"She was scared of my oldest brother," she said quietly.

"But your brother snapped. He fucked your moms up. Damn!"

"He beat that bitch with everything she ever beat us with, then he sodomized her, just like he had been done. Then hit her in the back of the head with that same hammer three times like she did me. Bitch deserved it," Niecy said, going into a deep stare.

"Naquel wrote me when y'all moved out Lake Edward. Then when she moved with y'all other sister. I got, like, five disturbing letters and that was the last time I heard from her. I didn't find out for days that the nigga killed her," he said angrily.

She looked at him, surprised. "Everybody thought it was suicide, but I always knew, Poppa, I always knew. That's why I was glad when they found that nigga fucked up and tortured, body tossed out Ingleside."

"Beaten, cut up, burnt up to his motherfuckin' head, then they tossed his ass in the back of the projects."

She looked at Poppa wide-eyed and surprised.

"He'll never do that shit again. When I came home, I became the judge and jury. And, motherfucker, I find you guilty," he said, standing up and sipping his Remy. "See, Naquala, we both fucked up and scarred for life. We need to find sane people, you and me would be headed for disaster before it began. You're beautiful and sexy, even while you pregnant, but I've learned to look past the physical and see the real side of things. So after I get my nut, what do I want with a woman. I got to feel a bitch now, connect on some other shit."

"I can respect that, and I feel you. But I want you to feel me," she said. She could no longer control her urge. She looked at him as that strong man she needed all her life. She walked into the room, lay across the bed, and began to cry softly. She was fucked up inside, but she could deal with real love; where and when was it gonna come her way? As she drifted out, she felt her body find a place to relax. Her entire body leaned back and found support as she felt herself being comforted into the arms of love. She fell into a deep, deep sleep.

"Oooh! Oooh!" Poppa said, exhaling as his head leaned back. *That dream felt so real,* he thought as he woke from his sleep. The Remy was still having an effect as he tried to focus on the figure giving him head; the darkness was preventing the picture from coming clear. All of a sudden, it stopped. The figure stood on the side of the bed and removed her clothes. Niecy's silhouette instantly made his dick harder. The full big breasts, and that big ass that jingled with her every move. She climbed on the bed with her back to Poppa and eased back until her warm, soft ass smothered his rock hard dick. The warmness of her body made him wrap his arms around her and squeeze. Niecy lifted her leg and reached back, guiding Poppa into her hot, wet, snug vagina. Poppa never let her go as he moved in and out of her slowly. He eased his hands to her breasts and massaged them, while holding her nipples firmly between his fingers. With her mouth held open, all she could do was gasp for air while sticking her ass out. He sped up as he massaged her ass, then gripped it as he bounced off it. His body began to tingle, then a feeling of ecstasy rose in his groin and slowly flowed through his entire body for about five seconds before his body began to jolt. She waited for him to get up, but he never moved. Not a word was spoken for minutes, then he began to move in and out of her again, grinding until he was hard again. She just stuck her ass out and let Poppa enjoy the love she was able to give. Before he knew it, his body was shaking again.

"Damn, I can't last in this ass. This shit is ridiculous," Poppa said, rubbing her butt. She waited for him to get up since he was finished, but he pulled her to him, stretched out his left arm so she could relax comfortably against him. Then he reached around her and placed his hand on her belly, kissing the back of her neck. "Damn, you got some good pussy and sexy as shit," he said. "You're a wonderful woman and I enjoy all the time we spend," he said, smiling. She smiled and fell into his frame, and went back to sleep feeling wanted, happy, and not used.

* * *

The following day, Choice and Janelle were out rolling around town trying to figure out the game plan.

"What's the deal, ma?" Choice asked as he drove down Virginia Beach Boulevard in his Escalade, pumping Plies's new shit.

"Whatever, long as I'm rolling with you. You said we was chilling all day," Janelle said with attitude.

"I just said what up? And you flippin' already. I don't want you to go nowhere, right here beside me. Right here," he said, smiling and reaching over to his hand on her leg. He stared at his girl and took in all her cuteness in just a glance. Her tight black jeans, her snug short white T-shirt, and the new black-and-white Jordans. *I love that look*, he thought.

"So what up? Thought you said you needed a cut."

"You right. I hope this nigga up here don't got a lot of people. I got to go," he said.

"I heard that, Mr. C-Rich ain't got no pull, he gots to wait," Janelle joked. "Wait 'til I tell Shakar Akbar Allah Mohammed God," she added, laughing. He started laughing too. He knew she was talking about his brother, who had changed his name from Anthony to Askia (Ahmad).

"You know Sherman don't give a fuck, every customer the same." They continued talking and joking, enjoying the warm feeling they gave each other, but their attitudes changed as they pulled up and saw Jah, Nitty, and Los standing up front, with two more cats. "Hold tight, let me see who Sherman got," Choice said, opening the door, and letting his new Jordans hit the concrete. He adjusted his new white T-shirt to conceal the chrome 9 mm with the wood-grain handle, but exposing his new Blackberry. He walked up and gave Pop a pound, then Big Herb, then Los. "What up, son?" Choice asked Los. He never acknowleged anybody else. Niggas stood around, cautiously wondering when he had gotten out. They knew of the beef his girl had with niggas, so anything was subject to jump off.

"Making it do what it do, C. When you get home?" Los said, hoping his friend would move on. He had a funny feeling.

"Couple days, my dude. I had to get a few things straight before I stepped back on these Norfolk streets, know what I mean?"

"No doubt, partner." Los said, not knowing what Janelle had told Choice, which kind of had him feeling uneasy.

"I'ma hollah in a few," Choice said, easing off.

As Choice walked into the barbershop, he heard Nitty say to Janelle that she could get out, she ain't gotta be scared. Choice quickly turned around. "Fuck she got to be scared of?" Choice asked, looking at Nitty and Jah.

"She know the deal," Nitty said.

"As long as I'm here, she ain't never scared, believe that shit."

"Yo," Jah, said getting Choice's full attention. Everybody stood, staring in silence. "Fuck your girl," Jah said, pointing at Janelle. "And fuck you, too, partner."

"Naw, son! Fuck with me. If you think you built like that," Choice said, stepping closer, ready for whatever. Or so he thought, until he was caught with a two piece from Jah. But Choice rolled with the left punch that landed on his right jaw, and the right was too weak to be recognized. Jah was totally caught off guard when Choice came back, throwing a fury of punches that landed to the face leaving Jah dazed. But the surprise punch to his left jaw from Nitty almost dropped him. He felt his knees buckle, and that was just enough time for Jah to get his composure and throw a body-crushing punch to Choice's chest, causing the air to shoot from his body. He tumbled backward with Jah and Nitty still coming at him. But when most would have tried to catch their fall, Choice fell back and concentrated on wrapping his hand around the wood-grain handle of the 9 mm. When he hit the ground, the shiny chrome caught the two men off guard, but it was too late as Choice let it go. The shots made niggas scatter like roaches. One shot hit Jah in the stomach, the other in the chest. Nitty had stopped in his tracks and made a dash to get in the barbershop door, but one of the stylists had locked it when she heard the commotion. Two more shots rang out, one catching Nitty in his thigh and the other going through the barbershop door. Choice heard the sirens coming fast; he was in Virginia Beach and had forgotten how fast their reaction time was. He hit the side of the building in full stride. Janelle slid into the driver's seat and slowly pulled away. Her heart was beating fast. She was so confused she went the opposite way of Choice. As she turned the corner on the side of a 7-Eleven, Choice came running from behind the building.

He jumped in. "Hit the interstate," he said. "Quickly, but cautiously. I didn't get in the truck because I didn't want to involve you, especially on no highway chase. I ain't never getting locked up down here again."

"How did you know to come up behind the building? Anyone else would have run into the neighborhood," she said.

"Instinct, ma, maybe I knew you'd be there," he said, smiling.

"I was there, baby." She looked over at her man as they flew down Wesleyan Drive. She was doing seventy in a thirty-five.

"Slow down," he said. "Slow down."

"My bad. I'm over here scared as shit. Mind racing, heart racing. Whoa!"

"Go right," he said as she made her way onto 264, headed toward Richmond.

"Where are we going?" she asked.

"New York, baby. I'm going home."

Janelle kept driving with all kinds of thoughts roaming through her head. *Damn,* she thought, *my life just did a 180 in seconds.* What about her place, her clothes, her sister, and her baby? Damn! Would Niecy be all right? She convinced herself that Choice had her best interest at heart, at least she hoped so. Choice hadn't said a word in the last three hours.

"What way I go," she asked as they came up on Washington, DC.

"Stay on 95, follow Baltimore signs."

"Relax your mind, baby. I'm trying to and you shocked the shit out of me. That shit happened so fast."

"Can't relax 'til I get to New York," he said shortly.

She reached out toward him and held out her hand; he looked over into her face. She could see the confusion in his eyes. She wanted to get somewhere, wrap her arms around him, and tell him everything was going to be okay, but she knew this nigga had just caught two bodies and she could only imagine what he was feeling.

"That big motherfucker was soft. That nigga was straight weak. I was gonna fuck him up. Then go to his boy ass. Weak-ass country niggas. Took two of them to handle a little nigga," he said, frustrated.

"I saw that shit. When Nitty got in it, I was jumping out the truck to help you. By the time I got out," she said, hunching her shoulders, "You, you, you . . ." she said, holding her palm up as if to say, "You know what stopped me."

"I was gonna shoot a fair one. Me and him," he said as she paid the toll.

"Choice, you had no choice. You know they would of

stomped yo' ass out and probably fucked me up, too. You would have been laid out in Bayside Hospital, fucked up. That would have had me feeling worse than I do now. Is that shit fucking with you? If it is, don't let it, that shit was self-defense, they both had you by one hundred pounds."

"Baby, I'm worried about getting caught, fuck them niggas. It is what it is," he said calmly. He reached over and turned up the radio, leaned back, and let the best of Jadakiss take him down the New Jersey Turnpike. He began to relax. Jadakiss had taken him away, and by the looks of Janelle, she had relaxed a little more. Actually, thoughts of Niecy, Lowe, Danyelle, and Reece penetrated her thoughts. Things were good just a few months ago. Now they were all distant, all over their men.

"Take exit thirteen towards the Verrazono and keep straight 'til you see the BQE."

"BQE? What's that?" she asked, confused

"Brooklyn Queens Expressway, you'll see it. When you do, wake me up," he said, and within minutes he was out. When Janelle whipped the Escalade right on to the BQE, she woke Choice up and he guided her into Brooklyn, where Fort Greene projects became home.

It had been a couple of weeks since their first sexual encounter. And it had happened three more times. Niecy stared into what would soon be her baby's room. The crib, the dresser, the changing table, pampers, and all the accessories any newborn would need were there. Poppa had made sure that she had everything she could possibly need. He was treating her the same, and she was there to listen, console, and not judge. And that was what he fell for. Even though things were okay, she still got depressed, and worried about her baby being late; they were going to induce labor in two days and she hadn't heard from Janelle. Her phone and Choice's phone were off and that had her in a frenzy. She went and picked up her phone to dial Danyelle.

"What up, girl, is it time?"

"Hell, naw. Just called you."

"No, you didn't. You wanna know if I heard from yo' sister," Danyelle said. "Hell, no, but that bitch know better. She know she suppose to find some way to hollah and let us know what's going on. He could have killed her, we don't know shit," she added.

"I know. I need her Danyelle, I need my sister," Niecy said, crying.

"She know, she'll be back in time. Just chill. Let me check a few things and I'll call you back," Danyelle said. She hated to hear anybody crying.

"What the deal?" Lowe said, answering the phone.

"You know what it is, Niecy just called me."

"She in labor yet?" Lowe asked, excited.

"Hell, naw, she upset and want her sister. She crying and shit and I don't know what to say."

"Tell her shut the hell up. Janelle just being selfish and thinking about Janelle. She up in Choice ass because she want to be; she ain't shoot nobody, she ain't gotta run. She on some bullshit. She know where she need to be. Selfish bitch. Tell Niecy we here, fuck Janelle. And I'ma tell her about herself when I see her instead of ignoring her ass."

"If we see her. She might be dead. Girl, you know them New York niggas crazy," Danyelle said.

"Don't say that shit. She all right. Speaking of crazy, it just pulled up. Later," she said, hanging up the phone.

"Who was you talking to?" Dundee asked.

"Danyelle."

"What you know?" he asked firmly.

"Nothing."

"If you knew, would you tell me?"

"No, I keep telling you, your business is yo' business. I don't get involved; my girl shit is our' shit. Girl shit that we been fucking wit' for years don't got shit to do with y'all niggas. And being that she ain't hustling, she ain't got shit to do with you. Now get the fuck out my face." She was tired of his controlling acts and his questions. She braced herself as he punched her in the back of the head and lifted her off her feet by her neck. She fought until her body went limp, then he tossed her ass on the floor.

"I usually beat yo' ass, but now I'm on some new shit: choking bitches out. That's my new shit, choking hoes out," he said, heading upstairs and leaving her on the floor. "I'm taking care of yo' dumb ass, and you telling me you ain't gonna tell me about the nigga who fucked up my money. You must be out yo' mind." Dundee stripped down and jumped in the shower. When he returned downstairs, he saw Lowe sitting on the couch, crying.

"I can't take this no more. You gonna fuck around and kill me. And I ain't did shit to you. I'm here for you to love and cherish, not fuck, beat on, and treat like shit. Where did all this shit come from? You act like I did something wrong."

"You be on that bullshit, like you can do what the fuck you want and it don't mean shit. Yeah, you nice and shit, but no bitch run me or own me. You need to recognize who the fuck I am."

"Nigga, I'm grown, with kids of my own. You don't run me, I ain't yo' child."

"Then don't act like you are. Stop sitting around this bitch waiting for me to take care of yo' ass and do something for yourself," he said, looking in her face.

"I was fine before you and I'll be fine after you," she said staring back at him.

"You was fine at yo' momma house, with no car, no job, just getting assistance and fuckin' niggas for dough? Bitch, please, if you don't like how I do shit, leave with what you came with."

"This my shit, in my name," she said.

"But my money got it, don't get it twisted. Just leave if you ain't happy, anything more and they might find you floating in the lake out the way." Those were the last words she heard before hearing the door shut. She wanted so much to show him she didn't need him, but she did. Leaving just wasn't an option. He provided everything for her. She wasn't about to give it up and go back home and sleep in one room with both her kids, go back to scrambling for rides and giving herself to niggas so they would give up dough to find out most niggas already had a girl and they had no dough to provide. She sat there, beating herself up, until the ringing of the phone disturbed her.

"It's time, Lowe," Nicey yelled. "They said they were going to induce in two days but I think its happening. I don't know what to do."

"You gonna have your baby, girl. It's time; they had you fucked up. You packed?" Lowe asked, grabbing her bag and keys.

"Yeah!"

"Breathe and relax, I'm there in five minutes," she said, jumping into the car and taking off. When she arrived, the door was unlocked. Niecy was on the phone with Poppa. He was across the water in Hampton trying to make his way back to Norfolk.

"Lowe here. I'm on my way, please hurry," she said before hanging up. Lowe helped Niecy into the 1999 Grand

Cherokee that Dundee had copped for her, and headed to Leigh Memorial Hospital.

After six hours had passed, Lowe, Danyelle and Reece sat in the delivery room with Niecy as she waited to dilate. Between her contractions she cried, not from the pain of giving birth, but because she was alone. She didn't fuck with her other family. She didn't have a number for her brother, and Janelle and Poppa were nowhere to be found. Her mind was everywhere, she was hurting inside, she was sad, she cried real tears. She was truly fucked up as her baby made its way into this world.

"Love you, baby. I'll hit you later."

"Love you too. Be careful, Janelle. And lay low. Don't be on that ra-ra shit, ma," Choice said, hugging her as he leaned against the platinum CLK 500 drop.

"Naw, niggah, you lay low. You been going hard, Choice. First it was here to Richmond and Hampton, now you fuckin' with Baltimore and DC. Don't get me wrong, son," she said, smiling, "you and your team nice with y'all shit, but I"ve seen the best, the tightest cliques fall. I can't lose you, Choice."

Choice smiled as he stared into her eyes, and she softened at his good looks. He had just gotten a cut by the Dominicans up on Broadway. His shit was razor sharp, along with his brown skin, straight white teeth, mustache so neatly trimmed. Her eyes fell, then her head. She shook her head noticing the Red Polo falling on the dark denim shorts, all complemented by the fresh white Uptowns. The iced out Breitling sparked her attention, as he lifted her head in his hands.

"Janelle, I'm good, you know I'm always safe, baby. Don't worry about me. You stay out of shit and low. Now get outta here and check on your sister."

"Yeah, push me off," she said, getting on the Chinese bus leaving Manhattan. Choice watched her board the bus headed to Norfolk. It was a good way to ease back into town. He hopped into his Benz and hit Canal headed toward the Manhattan Bridge, when his phone rang.

"I can tell if another bitch been sitting in my seat. Don't get it twisted nigga, I know how niggas live when they getting paper. Don't fuckin' hurt me, Choice," Janelle said in a whining voice.

"Never that, ma. Never that."

"Be good! 'Bye."

" 'Bye," he said as he hit the BQE headed to Queens to catch up with his cousin, Jus. Jus's family had moved from Thompkins Projects when he was twelve. They had just gotten into the art of robbing niggas, when they up and moved to South Jamaica. Now, along with the robbery game, Jus had a serious murder game. "Yo, Jus, what the deal, my dude?" Choice said when his cousin answered the phone.

"You know what it is, son. Niggas trying to earth me, son. You know! I'm just trying to get paid."

"I'm on the Van Wyck now. Where you at? I need to hollah. On some real money shit. But it's down South, my dude," Choice said.

"Where, son? Don't say Virginia, son, I ain't fucking with VA. Niggas done told me, son," Jus said, meaning every word.

"Where you at, Jus?"

"I'm on the Avenue, son. But I got these hoes on the track now, son. We ain't talk in like a year, son. I got, like, four hoes, son."

Choice started laughing. "Damn, nigga, you doing it. I'll check you out in a second. One." The phones went dead. Choice met Jus in the mall section of 165th Street just off Jamaica Avenue. He had parked and come through the Coliseum. When Jus saw Choice, they greeted each other with open arms, then walked to grab a beef pattie. Choice ran down the last two years of his life to Jus in five minutes. He informed him of the bodies he'd caught, how he'd come up and needed his blood, the only nigga in the world who ran, thought, and moved like him, but had that murder game that only Southside niggas were known for. He was still all Brooklyn; wylin' out, beat yo' ass, fuck you and everybody out this bitch–type nigga. Not murdering cats, but he needed somebody outside of his team, who he could depend on to be there.

"I need you with me Thursday in Richmond," Choice said.

"Two days? Naw, son. Too quick. I got kids and business. If I'm rolling and you established like that. Ten thousand dollars for each body!"

"Done."

"Five thousand dollars a week straight."

"Three and you gonna put in some work."

"Done, I'm still a hustler, baby." Jus smiled.

"Thursday still too soon, cuz?"

"Ain't no cuz here, Blood!"

"My bad, cousin, real cousin," Choice joked.

They reached Choice's car, and Jus acted like he choked on his food. "Oh, shit, son got the 500 drop, new shit for the summer. Naw, son, I need five thousand."

"Fuck you, deal is done," Choice said. He reached into the car and opened the glove box, pulling out three grand to hand to Jus.

"That's what it is, son," Jus said, giving his cousin a pound.

"Thursday at ten, my dude. Need you, Jus." Choice said, staring seriously at his cousin.

"Got me, fam, you got me," Jus said, walking off and

gripping the three grand. *That's how you talk to a nigga*, Jus thought. It was come up time.

Janelle arrived at the bus stop on Newtown Road. She caught a Beach Taxi to her condo off Witchduck, got her keys, jumped in her truck, and was out. It was 1:30, and her nephew or niece had been born thirteen hours ago. She walked into Leigh Memorial and straight to the maternity ward. When she walked in, Danyelle was sitting on the couch reading the classic street novel, *My Time To Shine*. When their eyes met, they hugged the breath out of each other, then turned their attention to Niecy, who was sound asleep. Janelle walked over to her sister and grabbed her hand. Niecy opened her eyes and cleared her vision, only to let it be blurred again by instant tears. She opened her arms and Janelle fell into them, and they both cried like babies. In each other's arms they felt a sense of real unconditional love and security.

"Where's the new Brickhouse?" Janelle asked, going to the other side of the bed where the baby lay. The first thing she did was check the wristband for the last name. She smiled. "There's my little Brickhouse," she said in a baby-talk. Niecy watched as Janelle and Danyelle held the baby and talked.

"You can have it," Niecy yelled. "I don't want it, get it away from me. Aaah! Aaah! Where the fuck you come from?" Niecy said in a lower voice. "What is that? Huh!" she yelled.

Janelle and Danyelle moved closer to the door with the baby. They were escorted out of the room as members of the medical staff rushed in. A nurse took the baby to the nursery as the girls sat quietly in the waiting room.

"Where Poppa?" Janelle asked.

"I don't know. He didn't seem like a bullshit nigga, but I guess he is. Sorry motherfucker," Danyelle fussed.

"Naw, something happened, dude was real. Seemed like he was past the games."

"Right! You keep saying it, you might believe yourself."

"Fuck him. That nigga got his own kids. He probably want Niecy to momma them."

"Niecy can't momma nobody, not herself, not even the one she just had," Janelle said sadly.

"Nor the other one, don't act like I don't know. You gonna have to be here, Janelle."

"I got a life, D, and I ain't got no babies, and fuck what you heard." The doctor came out to speak with Janelle. She was told that Niecy was diabetic and her sugar had dropped real low, which caused her to lose her memory and act out. They had gotten it back up and she seemed to be doing better, but was resting. They needed to come back tomorrow.

They were going to the car when Lowe and Reece pulled up; Danyelle had called them during all the commotion. They stood in front of Leigh Memorial for an hour talking about good times, and forgetting the bad for just a minute. A while later, they all went their separate ways, promising to get together soon for a night out. Janelle walked Reece to her car. "What's this, girl?" Janelle asked, referring to Reece's new white Camry.

"Time to come up, girl, and handle my shit," Reece said. "I been running around partying, clubbing, fucking with mad niggas just having fun, and I'm tired, Janelle. Tired of being used and feeling fucked up, and these niggas don't give a fuck about nothing but a nut. I want my own like you, like Danyelle, but her nigga is ideal. Get money and cater to her. Never leaving her alone." Reece sighed as if she were reading a heartfelt card.

"Girl, what nigga done gas your ass up?"

"This me, I don't need a nigga to want more," Reece said.

"Reece, please."

"I been talking to Mansio," Reece said.

"Mansio, Mansio . . ." Janelle tried to place the name.

"161st and St. Nick."

"That real dark-skinned dude with the thin line beard, driving the Bentley coupe?"

"Yeah, that's how I got word to you that your sister was in labor. I told him, 'I don't know your business, but if you know Choice and can reach him, tell him his sister-in-law is in labor.' He said 'I don't know any Choice,' but you got the message."

"Choice never said who told him. He just said I heard your sister in labor. I heard that."

"So he brought you a car?" Janelle asked in a leading tone.

"Brought me a car, came here for a week and got me a rental with the option on a townhouse with a garage out Chesapeake. I moved in a week later, he came back down and paid everything to get in and laid it out. He stayed another week and raised the bar for all niggas. I will never in my life accept anything less."

"Them New York niggas are serious, they about money and take life seriously. These niggas in Norfolk wanna play 'til they forty and don't commit to shit."

They laughed. "Shit, I can't say shit. That day we spent with all them, they were all respectful, nice, and you could tell they had money. Choice was comfortable and relaxed so things must have been good."

"He's mad cool and this nigga got my closet tight. I went to MacArthur Mall and killed BCBG, BeBe, Coach, Macy's, and Nordstrom shoes. He catered to me and I catered to him every night he was here."

"You better, nigga giving you all that attention," Janelle

said. She never thought of Reece being on her level, but Mansio seemed like he was gonna upgrade her. Janelle felt a little intimidated but she smiled it off, said her good-byes, and made it home.

Three months passed pretty quickly and Niecy was in full swing. She had tortured herself for two months. She hadn't lost a bit of the weight from her pregnancy. She set up in her living room, nodding off from the heroin she sniffed and the drink in her hand. The system blasted Mary J.'s "Life" into her ears as her baby lay in the crib hollering. "I bet he don't call me," she said to herself. "He already called me," she said, again to herself.

"Who called you already?" the dude she'd invited home said.

"What, you still here? What did you do to me?" Niecy stood up. Her skirt was wrapped around her waist, and she didn't have panties on. Her bra was twisted and her breasts were hanging out. "Did you fuck me?" she asked, reaching between her legs, feeling wet with cum.

"Girl, you was with it all night, don't get crazy now, you invited me here," the dude said.

"You raped me, oh! My God, you raped me," she yelled reaching for the phone.

"I'm out, shorty. You left your car at Mystique, you were kinda nice and I drove you here. We came in, you got to snorting and we freaked and fucked and I fell in love. Now you don't remember." Niecy stood, staring at him. She couldn't remember anything since 11:00 last night when she left to catch a club. Now here it was, four in the morning, she was staring at a nigga she didn't know, and he'd had her any way he could think of.

"Please get your shit and leave," she said, shaken at the thought of him not using a condom. Did she catch something? Or worse, she could have gotten pregnant.

"Naquel, I'll hollah," the dude said, headed out the door.

Naquel? she thought. *Why would he say that?* She locked the door then ran to the shower. When she returned, she heard her baby. After a clean diaper and a bottle, she was back in the crib and Niecy was back on the couch, balled up in her robe. She reached over and lit a Newport.

"Who am I? Where the fuck am I going? What's going to happen to me? Lord, I'm talking to you. God, I'm talking to you. I don't like myself, I don't like me," she cried. "I don't want to be here no more," she said softly. "God, please take care of me, I don't want to hurt Naquela," Niecy said in a different but familiar voice.

She got up and turned off everything, lay back down on the couch, balled up and stared off into a daze. She wasn't crying, but tears ran from her eyes. Inside she felt disgusting, sickening, and worthless. Getting high eased her pain, just like when she got the call that Poppa was locked up. He got locked up speeding from Hampton to get to her. Driving on a suspended license and reckless driving got him a violation of his parole. They gave Poppa six months and he was gone in a moment. Then the day she got the papers saying Jeezy was not the father, she almost overdosed trying to deaden the pain. Not knowing who her baby's daddy was ate at her soul and sickened her insides. She knew a woman couldn't get any lower than that. And she had to tell Poppa when he came home. She closed her eyes and began to pray, "Now I lay me down to sleep, ahh, ahh . . . I pray to You my soul to keep. If I should die before I wake . . . God, that would truly be okay."

It was Saturday evening and Janelle had decided to have a dinner party that would lead them to the club.

Things had gotten back to normal since she found out that nobody talked about who shot Nitty and who killed Jah. It was just that nobody knew where Dundee stood at this point. Nobody knew what he was gonna do, but he allowed Lowe to do her thing.

"So what are we celebrating?" Lowe asked.

"Being here, alive and happy," Reece said, dancing to Lyfe's CD. She was winding to the joint with Wyclef.

"Sit your ass down, Reece," Danyelle said, getting her champagne glass.

"What the hell is that gold shit?" Lowe asked.

"This is Armand de Brignac, $300 a bottle," she said, popping the gold bottle with an ace of spades embedded on the side.

"This shit good. Taste elegant," Janelle said, smiling.

"Shit all right," Danyelle said, setting down her glass to get some fresh fruit that Janelle had prepared at Farm Fresh.

"You need to get $250 back. Go back to Farm Fresh and get a bottle of Moët for fifty dollars. Buy some weed and pocket the rest," Lowe said seriously. Everybody laughed except Janelle.

"Take that $250 and buy some boots." The other girls agreed.

"Y'all bitches ungrateful. Guess what. I brought $300 champagne and still got money to buy $300 shoes, boots, or whatever tomorrow," Janelle said, defending herself.

"You ain't got to go there, Janelle, this ain't about dough."

"Fuck that, y'all talking shit," Janelle added. The daiquiris they'd had while sitting around talking before they popped the champagne had them feeling nice.

"I know you ain't talking to me, because I shit on yo' money. My man got shit locked from Virginia Beach to the Miami bitch." Danyelle said, going to her Coach bag. She pulled out $3,000 in hundreds and fifties, and laid it on the table. "Play money," she added.

"Excuse me," Janelle said, reaching into her back pocket and pulling out a stack of hundreds that equaled about five grand. "Newport News, Richmond, DC, Baltimore, and Brooklyn. My nigga stay getting, ma!" Janelle smiled.

"And my man run New York. What you wanna do?" Reece asked, pulling out $2,000 of the $10,000 she had of Mansio's money.

"Bank $2,000," she said, shaking the dice.

"Fuck it, I got $100," Janelle said, throwing it down.

"Fifty," Danyelle added.

"I got twenty dollars," Lowe said. "I got something."

"You said you wanted him out your life."

"I know and I do, but it's hard out this bitch," Lowe said, shaking her head.

"You'll be all right. You don't need a nigga beating yo' ass," Danyelle said. "Here's a hundred to help you out, baby," Danyelle added, holding out the money.

"You look better and happier, here's another hundred for the kids," Janelle said.

"Shit, I'm done," Lowe said, picking up her twenty dollars. "Got my rent, and change for some food."

"Nigga left you with no food and no money, damn!" Reece said. "I'ma call you tomorrow and you can meet my sister at Food Lion. I'll give her, like, fifty or sixty dollars and you can spend, like, one hundred twenty on her card."

"Thanks, Reece, for real."

"Yo, that bad-ass son of yours, don't feed him. Don't give him shit. That nigga bad," she said, throwing the dice . The girls played ce-lo for an hour. They liked to imitate niggas on the block. They never bet over $100. They drank, smoked the haze Janelle had, ate the veggie tray, fruit tray, drummettes, meatballs and cheese and crackers. Nobody felt like doing anything, but the radio station, 102.9, was broadcasting live from Entourage downtown, and the crowd sounded live.

"That's my shit." Janelle jumped up as Lil Wayne came jamming through.

"That nigga the best that ever did it," Reece yelled. "Where they at?"

"Entourage, what up?" Janelle asked.

"Got my keys and my bag, what up?"

"You driving?"

"Yeah, but I'm staying here when I come back. I am not driving to Chesapeake tonight. That shit far, for real."

"Far from what, Reece?" Janelle asked. "All the bull-shit uptown. These streets gonna be here, lay your head where you can rest and get a peace of mind."

"True, it is quiet," Reece said. Soon, they were driving up Witchduck, hitting 264 headed downtown.

"What they gonna do?" Reece asked.

"Danyelle said she going home to go to bed and Lowe said she was going upstairs to go to bed. She all fucked up over that crazy-ass nigga."

"Who, Dundee? That's a funny nigga. He crazy though. Lowe sweet. She get firm at times, but she ain't with all that bullshit."

"I wish she could find a decent dude, a dude who show her some respect and love. A nigga who work, like, seven to five. Come home, look at the game, hold her, look at a movie, fuck, and go to sleep."

"Don't that shit sound good."

"Good as hell," Janelle said, dreaming of the day she and Choice could live like that again. At that moment, Reece pulled up to Entourage and left the car with the valet. They entered Entourage fucked up, and that's when the party began.

* * *

Niecy fixed herself up as she waited for Poppa. She had given up her place two weeks ago when Poppa told her rent on both spots was a little too much. She had completely moved into his place except for the couches and beds. She had slowed her fast ass down after an abortion five weeks ago. She was going hard, still getting high; sniffing and smoking were everyday things, but she hadn't lost weight. Actually, she had gained some from the late-night eating. Every nigga wanna eat.

Ponic pulled up to Poppa's house in Alexandria. Poppa thanked Ponic and gave him a pound.

"Next time, let your babe get you," Ponic said.

"Naw, I do my time. Bitches don't need to come see me, or pick me up. Get home when I get home."

"I hear ya, but it don't stop her from doing her."

"I don't need to hear that shit right now. Not today!" Poppa said, looking at his cousin.

"Everybody knows she ain't shit. The girl is a jump-off, Poppa. She nice, but she is a jump-off, and you wifing that bitch!" Ponic said. Poppa looked at Ponic.

"You done?"

"Yeah, cousin, I'm done. See you later."

Poppa walked up to his house. Niecy greeted him at the door, throwing her arms around him. He hugged her tight, actually enjoying the extra weight and the way she felt. He looked into her eyes, then kissed her. He could tell she was high, and the old T-shirt and old sweats was not the answer.

"Where the baby?"

"With Janelle, she knew you were getting out and said she had 'em so we could spend some quality time." Niecy smiled.

"Let me get a shower, baby, first things first."

Niecy gave him a moment, so the reality could sink in

that he wasn't locked anymore. Then she stepped in front of him in only a gold bra and purple panties. "Behold the purple and gold, nigga," Niecy said. She put her gold open-toed high heel in his crotch.

"What the fuck you gonna do with this?" she asked, staring at the top of Poppa's head as he grabbed her foot, ran his hands up her leg to her crotch, and rubbed it. He laid her down, and pulled his towel to the side. He slowly eased his dick into her. It was snug, but wet. She cringed from him trying to force his way in, so he worked it in and moved slow, enjoying the feeling of his woman. She put her arms around him and knew that through all the bullshit, this nigga was here for her. As she fell deeper into Poppa's rhythm, the thrusts came faster and harder and she felt his body tense and his back arch, before he let out a deep groan. He pulled her up, with his dick still hard and dripping cum, and walked to the bedroom. He pulled off the gold and purple, laid her down, and fell right back in that warm, wet love that only Niecy had to offer.

"Had to get that first one outta there, now I'ma show you what I'ma do with this hit." And he hit her every way that he'd thought about every night since he'd been locked up.

The next couple days were routine. Niecy and Poppa were in pure ecstasy. Poppa did notice her mood swings, but he put it on her mental state. He knew the things she'd been through and knew that they couldn't disappear in the few months he'd spent with her. So he just continued to love her and work hard at putting the pieces in the right place to make her the woman he needed in his life.

Poppa began grinding and he allowed Niecy to be his road dog. He let her into his real circle. He made money, but not lavish money. His paper supplied a good life but opening his own club was gonna be his glory and his shine. Niecy kept him on a tight leash, with his kids, her kid, and one on the way. As the months passed, she got bigger and Poppa made her stay home. Her insecurities had her calling his phone forty times a day. He began putting it on silent because of the interruptions, and he couldn't afford no more problems. But he started going through pure hell after she had their baby.

It was now three months into their new baby and Niecy had started disappearing for days at a time. The last time was the first time he'd put his hands on her, and all hell broke loose. Janelle, Choice, and Jus were at the house because they were supposed to meet the third investor. Niecy never came back and fucked up the progress. Since Janelle heard about the club Poppa was opening, and he wanted two more investors, she talked to Choice and he gave her what she needed. Choice had been spending more time in Norfolk lately. The last nine months he'd gotten closer to Niecy, and he and Janelle had seen what was becoming of her. The bomb-ass Brickhouse was running around looking damn near nasty. Her ass had dropped so it was swagging, not swaying. Her breasts were sagging and wrinkling, not full and pretty. Her smile had hardened, her yellowish teeth no longer sparkled, but Poppa continued to love her, continued to hold her, comfort her whenever he could. Being true was never a doubt; he was a man who was tired of the streets, and the love he had for Niecy, he felt, was a blessing, so he allowed himself to be blinded to the facts.

To Niecy, he was becoming a trifling, no-good fucked-up nigga, which she had clearly let him know on many occasions. Then twenty minutes later her whole demeanor would change and she'll be all on him, giving him the sex that she wanted so bad, and the love that he desired and needed from her.

Now that the club was getting ready to open in two months, the third and silent investor came through and told Poppa he had ends. Everything in life was going well. He was on top of the world, if only he could connect more with Niecy. But he was coming to his last straw, the blinds were lifting. As he threw on his new white T-shirt over the wife beater, he came down the stairs. His sons were off to school, but the one-year-old was pulling himself up, trying to get to the baby as Niecy sat flipping through the TV.

"What them little niggas eat this morning?"

"I don't know, I was asleep."

"Goddamn! Ain't a clean glass in this bitch," Poppa said, trying to find something to get some juice. Niecy ignored him, turning the TV up.

"Turn that down," Poppa said, frustrated. "The same shit everyday. Getting tired of this shit."

"Tired of what? You tired of what, nigga?" Neicy jumped up yelling, scaring the babies. They began to cry, aggravating her more.

"Niecy, you need to calm down, this ain't the day," Poppa said, downing his juice as he headed for the door before Niecy had one of her tantrums. Niecy blocked his path.

"Fuck you mean, Poppa? Say it again if you a man," she said, standing in front of him.

"Niecy, you need to . . ." was all Poppa got out of his mouth before she slapped him across his face.

"My name is Naquala, that's what you call me from now on, bitch," she stood in front of him like a dude in a long T-shirt with a serious look, ready to fight.

"You don't do shit. All you do is run the fuckin' street, doing nothing. You ain't got no money, broke-ass nigga. Carry yo' ass. Talking about you tired. Tired of what?

Nigga can't do shit, 'cause you ain't got shit." She smirked at him.

"Tell me a bill you pay, you tell me what you do besides change a pamper every time you pamper your nose? Girl, you getting trifling and you need to check yourself," Poppa said with mad attitude, ready to snap.

"That ain't shit. You getting tired of me after you give me a baby. After you see I got one, then you get me pregnant again, and you expect me to take care of your other two that you had with another bitch! Suck my ass, nigga!" she yelled, running to the bedroom. She came out with her sweats, T-shirt, and sneakers on in minutes.

"Now, you stay your ass in here and take care of babies all day," she said, trying to rush out the door. Poppa's whole attitude changed as he grabbed her.

"Look, I need you to chill. I'm tired of all the bullshit. Not you. I need for you to get yourself together, man, and start keeping better house, taking care of your home. Come on, I'm doing everything I can to keep you happy and satisfied, but I gots to get this paper."

"Fuck that, you fuckin' bitches in the street. I know you got other bitches, you ain't never home and you ain't fuck me in weeks," she said, staring him in his face.

"Because you look like shit and yo' pussy stank. Now get your trifling ass together before your ass be looking for a new home, bitch. I'm done fuckin' with you. The more I bend, the harder you go. And believe me, that shit about to stop."

"I'm gone, nigga," she said, trying to leave. Poppa grabbed her and pulled her back. She tried to push away, so he threw her onto the couch.

"You don't put your hands on me motherfucker, no man gonna put his hands on me," she said, grabbing a knife off the counter and coming at Poppa. Poppa didn't believe she would do it, so he moved slow, but the sharp knife penetrating his skin let him know otherwise. He grabbed her arm as she came at him again. The look in her eyes let him know she was someone else, and she had gotten strength from somewhere, because he couldn't hold her. She broke loose, cutting his hand in the process.

The new white T-shirt turned dark red by his shoulders and his hand dripped blood from the deep gash. He looked at Niecy as she stood there with a devious frown and said, "I hate your ass, and I wish you would die." She came at him again. From the blood on his hand and the pain in his shoulder, Poppa knew he could no longer try to get hold of Niecy and make her calm down, and that scared him. His adrenaline kicked in from being scared, and his size-eleven Tim slammed into her chest, taking her breath away and stopping her in her tracks. But the right fist that opened the second before it caught her jaw still did more damage than Poppa expected. Her body crumbled to the floor as the knife dropped from her hand. She sat on the floor wobbling, seeing darkness and stars, trying to let out a scream that wouldn't come out. And as Poppa brought his Tim back, ready to take her head off, he snapped back and tumbled past her. With his teeth gritting, trying to control the anger inside him, he looked at her as her hands came up to her face. She let out a scream that was deafening to the ears and heart. Poppa looked at the babies crying, then he looked at their mother as she lay balled up on the floor, crying. His heart fell and his eyes filled with tears. He went to his room and got a wife beater and a new white T-shirt. He threw on an old sweater coat and headed out the door, straight to Patients First. The wounds weren't life threatening. Four stitches in the shoulder and twelve in the hand. He wasn't ready to answer a lot of questions, so he covered his shoulder and bandages under his shirt, but his hand was another story, he couldn't cover that.

* * *

"This has been all that. I have never in my life seen anything so beautiful," Janelle said, staring into Choice's eyes. "And this is a time in my life I will never forget."

"Better not, I brought you all the way to Hawaii to ask you to be my better half forever."

"Lanai, not Hawaii, the most beautiful of all the islands," she said, smiling and excited. She tried to hide it, but the butterflies in her stomach wouldn't allow her to calm down.

"Lanai, with the white sand beaches. Goddamn!" Choice said. "This shit is something, far from Brooklyn," he added, laughing.

"Shit, far from Virginia Beach. Don't get me wrong, our shit nice, but this shit here is a sho nuff memory! And I got pictures!" she said, smiling as they exited the fabulous hotel room they'd called home for the last week. Choice had decided he wanted to ask Janelle to marry him. He was straight now. He had the game down and things were so lovely that he was only doing Baltimore, DC, and Richmond. He'd given his cousin the upper hand on the Brooklyn to Hampton thing and it was working. Jus had come in running things with an iron hand. He was doing so well that he added Portsmouth and Newport News to his list. Choice was proud; Jus being on the grind and holding him down gave him a little more time for Janelle. So when he saw the commercial, he called Janelle and told her to call a travel agent, so they could go to Lanai. The marriage thing would be a surprise. When Janelle got involved in the club, Choice's eyes opened. She got a lawyer who had formed a company and named herself president. That company went 50/50 under a corporation that was also set up by the attorneys. She was covering herself and Choice against any shady bullshit. Then she figured out how to buy the house they were renting. She put down 5 percent and with both of their names on the deed, they closed. She was doing things he had never expected, but he loved it, and never wanted to lose her or the security of him being held down. So the 1.2-carat, Princess-cut, platinum diamond ring that he put on her finger was worth every penny.

After a long flight, and crazy layovers, they were back to reality. They gathered their bags and made their way from La Guardia Airport.

"I'm not ready to leave you," Janelle said, leaning on Choice.

"So what you wanna do, ma?" Choice asked directly.

"I don't know, what you want me to do?" she asked in her little girl voice.

"Come on, Janelle, we got to tell the man something."

"I'll go home in two days, Thursday. Poppa got things under control. The club is ready, just waiting for his liquor license and occupancy permit. I know you got business, but give me one more day. I love you," she said, smiling.

"Marriott, downtown Brooklyn," Choice told the cab driver. "Hell yeah, need me some fresh Uptowns. And whatever new that dropped," Choice said, grabbing his girl around her shoulders and pulling her to him. "You were made for me, ma."

"Naw, you made me like this. I use to buy things I needed and keep it up. You buy shit just to have it. Sometimes a waste," she said.

"You crazy, I wear everything I buy. But we came up different. You had a real fucked-up childhood. You went through mental and physical abuse, but you had all your necessities: food, clothes, water, and shelter. We didn't have no abuse going on, but we ain't have shit. No water and lights off most of the time. No food all time and clothes and shoes was out of the question. And if we did get them, they were hand-me-downs, until my brother Boo-Bee started hustling, then it was all over. By the time he caught his case and got sent upstate for fifteen, my other brother Ray was already running, and when he got knocked for running a criminal enterprise down south, they gave him twenty-five years. Now I support my family. But I'm not going nowhere. I buy myself nice shit, but I've learned from those before me, O.G.s say invest and get out. If this club jump, I can get into promotional shit. Give this shit up before something happens, I had a good run, damn good run. If things fall the way they should, six months and your man will be good for retirement." He smiled.

Janelle looked at his smile and lips, taking in every word. It was important to know his plans and know where Choice was headed; these things kept her on point ahead of the bullshit. They checked in and relaxed for a few, but it wasn't long before they were out on the train headed to Manhattan. They shopped, ate, and had a great time. They stopped at the liquor store, and got a bottle of Ciroc, and called it a night. The following day was spent in and out of shops on Fulton Street. They had bags over bags, sneakers and boots mostly, but they were happy.

The following morning, Janelle woke to a big comfortable bed alone. As she rolled over squeezing the pillow, her thoughts ran to Choice. She remembered his kisses, then she heard the room door shut behind him. It was six in the morning and he had to be in Baltimore before noon, and he had to see Jus and the rest of his team before he left. Janelle wasted the day away relaxing, before heading to Chinatown to catch the Chinese bus back to Virginia Beach. She arrived in Virginia about 11:30. Lowe picked her up and took her home. She was the first one to congratulate her on her engagement.

"Danyelle told me to call her when you got in," Lowe said, dialing her phone.

"I ain't fuckin' with them tonight," Janelle said not wanting to be bothered. "And why you all dressed up tonight? Tight jeans, tight top, new fresh whites, damn! You look cute."

"Went out with this nigga from out Green Run. He cool, had a good time."

"Got money, what he do, what he driving?" Janelle asked quickly, surprising Lowe.

Lowe hung up her phone. "She ain't answering. Ooh! He was driving a new 300M, or is it M300? You know, them new Chryslers that look like a Bentley. He was all jeweled up, rocking new shit from head to toe each time I saw him. He say he fuck with Plexico. That's his peoples."

"Damn, that's some different kind of dough. So you gonna see him again?"

"Know what, girl?" Lowe laughed. "You know I moved back home with my momma to save up my money right. So I've been out with three niggas since then. They all had nice whips and shit. But it seem like they were all trying to be Dundee. What he do so natural, these cats was trying and talking like they the shit and I can see the fakeness all up and through 'em."

"Girl, I can say you still love Dundee, or I can say, you just the type of bitch who want and need a real nigga to handle that ass. And them niggas ain't real, but you don't need him beating your ass. There's a difference between being stern and being crazy," Janelle said.

"True!" Lowe responded.

"Look! You got this nigga who will ask for pussy nicely, 'Please can I have some please?' and then you got those 'Pull that shit off, I need to fuck' type nigga. And it's sad, but we want that ignorant one."

"Why that nigga just leave me, Janelle, instead of changing and showing me some respect?" Lowe asked.

"Because that's what you wanted. You stood up and demanded respect, something you had to do, he wasn't doing right, Lowe. You didn't deserve the bullshit, don't sell yourself short. Even if you run into him and you fuck him 'cause you miss him and want dick, he'll know you still ain't the one if you don't put your foot down. Bitch got to demand respect. That's what you did when you said 'fuck him.' Even though you moved back home, you still put your foot down and some niggas can't handle that, so they try and go to yo' ass to change you. If they can't, they leave, then they realize the strength you had, and they begin to admire you. Some ex-couples become the best of friends."

"I miss him. I need to hold him."

"Girl, you need some dick," Janelle said, laughing. "Just say it, you need to be fucked and you ain't giving yourself to no lame-ass nigga, you wanna go back where you feel secure."

Lowe laughed at the fact that Janelle saw right through her. She hadn't been with a man since he'd left.

"I know you, Lowe, and I know you gonna end up calling him, but you got to be smart. You can't allow him to treat you any kind of way. I keep saying this because I know you gonna give in sooner or later. I don't want to see you in a fucked-up situation again. Do you, girl? Now, if you do call and he don't answer, then he fuckin', if he answer and say he'll get back, he already got pussy. But if he say, 'Let's get up,' or he hungry or you hungry shit, he want the same thing and he had too much pride to call beggin' and crying, but if you open the door, he will bust it down." They laughed as thoughts of calling him ran through her mind. The ringing of the phone disturbed her.

"What da deal?"

"Where you at?" Reece asked.

"At Janelle spot."

"We at D'Frazier's, y'all come on through. Danyelle phone about to go dead. Hit me when y'all outside."

"All right. Yo, they up at D'Frazier's, what you wanna do?" Lowe said, hoping Janelle was ready to hang. She had given up her place and moved back in with her mom and brother, and she needed to get out. She wasnt' ready to go back home.

"I ain't gotta change for D'Frazier's, do I?"

"Hell naw, they ain't Luxury Brown, strict-ass club," Lowe added, laughing.

"We out," Janelle said, grabbing her small Prada purse, while holding the door so Lowe could get out and she could set her alarm.

"I'll drive," Janelle said. She hit the garage door opener and happiness came over her body. She began to shake and tears formed in her eyes.

"Damn, that Choice shit. I ain't even seen that shit yet, GS350. White, clean as shit."

Janelle walked over to the Lexus and opened the door. There was a card on the front seat. She opened the card:

> *To my wifey-to-be*
> *I don't want to shine alone*
> *Enjoy your shit, ma!*

"Get the fuck in, girl, this my shit," Janelle yelled.

"Stop lying, Choice gonna get yo' ass," Lowe said, closing the door and allowing the leather to surround her. *Just like in Dundee's car,* she thought. Janelle hit the button to close the garage and pulled off, throwing the card in Lowe's lap. Lowe read the card.

"That's some shit, girl," Lowe said in a low voice, amazed. "You doing it, Janelle. Getting everything you said. My life ain't gonna be fucked up," Lowe said, smiling.

"Know what, Lowe?" Janelle asked. "I was determined. My whole family fucked up: addicts, mental illnesses, faggots." Lowe shot her eye at Janelle. "Is what it is. Love my brother, but the nigga a faggot and I'll never understand that shit. Niecy say she understand him. She fuck with him, but they been through a lot, let them tell it, I don't remember that shit," Janelle said.

"Your choice not to remember," Lowe said, turning on the radio. Janelle hit five on her speed dial.

"What up, ma?" Choice said with music in the background.

"I love you, baby, thank you," she said, smiling.

"Don't thank me, just act like you got some motherfuckin' sense."

"You know I am. Where you at?" she asked, wondering, if she wanted to know.

"DC," he said.

"Where in DC, Choice?" Janelle asked bluntly.

"Dream, Club Dream," he said, frustrated.

"Dream is closed, Choice, why the fuck you lying?" she yelled.

"Girl, I'm in the club all fucked up and you coming with a thousand fuckin' questions. I'm wit' these niggas, shit, I don't know, where the fuck I'm at?" he asked Jus.

"Love," Jus said, sipping his Hennessey VSOP while this fly-ass mami with body for days sat up under him, sipping Chicito.

"I thought this was Dream," he asked Jus, Boe, and A.

"It use to be Dream, now it's Love," Boe said, turning the Crystal bottle up to head. Boe and A were two cats

Jus knew from New York who were in DC doing their thing.

"See, girl, they changed the name. You be killing me with that dumb shit."

"My bad! Love my Lex, baby, and I love you too," Janelle said, trying to change the subject.

"It's one o'clock, where the fuck you going?" he asked, concerned.

"Me and Lowe going to D'Frazier's. Reece and Danyelle already up there."

"What the fuck is D'Frazier's, they closed that shit, why you lying?" he said, laughing.

"Martini Blue," she said, pulling up. They shared a moment, and inside he felt his girl was right there. She stopped laughing. "I love you, Choice. Be careful, baby, I need you more than ever. You are my heart," she said, letting him know she was truly feeling him.

"Me too, ma. Me too. Hit me when you get home. One." And the phone went dead.

"Come on, girl, all that lovey-dovey shit," Lowe said, closing the door.

"You jealous, bitch, all y'all bitches jealous of Janelle, the fly-ass diva," she said, laughing slapping Lowe on her back.

"Well, come on up front Ms. Diva, so you can get us in the club. You know I ain't got no money."

Janelle walked through the door. They only wanted ten dollars, but she handed Security a hundred. Once inside, she ran to Reece and Danyelle with her hand in the air, showing off her diamond ring. "Congrats, girl," Reece said, excited.

"I won't be the only bitch who got to go home because her husband call." They all laughed as Lowe walked up and hugged Reece and Danyelle. Janelle leaned over to her.

"That bitch gave you my change, right. I gave her a hundred."

"Naw," Lowe said, dumbfounded, throwing her hands up. Janelle was getting ready to take off when Lowe laughed and said, "Yeah, I got it."

"Okay!" Janelle said, and began talking to all her friends. They ordered rounds and a bottle of champagne, and as they got into celebrating Janelle's engagement, her phone rang.

"What up, girl?" Janelle said happy, excited, and a little tipsy.

"What you doing?" Niecy asked, dragging.

"At D'Frazier's."

"Sound like you having a good time. Who you wit'?"

""Lowe, Reece, and Danyelle, you know who I fuck with."

"You ain't even call me and let me know you was back from fuckin' Hawaii?" Neicy said, frustrated.

"Girl, I been back. I called you when I got back to New York. And I just got back here an hour ago. We talked the other night. You need to leave that shit alone," Janelle said as a joke.

"I ain't fuckin' wit' shit. I'm just tired of everything. Sometimes I wish Naquel was here and I was gone," Niecy said sadly.

"Here you go with that bullshit, carry yo' ass to sleep. 'Bye," Janelle said, closing her phone. Trying not to let her sister get to her, she filled her champagne glass with the Red Moët, they'd decided to try, and they toasted once more.

"To you, Janelle, may you and Choice be forever happy," Danyelle said.

"And may he continue to take care of you like he doing," Lowe added.

"Amen to that," Reece said, and they drank up. "Where Niecy these days?"

"Taking care of them kids. Running the street is over," Lowe said.

"Shit, she still running, still getting high, and giving Poppa hell. I don't see how any nigga put up with her. That's my sister and I love her ass, but she come with some shit and she seems to be getting worse," Janelle said with a spaced-out look.

"My momma said she having those babies too damn close, she ain't giving her body a chance to heal before she fuckin' again. It can fuck her up physically and mentally, you need to tell her ass to slow the fuck down," Danyelle said.

"That bitch already three months pregnant again!"

"That nigga stay riding her ass," Reece said, laughing.

"So what's up with you and Mansio?" Janelle asked. Reece began to laugh. They all looked at her. She couldn't stop laughing, when she got her composure, she finally made them swear to never repeat what she was about to tell them. They agreed.

"Ok, I'm a freaky-ass girl, y'all know this, but I gets off. Now I'm fuckin' dude and he ain't really doing it, so when he throwing dick, I start rubbing my clit to cum. After I cum, I'm still horny, so I ask him if he want to go in my ass. He gets all excited. I get my dildo out, I put it in my pussy while he in my ass." She had their undivided attention. "Now, he figure I'm a straight freak, so we laying there and he ask me was there any fantasy I had that I hadn't done. I told him I wanted to find a man who was so secure in his manhood that he'll let me fuck him." They burst out laughing, which made her laugh.

"No, he didn't, I know he didn't," Janelle said, surprised as her eyes popped open wide.

"Yeah, he did. I freaked the shit out of him. Sucked his neck, ears, chest, nipples, fingers, toes, dick, and licked his ass, he was panting like a bitch, then I threw my strap on and fucked the shit out of him. It was all that, but now I'm done. Fantasy has been fulfilled."

"I got one question, where the fuck you get a strap-on?" Danyelle asked with no facial expressions.

"That's always been a fantasy, and every now and then I come across a nigga who wit' it, but this nigga want me to fuck him every time I see him. If he stay a week, he want me to freak and fuck him every night. Last time I told him no, and asked if he was gay or bisexual. Shit, this nigga stopped fucking me," she laughed. They followed, still amazed. "We talked, but I told him I wasn't wit' that shit no more. I needed real nigga to put it down. Guess he took it the wrong way. Fuck him," she said, sipping her champagne. All they could do was shake their heads.

"How the fuck you gonna pay for all that shit, house, car, damn girl," Danyelle said.

"Girl, please, unlike some hoes, I know what my pussy worth, and I ain't scared to fuck and get my money," Reece said with attitude, looking at Lowe.

"Girl, I can put this pussy and phat ass on any nigga out here, have him stalking me and ready to buck on any guy that look at me. But he only gonna get that out of me if I like him. Not for his money, nigga can't buy me. You tell a nigga, fuck him and his money, then he see he can't run you with his money, then he wanna beat yo' ass. Fuck these niggas, pour me some more bubbly!" Lowe said with a smile. They laughed, downed their drinks, and headed to the car. When they reached the parking lot, they fell right into the parking lot party. They hung for a bit, talking to guys chilling with nice cars and playing loud music. Then they saw Dundee coming across the parking lot in his black Rocawear jeans, black Rocawear T-shirt, and black D.C.s with his iced out chain that read LEP, with his signature black bandanna tied around his right wrist.

"What up, gangsta girl," he said, looking at Janelle. "Yo' shit stink, just like everybody else's," he added, looking at Danyelle. "Raggedy-ass Reece," he said with his nose turned up.

"Fuck you, nigga and yo' team. Going to my car right now," she said, walking off. He turned to Lowe.

"You gonna let her talk to your man like that?" he said, looking at her and seeing a young woman, not a gold digger. He actually missed her. He figured if she won't shit, that another nigga would have replaced him and she would have kept her house and anything else she had going. But she didn't, she tried to hold it down herself and fell, and for that he felt like shit, but looked at Lowe different.

"You my man now?" she said, staring into his eyes. He just looked at her. "My man don't fight me and my man don't let me fall. I loved you, Dun, and you shitted on me. Why?"

"Because I was young and stupid," he said with his head down.

"Nigga it was just six months ago."

"I know, tell your girls you with me. Let's go talk," Lowe looked at Janelle with her eyebrows up.

"Hollah at me later. Love ya!" Janelle said.

"Love you too," she said. She grabbed hold of Dundee's hand and walked off.

"If I were her, I wouldn't give that punk the time of day," Danyelle said.

"She love that nigga. Give her a chance. She might learn how to handle that crazy motherfucker," Janelle said.

"When you become his fan? What about that shit with you and him? Him snatching you out the car and Choice doing his mans and them? You act like that shit all good," Danyelle said, looking at Janelle for explanation.

"It was all business, Danyelle. It was business and that shit with him and Lowe ain't our business. I don't like that nigga for her, but what can we do? She lonesome and want that nigga in her life. Hope he changed. I ain't out there wit' that shit no more so I ain't got no problems with nobody. I'm a club owner, an entrepreneur," Janelle said, smiling and getting into her new Lexus. Danyelle just walked away to her car, thinking that everybody needed to slow down.

It was the grand opening of Reign . . .